GOLDSONG

by Beth Hudson

Book One of The Sagathas Bard

This book is dedicated to the memory of my mother,
Vivian Kay Hudson
1937-2020
Whose creative spark lives on
in her children and grandchildren

And, as always, to the kids
Dylan, David, Gabbie, & Alex

A special Thank You to my generous patrons:

Laura Hudson Kittrell
Bob & Roxanne Quinlan
Eleanor & David Ray

Additional Thanks
To others who have helped me with this book:

Nigel and Susan Ray
Eleanor and David Ray
Amelia Kibbie
Andy Wheeler
Jason Hooton-Tuscher

TABLE OF CONTENTS

Chapter One
Reunion

Sunlight streamed through the window like liquid amber, filling the makeshift office with a warmth Traedis did not feel. For one thing, it was still winter in the mountains, and for another, she had just found herself an unexpected king. The second of these gave her no more cheer than the first.

Sitting quietly in a corner, her friend Ruth thumbed through a heavy tome, fluttering the pages. A cardinal trilled from its perch on the stone lip of the outside masonry.

The door crashed open, letting in a woman Traedis knew very well: her sister Vandeyr, a black-bladed dagger in her hand.

"Curses, Trae, what do you think you're doing?" shouted Vandeyr, and threw the knife.

Traedis froze while the black blade cut the air next to her cheek, sticking with a solid *thunk* in the plaster of the castle wall. If Vandeyr meant to hit Traedis, she would; this was a warning, not an assassination.

Ruth surged to her feet, her own weapon in hand. Though she stood only as tall as Traedis' thigh, the brunaidhi woman was not the sort to back down when a friend was threatened. The white leaf blade she brandished was identical in shape and size to the black dagger that now protruded from the wall.

"Oh, leave it!" snapped Vandeyr without even looking at the tiny woman. "If I'd meant to kill her, she'd be dead."

"She's right," Traedis managed to croak, though her voice felt half-strangled. A warm sensation spread through her chest at Ruth's expression of loyalty, but she knew her friend was no match for Vandeyr. Traedis' sister was one of the deadliest killers in a city of killers, and she had been an active assassin for the last ten years.

Ruth remained standing, muscles tensed; even her close-cropped gray curls seemed to vibrate.

"Sit down," Traedis told her sister, and gestured to the chair that faced hers across the desk that bisected her office. Vandeyr seated herself with a panther's grace. Ruth also relaxed and dropped back onto the three-legged stool in the corner, though she kept her dagger in hand.

The southern daylight streamed through the window, bathing the three of them in a warm honey hue. Traedis lifted her eyes to Vandeyr's face for the first time in six years, a sharp pang in her heart. They had been close once, despite Vandeyr's mercurial temper.

Her sister looked no older than Traedis remembered, certainly not like a woman approaching thirty. Her white-blonde hair was wrapped in a tight coil around her head, the strands firmly tamped down as if they feared to stray. Her fine-boned features were twisted in a furious expression below an equally furious blue gaze.

Traedis brushed back a few copper tendrils of her own hair and wondered what her face betrayed. She had never been good at hoarding her emotions, to unleash them only when and where they would have a calculated effect. Honest speech was not valued in the city-state of Tolin, which the world beyond called 'The City of Assassins.'

Now she was its king, and she must rule, despite the scorn of its citizens. She must turn the course of a river that had cut a passage into its bedrock for two thousand years. It was like trying to dam that river with cupped hands.

The truth before her was manifest; she loved Vandeyr, and would no matter how estranged they were.

"What do you mean, 'What am I doing?'" she asked, her voice emerging plaintive and young. Snapping her mouth shut, she immediately berated herself for showing vulnerability.

Vandeyr glared. "Why did you pull the assassins off every job we contracted for? Trae, we need those contracts! The City can't survive without them. You should know that – you had the same teachers as I did. You're going to destroy the City, and for what? Revenge? A need to show everyone that they were right to put you in prison?" Her words poured out, hot and bitter. "For once in your life, look beyond what you want, and do what's right for the country that birthed you!"

Vandeyr's words cut into Traedis' fragile sense of stability. Perhaps Traedis was wrong; perhaps her course was ill-advised. She did not know how to rule a country. She had never been able to understand the intricacies of City diplomacy. How could she lead a people she barely knew? Her thoughts whirled, tried to fit the future pattern of Tolin while her stomach churned.

Ruth cleared her throat loudly and leveled a sharp glance at Vandeyr. "That argument would be more convincing if Tolin had ever done anything for her *except* put her in prison," she said firmly.

Like cold water on burning embers, her voice brought Traedis out of the thick morass of self-doubt. Perhaps she was not qualified to rule, but she knew what was right. Assassination was an abhorrent practice, and though she had ruled only for a week, recalling the assassins had been her first decree.

There were other reasons to change Tolin's path. "Vandeyr, we can't survive *with* the contracts. Look at us; we're surrounded on three sides by Telardur, a closet in the heart of a mansion. King Kenrydh won't tolerate assassinations anymore, and Haven has a new king who broke with her own people over their willingness to deal with us." Her tone still wavered, but she knew she was speaking the truth. "We don't have the military power to withstand them if they declare war. We've only survived so long because the weight of tradition was on our side. That stopped being true last week."

Vandeyr scowled. "So you'll give in? You won't fight for us?"

"I *am* fighting for us," Traedis said quietly.

Vandeyr blinked, then refocused on Traedis, the curl in her lip straightening into thoughtfulness as she studied her sister. Traedis

refused to look away. She had been a child when she fled the City;
now she was a woman, and one with experience both brutal and
powerful.

"You believe that," Vandeyr said. Her voice dropped to a sour
register. "You would rather cave to Kenrydh and the King of filthy
Haven than support your own people." She glared at Traedis with
narrowed eyes. "I'm ashamed that you're an Atenel."

Traedis took a dizzying lungful of air and assessed her
breathing. Her inhalations were too quick and shallow; she slowed
and deepened them to make the lightheadedness pass.

For reassurance, she touched the harp by her side: carved of
crimson cherrywood with intricate climbing roses, it was a work of
art as well as a master's instrument. Gold coated the strings to hide
the far more valuable *sagathas* which lay beneath; 'dragon gold'
was one of the most precious and magical substances in the mortal
world. Her harp might be worth more than Tolin's entire treasury.

Lifting her chin defiantly, she met Vandeyr's gaze. "You may
wish I weren't part of the family, but I am. And whatever you say –
" She clutched the edge of the desk for support. "I am glad to see
you, Vandeyr."

"I wish I could say the same. But you've always done
whatever you want. Why should now be any different?" Vandeyr
threw a glance over her shoulder at Ruth. "Stay sitting, will you? I
won't harm her." She rose and walked around the desk and yanked
her knife out of the wall, leaving a deep gouge in the plaster.
Tossing the dagger from hand to hand without appearing to watch

what she was doing, she returned to her own seat.

Ruth's eyes narrowed.

"Very well." Vandeyr said to Traedis. She flipped the dagger into the air, where it somersaulted, coming down in her other hand hilt first. "What do you want me to do?"

"What do I – " Traedis could not make sense of the words. They echoed in her head, coiling back on themselves like the *quixil*, the serpent which swallowed its own tail. She could not make them resolve into any sort of coherency. Staring blankly at Vandeyr, she asked, "What do you mean?" Her tongue felt stupid and slow.

"What do you want me to do?" Vandeyr's voice was honey and poison. "If you don't alter your course, you'll be the target of every half-trained assassin in the City. You may be a fool, but you're still my sister. I don't intend to let anyone harm you."

Traedis blinked. The words still circled, starting and returning to a place she could not find. "You don't intend to let...?"

"Try not to be too stupid." Vandeyr frowned. "What do you need? You'll want me to set up bodyguards – a palace guard as well. A poison tester, or some sort of magic you can carry to keep yourself safe. You'll need intelligence about your enemies." Resentment trickled back into her voice. "Since your enemies are your own city, instead of Telardur and Haven." She cleared her throat. "I can do all of those things – and much better than some would-be assassin avenger with a pretty, white-bladed toy. I'm surprised someone hasn't already picked you off like an apple."

She expressed her contempt for Ruth by the set of her shoulders and the angle of her head.

Traedis could see Ruth tense, but the brunaidhi woman did not respond further.

The spinning thoughts in Traedis' mind finally began to coalesce into shaky comprehension. Vandeyr was offering to help her, and in a significant way. Traedis' nose prickled, and the strangled feeling returned to her throat; no matter what she had done, Vandeyr still loved her, too.

"Do you really trust her?" Ruth leaned forward. "None of your family visited you in prison. If she was worried about you, she should have done it then."

Vandeyr slapped the desk with the hand not currently holding the dagger; Traedis startled.

"You don't understand the City," Vandeyr said over her shoulder to Ruth. A crease gathered between her eyebrows, and her voice softened. "Trae, I didn't even know you were back for six months. No one told me. No one. When I found out, I went to Mother and asked about you."

"She knew I was there," Traedis responded, certain that she was right. "Mother knew, didn't she?" The prickling in her nose crept to her eyes, which began to fill with tears. Blinking, she forced the outward expression of her misery down into her core of self, where she kept the concentrated pain of years contained in a hard, tight knot.

"She told me not to visit you." Vandeyr's words skirted the

question, which was an answer in itself. "And told me not to bother Uncle Cordelayne with it." Her lips firmed into an angry line. "I ignored her and went to him anyway."

"What did he say?" It was obvious to Traedis that their uncle had not agreed; what she wanted to know was why.

"Does it matter?" Vandeyr set the dagger down on the desk in front of her, watching Traedis intently. Then she sighed. "I suppose it does. He told me that he was working on you, and that visits from family might disrupt what he was trying to accomplish. He forbade me to speak of it to anyone."

Traedis' stomach roiled. She had spent four years in the City's prisons for the crime of desertion; the Council had told her she would spend the remains of her life there. During that timeless span she had struggled, clutching any thread of sanity that could keep her mind from playing the endless years ahead over and over in her imagination. She had lost her fragile hold on reality more than once, regaining it just to have it swallowed once again by the yawning void stretching before her. Only the discipline of her music had prevented her from cracking open like a raw egg.

Knowing that Cordelayne and her mother meant she must be broken and remade did not surprise her, but it was a soul-deep wound. She loved them still, but all of her trust had been shattered long since.

"I'm sorry." Vandeyr's expression became gentler. "But they were doing what they thought was best. I wasn't in a position to disagree."

Ruth stood angrily, bristling with outrage. "What was *best*? Four years alone in prison?" Like Traedis, she did not sound surprised; she had also been a victim of the City of Assassins' need to control and shape others to further their work. "How old were you when you left, Trae?"

"Fourteen." Six years ago. It seemed like the memory of another life.

In some ways, it was. Traedis had redefined herself in the surrounding kingdom of Telardur, had become a bard, a friend of Powers, and had spoken with gods. She had been snatched back to the City two years after leaving, returning with a wealth of enchantments: the forms of a wren and a wild gray fox; spellsongs that only she could play; a gift from the King of Winter, and a deep connection to him; and a magic harp made for a legendary bard.

An understanding of Vandeyr's previous words, which had tumbled like river stones into the back of Traedis' mind, settled into a startling pattern; her sister had brooked her mother on Traedis' behalf. Traedis could not remember another time Vandeyr had done so. That she had gone to their uncle anyway was heartening. "You tried to see me. That means the world." It was a gift.

Recalling Vandeyr's questions, Traedis added, "I know I need a bodyguard, at least for the time being." She cut off Ruth's blossoming protest. "You can't be awake day and night, Ruth. You have to sleep, and eat, and use the chamber pot. Vandeyr is right." Again, she touched her harp for reassurance. "I hadn't even thought

of a palace guard. I mean, I've only had a palace for three days."
The mansion that Traedis now occupied had been emptied by its owners fleeing the new reign. It was well-suited to her needs, but as of yet, sparsely staffed.

All of Vandeyr's suggestions were good ones. "Poison tasters?" That was a wrinkle she had not considered, though it should have come to mind; among other things, City assassins were familiar with both common and esoteric poisons.

"If you want to make it past your next meal." Vandeyr leaned back in her chair and crossed her ankles.

After a moment, she said, "Trae, you need to go see Mother."

Traedis felt the old, familiar dread descend as she contemplated this. Echoes of a cutting voice filtered through the sieve of recollection, each grain a memory of shame. Traedis had never been able to meet Mitheira Atenel's standards, and the current situation was unlikely to reconcile them. Especially after what Vandeyr had just said.

"I've been busy." Even to herself, the excuse sounded pathetic, exactly the sort of defense her family would expect. "There was so much damage when the Storm Eagle died, the avalanche that carried off the Council Hall, and the demon Toledru rising from beneath it..." She trailed off as her sister's brow lowered. "It's true," she finished haltingly, heat rising to her cheeks.

"I know it is. Still, you're making excuses." Vandeyr picked up the knife again and tested the edge carefully against her thumb.

"Go and see her. She deserves more from you than to be treated like some embarrassing poor relation. I don't care how difficult your relationship has been – she's still your mother."

Shame flooded Traedis. "I know," she said. "But I really have been patching Tolin together as best I can, and no one else can do it as well as I." The *falmyros*, the godsgiven bond between the lord and the land, had overwhelmed her with the sheer need of what her new realm demanded. The magic which flowed from that bond could be used to heal the land, and to protect its people.

"Excuses," Vandeyr repeated. She stood and slid the knife into a sheath at her belt. "Go see her, Trae. It matters." Without another word, she turned and left the room, letting the door bang shut behind her.

Traedis sat, stunned, and looked fixedly at the door. She had not expected this. When she had gained the *falmyros*, her uncle had fled the City; her brother Otenemar had refused to receive her. That Vandeyr, one of Cordelayne's most avid pupils, intended to throw in her lot with Traedis was a boon and a blessing.

"That was your sister?" Ruth sheathed her own blade and hopped into the chair Vandeyr had just vacated. Her legs dangled over the edge; she swung them back and forth like a child. "She really doesn't need the knife, does she? That tongue of hers has got to be several times sharper." She grinned at Traedis, clearly hoping to ease the tension of Vandeyr's whirlwind visit.

Traedis nodded. She had been thrown badly off-balance by Vandeyr's lightning changes in mood and her offer of assistance.

"She's right. I do need a guard. And – " She forced herself to say the words. "I need to visit Mother."

Ruth looked at her sharply. "Are you sure?"

"Yes," she said reluctantly. "Vandeyr was right. I do love Mother, even if she thinks I'm the biggest disgrace the family has ever produced. I'll go." Dread of the commitment she had just made hung over her, shadowing the rest of her day. She would be glad when it was over; she wished she could already be on the far side of it, remembering rather than anticipating.

From the seat, Ruth gave her another long look. "Do you want me to go with you?"

A surge of gratitude rolled over Traedis. "Would you?" Then she shook her head. "I'd hate to ask you to do that. Mother can be – difficult."

"You didn't ask me. I offered." Ruth's air of cheerfulness was heartening; Traedis was not sure how lighthearted the other woman truly felt, or whether it was a façade intended to encourage her friend. Either way, Traedis was grateful.

"I would," she said, her voice cracking like a novice. "Thank you."

Ruth smiled. "I expect it to be an interesting afternoon."

"Oh, it will be," Traedis said, the sense of dread still heavy and stifling. "I can promise you that."

Chapter Two
Mitheira

The carriage route from the palace to Traedis' childhood home was bumpy, uncomfortable, and required a long detour through snow-bordered streets that were sufficiently open to permit access to four wheels and a pair of horses. Traedis sat across from Ruth, her mind spinning between the inevitable confrontation with her mother and the impact of the damage the demon Toledru had done to the City.

Ruth knelt on the seat and stared avidly out the window, bobbing with the motion of the carriage. "Everything is orderly," she said without turning her head. "In spite of the mess, the streets are straight, the colors all blend together, and each building looks like it's engineered more or less the same way. Your people must be very organized."

Traedis nodded. "They are. The Mastery family takes care of housing and building for the City, and they make sure nothing is too far from the original style. It's considered a strength for the City to have continuity – it helps us remember that we are one people, and that all of us are responsible for Tolin's mission." It was a biting reminder of how she had never been entirely part of that people.

"Oh." Ruth sat back on her haunches. "It helps me understand this city a little better – though some things I'd rather *not* understand." She returned her attention to the window.

On both sides, there was evident and widespread devastation.

The demon Toledru had been imprisoned below the city, held in check only by the power of the Storm Eagle, previous ruler of Tolin.

The Storm Eagle's great, gray form descended, claws outstretched, stooping over Traedis like a tempest. Traedis' heart gave a quick jolt; she rubbed her eyes fiercely, trying to eradicate the vision from her memory. He was not the author of her mind's worst darkness, but he had been entwined with so much fear that even a glancing recollection was enough to send her pulse racing.

"Are you all right?" Ruth's anxious expression also held a realm of compassion. "This has got to be a tangle of knotted yarn, considering you were in prison just two weeks ago."

"That's all? Two weeks?" It seemed like two days, and simultaneously like it had happened months since. Traedis' life had been overturned so thoroughly that she could barely make sense of its new shape. "Yes. It's a great deal to comb out into something straightforward." Her gaze flickered to the scenes outside the window. "Of course, unlike the streets, straightforward isn't the City's way."

Most of Tolin's buildings were gray mountain stone, slate or granite, constructed of large blocks mortared together; some of them rose three stories high. Many had been durable enough to withstand the shaking earth when Toledru had risen from his grave. Still, fallen stones littered the street, stucco and plaster had cracked off, and dust grayed the snow where they had fallen.

The cobblestones here had been cleared, with stone and wood

in great piles alongside the road so traffic could flow. Pieces of broken statuary lay in heaps: half a wing; the foreleg of a horse; the bottom half of a stylized beetle. Charred timbers and scorched ruins marked the aftermath of fires, though Tolin had been spared the worst of those by the winter weather.

Now that the Storm Eagle had entered her mind, she had difficulty refocusing her attention. He had been fearsome, but also had been trapped in his own *falmyros* by those who had forged the City into a potent weapon. When he had been assassinated, his suppression of the demon below Tolin had been lifted.

In hatred and rage, Toledru had turned his intent to destroying the city he had founded. Traedis had defeated him with the help of the Storm Eagle's spirit, sending him to his final rest. She shuddered, her mind shying from that memory.

The demon, his material form reduced to bones after almost two thousand years of imprisonment, threw his skull at Traedis. She felt a splintering pain as Toledru burst into her mind, seizing control of her body. Horror erupted within her head: the long corruption of her worm-devoured flesh, the scouring of bone, rotting into nothing as her consciousness forced her to see and hear and feel everything above her.

No! That was not Traedis. She was not the tortured soul who had persisted under the earth since the City's founding. She swallowed down sickness and made herself look at the scenes outside, cataloguing them as a litany against remembrance.

They were passing through a shop district, which showed less damage than many of the larger houses near Tolin's center. Waterfowl hung outside a poultry merchant's door; a woman in several overlapping skirts hawked bright scarves tied to a pole; a window held rare clockwork treasures behind equally rare leaded glass window.

The simple, everyday activity was a balm to Traedis' heart, but also vital to the City's recovery. Now that the assassins had been recalled, it was important to keep Tolin operating internally until Traedis could find them all some other purpose. It was something she must address soon.

"Still hard?" asked Ruth. She had turned away from the window, and was watching Traedis with a keen glance.

Traedis nodded. "More than I had any idea of. I thought that perhaps with the *falmyros*, my people would support me, even if they didn't agree with my changes. I don't know why I thought that. I know Tolin. We're likely to argue with the gods if they disagree with us. Politely, of course."

Ruth snorted. "Politely indeed! While they're busy planning how to reinterpret the gods' express word so it's in their favor. I'm not sure I'd call it politeness, but I suppose there are some who would."

Traedis gave her the shadow of a grin. "I can't say you're wrong."

The carriage hit a hole with a teeth-jarring jolt, sending the two of them scrambling for balance. When Traedis recovered and shot a quick glance outside, she saw they were nearing their destination. "Here's where I grew up," she said, more quietly. "Not far now."

This part of Tolin had changed little since she had left. It was easy to imagine herself a child again, traveling through the dull streets, staring up at the great gray buildings that squatted like monsters and peered with malice through half-shuttered windows at those who passed. She had been afraid the edifices contained malevolent spirits that might attack her, sensing that she was the flawed daughter of the Atenel family. They had prowled through her frequent nightmares, squeezing into alleys and rooms where they could not possibly fit. In those dreams, the windows had teeth.

Even the buildings were dwarfed by the twisting peaks of the Dragon Mountains which rose just beyond Tolin's border, hands of stone stretching toward the stars. Traedis could just glimpse them from the street. Sometimes clouds lowered over the summits, filtering the sun and turning the peaks amethyst or crimson or some hue of fluid light that had no name. Rarely, dragons could be seen flying overhead, though Traedis herself had never been able to tell if she saw one of the great creatures distantly, or whether she was watching some massive bird riding the wind above Tolin.

"This is as near the mountains as Kaelennar is," Ruth said thoughtfully. "What does that border feel like to your *falmyros*?"

"'It itches." Traedis reached to scratch the back of her hand, as if the *falmyros* was part of her flesh as well as her spirit. In some ways, it was.

Ruth raised an amused eyebrow.

Traedis leaned back in the carriage to compose herself for seeing her mother. She was not the child who had left. Calling upon the poise learned in the city of Kaelennar, where she had reinvented herself, she firmed her chin and straightened her spine. She was a trained bard now, and words should come easily to her. She should not have to stand, unable to speak, while her mother berated her for using the wrong-colored thread in a sampler, or for practicing harpsong when she ought to have been doing her lessons. She had nothing to prove now.

The gnawing sensation in the pit of her stomach told her otherwise. Regardless of Traedis being a bard and a king, she knew her mother could quell her with a single stern look.

As they reached the quadrant where the Atenel estate lay, Traedis felt the years peel back, exposing the lonely child within. Here was where she had learned to play harp, where she had read forbidden books and dreamed of a future outside of Tolin's walls. It was to here she now returned, once a deserter, now its king. Her two identities created dissonance, a pair of clashing notes played together.

The carriage passed through tall wrought-iron gates and into the front courtyard. The house itself was massive and ancient; it had stood in this place since the founding of Tolin. The main structure was gray granite, with large double doors of centuries-old oak. Over time, the family had added on, and it now sported an east and west wing, both somewhat smaller than the central edifice. Despite the solidity of its construction, it had an odd grace born of simplicity and austere design. Neat rosebushes and hedges of mountain laurel, now dormant for winter, gave a ghostly effect to the house's sharp lines and angles, though in summer they softened and brightened the estate.

They were ushered into the house by the steward himself, a graying man with a blade of a nose whom Traedis remembered from her childhood. He was stiffly and faultlessly polite, but still managed to make her feel as if she were a scruffy youngster with mud on her shoes. She even glanced at her toes just to make sure.

The steward showed them to a sitting room elegantly appointed with silk-upholstered cherrywood furniture. Traedis sat down, setting her harp case beside her. One of the chairs was the perfect height for Ruth; Traedis, knowing this room did not normally contain such a chair, took note. Somehow, her mother knew who was visiting, and had ordered it to be added. Someone was telling tales. Ruth, who did not know, took her seat.

A maidservant promptly brought a platter of delicacies from the kitchen – small cakes, finger sausages, and wedges of fine cheese – and placed it on the table between them. Another hustled in after her, bearing a teapot, cups, and saucers with a simple pattern of blue birds. Before they had time to reach for anything, Traedis' mother entered.

Mitheira Atenel had changed little; a few more lines at the corners of her eyes, and her lips were thinner than Traedis remembered, but no gray streaked the red-gold of her hair, and her heart-shaped face and features still held the sculpted beauty of an artist's masterwork. Traedis had been told she looked like her mother – the same heart-shaped face, the same wide, long-lashed eyes – though her chin was smaller and more pointed, her eyes green, and her long curls more red than gold.

Mitheira stood for a moment, watching, her arms at her sides. "Traedis," she said in the cold tone that meant Traedis had done something very wrong indeed. "You have finally come to see me."

Heat rushed to Traedis' face. "Mother." She put down the teapot, rose, and faced Mitheira, who topped her by four finger's span; Traedis had remembered her as taller. "I am sorry I didn't come to you immediately – I had to deal with the damage to the City, and to accustom myself to the *falmyros*..." Her voice trailed off as she watched her mother's expressionless face. She continued, "I should have come to see you days ago."

"You should." Mitheira seated herself in the chair across from Traedis, who sat back down and looked at her, chest aching, remembering how exacting her mother could be. *You'll never be good enough*, said her own internal voice in her mother's tone.

"This is my friend, Mistress Ruth," Traedis said, her voice roughening as she spoke.

Ruth rose, bowed, and re-seated herself. "Greetings, Lady Atenel," she said cheerfully.

Mitheira inclined her head. "Greetings, Mistress Ruth. I hope you do not find my hospitality lacking." She poured tea for the three of them, as coolly as if she had strangers to tea every afternoon. Though Mitheira spoke graciously, Traedis knew that her mother was unlikely to be pleased at the friendship between an outsider and her daughter.

Reaching for a cake, Traedis looked down, and nearly dropped it. It was a sun cake, a cinnamon and honey confection stamped with a face, usually served at the year's turning. It had a special meaning for Traedis. Each year during her imprisonment, she had received two such cakes at Midwinter's; the only luxury she was given in an entire year's span. She felt momentarily unsteady; those cakes had come from her mother. She had suspected it, but had hardly dared to hope. Whether it had been sent out of duty or out of kindness Traedis did not know.

"Thank you for your welcome," Ruth responded to Mitheira. Traedis could not detect any obvious irony in her friend's words. "I'm sure your hospitality will be lovely."

Mitheira smiled graciously.

"Mother. It's good to see you," Traedis began again, forcing her voice through the slight roughness which had surfaced in her speech. The catch in her throat distressed her, reminding her that she was more vulnerable than she had thought. No matter what had transpired in the previous six years, she could not help being a child here in this place.

Mitheira sat straight-backed in her chair, regarding Traedis unfavorably. Traedis felt the silence stretch between them like a plain covered with flood waters. A step made toward her mother through the dangerous gulf now might well drown her in bitter recriminations. At least Traedis could let her mother be the one to navigate the waters.

Finally Mitheira said, "I suppose it was more than I could expect, that you would consider your mother as soon as you were free to go where you chose. But then, you hardly considered me six years ago when you ran away. That was a terrible blow to your father. Of course you took no thought for him."

The fight between Traedis and her father had precipitated her flight from the City. *If you were to fall into a lake and drown, I wouldn't grieve*, he had told her. She wondered if her mother knew the full story of what they had said to each other. If Traedis' flight had been a blow to her father it was to his pride, not to his feelings.

That was the last time she had ever spoken to him; he had died of a heart attack only months after Traedis' escape.

"I had no choice," she said softly. Ruth shifted in her seat, but did not speak; Traedis thanked the four gods that her friend was there. The brunaidhi woman's presence was a welcome reminder that the Atenel family did not rule over the four corners of the world.

"You were always one for excuses," Mitheira said sharply. "While your father lay dying, you were gadding about in Telardur. I hope you have taken sufficient thought since to the pain you caused Linden and me when you ran away. He was terribly worried about you, a young girl all alone in a strange country. How could you have done that to him? How could you have done that to *me*?"

With shock, Traedis realized that her mother was truly upset. The thought had never before crossed her mind that her family had been anything but relieved to find her gone, a problem and a burden removed from their shoulders. Traedis squared her shoulders, as if against a gale, and lifted her eyes to meet her mother's gaze.

"I didn't see anything else I could do," she said simply. It was the truth; the City would have crushed her if she had stayed. Remaining would have meant either marriage to a man determined to control her, or death at the hands of the City, when they had decided that she was a liability. Only her father's position as Council member had kept her safe long enough for her to flee.

They were interrupted by entrance of the steward, who stood quietly to be noticed by his mistress.

Mitheira looked up sharply. "What is it, Baldus?" she asked, far more mildly than she had spoken to Traedis.

"Pardon the intrusion my lady, but your son Lord Daymet is here and wishes to see you." The steward's movement was formal but not stiff; Traedis knew that he was her mother's most valued servant. "I thought perhaps that you might wish me to show him in."

"You were quite right," said Mitheira. "Do so directly, and inform him that his sister, Lady Traedis, is here as well."

"Very well, my lady." The steward bowed again and exited.

Suspiciously, Traedis looked at her mother. Mitheira did not appear to be surprised. It was an orchestrated plan, then; when Traedis finally came, Daymet would join them, supporting Mitheira. Traedis wondered if Vandeyr were involved in this scheme as well. It was not like her straightforward style, but she was quite capable of being subtle when she chose. And just now, Traedis trusted none of her relatives.

Traedis barely had time to steel herself for the new encounter before Baldus returned with Traedis' brother Daymet: the second of her three brothers, and the one she feared most. She had seen him more recently than most of her family. He had been the contract lawyer who had hired Traedis out of the City to pursue a quest that had ultimately led to the death of the Storm Eagle. Like their mother, Daymet had red-gold hair, but his eyes were the same green as shone in Traedis' face, and he shared the Atenel slightness.

He looked around as if assessing a battlefield, then went to Traedis and kissed her on the cheek. For a moment, superimposed over the present, Traedis saw her brother, somewhat younger, but still much older than she, as he slid her braid over a nail in a back hallway, where she stayed until the servants heard her shouting. Her cheeks flamed at the memory; Daymet knew exactly how to humiliate her, and was not averse to doing it.

"Sister," Daymet said mildly. "It is good to see you looking so well." Traedis cringed inwardly at his proximity, but feared to display discomfort lest Daymet seize on it like a cat before potential prey.

She was not sure if he had made a pointed reference to the last time they had met, but he might well have. She had been half-wild with even the limited freedom that the City allowed her after binding her with oaths that the gods would enforce, were she to break them. She had neither looked nor acted her best.

"…it's good to see you." The belated politeness stumbled from her lips, a lie she could not avoid unless she were to anger both her mother and brother. Her pulse beat in a staccato rhythm. Daymet looked at her just long enough to convey that he knew her thoughts before turning toward Mitheira.

Giving their mother the same kiss he had given Traedis, Daymet said, "Mother, it's always good to see you." He nodded to Ruth. "Mistress Ruth, greetings."

Ruth's eyes narrowed, but she nodded in return. "Lord Daymet."

As her brother seated himself on the settee, Traedis braced herself for words that would bite far worse than any animal's savagery. "Daymet," she said, though her voice caught on the name. "You also look well."

Daymet smiled warmly; Traedis could feel the sheer force of it tempting her to lower her guard and trust him. "I am well," he said. "The troubles which have of late befallen the City have fortunately passed me by. I count myself lucky that I was neither killed nor injured following the Storm Eagle's death." Though he spoke with no particular emphasis, Traedis wondered if his words were intended to sting.

If he meant nothing more than he seemed to – a premise which Traedis was unwilling to accept, given his skill with words – then he was being remarkably cordial to a sister whom he had seldom regarded with anything but disdain. Traedis liked that idea less than the idea of Daymet needling her. Her muscles surreptitiously tensed, as if she waited for a clandestine attack.

Daymet poured himself a cup of tea and leaned back in his seat. "Our family has been fortunate in many respects. Lang and Alluve sustained some minor damage to their home, but nothing serious, though I understand that Gavaya was frantic over the disarray in the City library."

Disconcerted by her brother's subtle goading, Traedis heard a rush of blood in her ears as her pulse quickened, She tried to stop it by breathing deeply and evenly as she had been taught. Gradually, the sound ebbed, though she still felt lightheaded. She touched her harp case, though it was closed; a calming melody threaded its way into the back of her mind.

She knew, though she had no proof, that Daymet had some intention toward her besides goodwill or even simple malice. But she had never managed to follow the intricacies of her brother's labyrinthine mind, and she feared the consequences of her own straightforward thinking. She stared at him blankly, unable to formulate any questions which did not highlight the fact that she taken his career when she recalled the assassins. With no more assassination contracts, there would be no more need of contract negotiators.

Daymet looked at her guilelessly and said, "The family has grown since you left home. Otenemar married Kai Desivel – do you remember her? She was about your age or a little older. They have two daughters now. Lang and Alluve have two daughters and a son, though you know about the eldest – Callivare was born before you left the City, I believe." He rested an enigmatic gaze on her. "I have not been so fortunate as to find someone so suited to me, but my work has kept me satisfied."

Traedis swallowed a bite of sun cake and focused her mind on anticipating his angle of attack. "You haven't married?"

"No," Daymet told her pleasantly. "I have had my work.' He took another sip of tea.

An awkward silence settled over the room. Daymet appeared at ease, but Traedis fidgeted covertly and tried to think of something else to say which would not lead her to discuss why Daymet no longer had his work. Ruth gave her an encouraging smile, but maintained a prudent silence.

Mitheira, herself adept at hidden meanings and innocent-sounding barbs, frowned at Traedis. "Though I would be very happy if your brother married and gave me more grandchildren, he has been serving the City, and I cannot fault him for that."

Traedis cringed inwardly, reminded of her childhood in this house. Powerlessness and guilt were her oldest enemies; they had followed her constantly in her youth. How could she still feel them so keenly when the *falmyros* danced in her blood? The land loved her: was that not enough? But it was not. Somewhere in a small pocket of her heart, Traedis had tucked the hope that the kingship would make her family approve of her. Now that hope shriveled into oblivion as she sat under the critical scrutiny of her mother and brother.

Daymet smiled his brilliant smile at her, the one which could convince a man that he could draw fire from a well. "And now that you are king, Traedis, what do you intend to do? I understand that your rule is very new, but I'm sure you will soon come to understand what the City requires of you." The slight emphasis on his last words struck Traedis as a well-veiled threat; intentional, certainly. Her brother always said exactly what he meant others to hear.

"If there is anything I can do to assist you in your new responsibilities, I hope you will call upon me, Traedis," he continued with studied gentleness. His message was quite clear; he did not intend to let her pursue the course she had begun by halting the assassinations. Traedis was not sure whether he could prevent her, but he had never been one to make idle threats. He had great influence in Tolin, and the approval of the family. Traedis had neither.

"It's good to see families getting along." Ruth smiled at him innocently over her cup of tea, looking more like someone's maiden aunt than the competent warrior she was. Daymet shot her a sharp glance and returned his attention to Traedis.

"Thank you, Daymet," Traedis forced from a throat tightening with fear. She was surprised how natural her words sounded. "I'll let you know if there is anything you can do." For once the words came out as she had meant them to sound, a cool dismissal.

Daymet's eyebrows raised fractionally in surprise. She had

learned something in her years in Kaelennar, then. If nothing else, her poise and outward confidence had grown despite what she felt inside. But Daymet had never known the Traedis who had aided Harfast, the Lord of Winter and fought the powerful and god-maddened Wingblade. Since Traedis had fled Tolin, she had walked with dragons and Powers, and had been possessed by Kyaan, the god of air.

She had also spent four long years isolated in a prison cell, fighting for her will and sanity. The woman who had emerged from that cell was not the same one who had entered it; she had learned truths about herself which she could never put aside. Daymet spoke to the child who had left, but it was a woman who faced him now.

Daymet gave her a long, probing stare. Then he nodded slightly and re-pasted the smile on his face, not noticeably flatter than before. "I look forward to serving you," he said without apparent irony. He put down his cup and rose to his feet. "Mother, I beg you to excuse me, but I have many things to do today. Traedis, it has been a pleasure." As he exited, Traedis felt the hairs on the back of her neck prickle. She had accepted his gauntlet, though she did not feel competent to fight back against the brother who had always bested her.

Daymet had declared himself an enemy. And this was a fight Traedis must win.

Chapter Three
Diplomacy

It was midmorning in the religious district, where churches and chapels vied for a patch of earth, their forms more varied than any other structures in Tolin. The sun had just scaled the mountains, sending the first flood of day into lamplit streets. Traedis had just finished a conference with Esduin Anliares, the Elder of the Meda church; now she was riding back to the palace to meet Ruth for lunch. Vandeyr and three palace guards accompanied her, all of them sporting highly visible swords.

A vague sense of disquiet churned in Traedis' belly, strengthening as she moved westward. Abruptly, a twitch in her *falmyros* alerted her as sharply as if someone had pinched her hard. Immediately, she pulled her horse to a stop.

Vandeyr joined her, scanning the streets around them. "What is it?" she asked tensely.

"Something's wrong," Traedis told her, trying to isolate the sensation, which was growing more intense as she directed her attention to it. Tolin seemed etched on her body, a map made of nerves and fine hairs and skin. "The western quarter, I think."

"What sort of wrong?" One of Vandeyr's hands dropped to her sword.

Traedis concentrated, trying to understand what the land was telling her. "Something's about to happen. Something is falling, and it shouldn't fall." She squeezed her eyes shut. "Something massive."

"Can you be more specific?" Vandeyr asked. Her mount snorted and whickered.

"I can find it. I'm almost sure." Opening her eyes, Traedis pressed a leg to her horse's side, angling it toward a different street. "The disturbance isn't far. I don't know where it is when I think about it, but I can lead you there."

"Don't go too fast." Vandeyr stayed beside Traedis, while the other three guards turned to follow. "I don't want you riding into an ambush."

"There's no ambush," said Traedis, knowing in that instant she was right. She had not known a moment before, but her *falmyros* was rising around her, clothing her in a thousand sensations she could not consciously differentiate.

She followed the mountain down its slope, knowledge crystallizing in her mind as the land sang its silent plea. She ignored the grime-splashed snow, the lamplighters dousing streetlights, the dripping ice hanging like daggers from every eave. Lives were at stake, she was sure of it.

As she neared the source of the disturbance, a building broke into sight. A behemoth of stone, it had once been a dwelling that supported several families, but its unlucky downhill location had caught some of the remnants of the Council Hall during its collapse. Cracks in its walls and a shifting foundation made it unstable. Now workers were razing it; they climbed along its roof line or labored on the ground to break up shorter walls with heavy tools. Some were faldrim sent by Kenrydh to assist in Tolin's reconstruction.

A crowd of watchers, perhaps fifty or more, had gathered, staring at the wreck with the numbness of those who had lost too much. A child darted toward it, and was hastily collared by a man in a tattered cloak; a woman wept tears that froze as they trickled down her face.

Another shiver in the *falmyros* signaled the danger. "Roof's going!" Traedis shouted, pitching her voice high and clear so that her voice would carry. "Get back!" A few of the crowd took up the cry, though they, too, were fanning away from the dangerous jumble of breaking stone.

Most of the crew spun around to see the danger; those on the ground scattered, leaping over already-fallen debris. The ones on top scrabbled for purchase, anchoring themselves against the sturdiest parts of what still stood. Only one man, farthest from safety, still wielded his pickaxe as if he had heard nothing.

In a sudden torrent of slate, wood, mortar, and nails, the roof crumpled like paper, plunging inward with a waterfall's roar. The ground trembled underfoot, and the horses whinnied, high and frightened. Traedis' mount rolled its eyes and shied.

Scanning the still-settling building, Traedis saw that the pickaxe wielder was gone. She dismounted, tossing the reins to Vandeyr, who was attempting to calm her horse. Dashing forward, Traedis headed for the place the man had fallen.

Vandeyr was only a step or two behind her. Traedis reached the rubble, her hood flying back to show her long, copper braid.

"Traitor!" someone called out from behind her.

Vandeyr's footsteps slowed, but Traedis was paying little attention. She knew where the man was as surely as if he were a fingernail or a scar. *Still alive*, she told herself, measuring her breath so she would not run short and be no good to anyone.

Somewhere between clambering over blocks of stone and ducking under fallen timber, her cloak caught; she shrugged it off and pressed on. Others were swarming into the wreck, but they were looking in the wrong place. She could hear muffled groans coming from the interior.

There: two beams had fallen crosswise, leaving a small pocket of safety where the man lay. Grime and dust covered him, making him almost blend into the ruined interior. He had not escaped without injury; a beam lay across his thighs, holding him in place. Traedis grabbed the pickaxe and moved to pry at the wood that trapped him.

A strong hand caught her arm. As Traedis swiveled to fend off an attack, Vandeyr said, "It's me! Don't try to cut him loose – Mintei is going for a healer. When limbs are crushed and then freed, it can kill."

Traedis filtered the information through a haze of fizzing energy before she could bring herself to lower her arms.

"We know where he is now, and we'll get someone in fast. You saved lives, Trae."

The strength which rushed through Traedis began to ebb swiftly, wringing her out like a sponge. She nodded, letting

Vandeyr help her out of the ruins of the once sturdy dwelling. They passed several people whom Vandeyr directed to the injured worker, while giving quick but firm instructions about waiting for the healer.

It took longer to get out than to get in. By the time they had extricated themselves, Traedis could barely stand, too full of her body's reaction to the disaster.

At first, she did not notice that Vandeyr was frowning. It was not at her; Traedis knew what that scowl looked like. Then she began to hear the calls from the people who still milled in the street.

"You call yourself king? King of Traitors!"

"Atenel bitch! That was our home!"

"This is getting ugly." Vandeyr put a hand on Traedis' shoulder. "We should leave. Unless there's anything else wrong?"

Traedis reached back into her *falmyros*, not sure what it could tell her. A wisp of something on the wall caught her notice, a hairline distraction, but her knowledge of the land was so new that she was not sure how to clarify the sensation. She decided to worry about it later; there was no great urgency in the land's draw.

Her ears were assaulted by more yells. "Filthy foreigners! Get out of our city, and take your cursed tools with you!"

Traedis looked around; the faldren workers stood in a tight knot, facing in all directions. A man threw a snowball at the nearest, a stout woman holding a hammer. She ducked, and the missile slammed into stone, shattering to display the rock inside the snow.

"We have to fix this," Traedis said. She gathered the threads of her kingship and strode out to confront the citizens who seemed dangerously close to rioting.

"Pouring oil on fire," Vandeyr muttered, hastening after her with a drawn sword.

"Folk of Tolin," Traedis shouted, projecting her voice to carry as far as possible. "Don't blame the ones who have traveled here to help us! Your anger is with me! I swear that I will see your home rebuilt, and those of your family and friends."

No one seemed pacified.

"May the gods witness my oath!" she called in a voice that rang out like a pealing bell. The *falmyros* stirred within Traedis; faraway thunder rumbled.

That seemed to do it. Just as the healer arrived, the mood of the crowd shifted. They broke apart into separate groups that either moved in to help the workers or retreated down the snow-covered alleys.

"I can't believe that worked," Vandeyr said. "Let's get out of here."

Traedis opened the safe embedded in her office wall, while Ruth kept guard outside in the hallway. Traedis took out a large, uncut ruby, hefting the rough weight in her hand. Of the tasks she was dreading, this was one of the foremost, but also the most important. The gem would link her to the oak and ruby crown of

King Kenrydh, ruler of the surrounding country of Telardur, enabling them to talk through the enormous distance between Faldrohaven and Tolin.

Though King Kenrydh had been helpful and supportive of Traedis' new reign, she was aware, like an irritation in her skin, of the *falmyros* of Telardur. That land surrounded Tolin on three sides, dwarfing her country both in size and population.

She could not continue to wait. As king of Tolin, she was responsible before the gods for governing as best she could, and that included the hard tasks. Kenrydh would want concessions from her, and she was unsure of what she was willing to concede. Some might cost her in personal terms. Still, she must do what was right.

Looking into the heart of the ruby, clouded with flaws and impurities, she let her vision blur, waiting for a figure to resolve out of minerals and light. A red haze rose and surrounded her inner vision, pulling her into harmony with Kenrydh's ancient crown. The light gathered his form and pulled it into the shape of a faldren man, young for his kind, with a neatly trimmed dark-honey beard and shrewd brown eyes. Taller than most faldrim, he also had the wide breadth of chest and shoulder that characterized his people. He seemed to be speaking to someone, but he immediately stopped and looked toward her.

"King Traedis," he said abstractedly. "A moment, please."

She nodded and waited as he spoke a few more words to an unseen presence. Then he refocused on her face. "Greeting, King Traedis," he said in a resonant voice with the pleasant rolling accent of his native tongue. "I am most glad to see you. How fares your city?"

He had sent engineers and supplies to aid Tolin immediately after Traedis had received the *falmyros*; she knew that his assistance was born of goodwill and not intended to obligate her. Still, she *felt* obligated as well as intimidated; the City had not depended on the charity of others in all its two-thousand-year history.

"Greetings, King Kenrydh," she replied. "Your help has been invaluable. Though the destruction is not as widespread as it might have been, it is quite enough, and it will take us some time to properly rebuild. Luckily, it did not touch all parts of the City equally."

Kenrydh nodded. "There are a few matters I want to discuss with you." He glanced over his shoulder at someone Traedis could not see. "Yes, of course." Turning his attention back to Traedis, he continued, "No doubt you can guess what some of them are. I hold you as an ally, and consider that we are likely to have at least some meeting of the minds on these matters."

Traedis felt her stomach clench. They might have a meeting of the minds in a personal sense, but she was now responsible for all her people, and her notion of their welfare might differ from what he wanted. She nodded slowly, and temporized, "I think it likely that we will agree on many things."

"Very good." Kenrydh gave her a searching glance. "I recognize your sovereignty, and hold it in high regard, King

Traedis. There are two specific subjects I want to discuss. The first and most important is that if we are to have any relations between our two nations, the assassinations must stop."

Traedis felt her jaw unclench; Kenrydh's declaration was expected but not certain. His first request at least, was easy. She nodded. "I have already ended them. All of the assassins have been recalled, and Tolin will no longer be that city."

The expression on Kenrydh's face was guarded, but lines smoothed around his mouth, and the skin of his cheeks loosened fractionally. "I am most glad to hear it. That lifts a burden from my heart." Though he spoke formally, there was a warmth in his voice that heartened Traedis.

"What is the other matter?" She knew what it was; too much blood had been spilled by the City for him to overlook simply because Tolin had a new ruler. There would be reparations to make. Some of those reparations might be a point of disagreement between the two nations.

Still, she must follow her conscience, not what was expedient. Her head began to ache as she waited for the answer.

Kenrydh's own tone was calm and steady; Traedis could not tell if it was surety of power, or whether it was simply long practice in the art of rulership. Some of both, most likely. "For the whole of my reign, and for my father's, the high faldrim have demanded redress for Tolin's crimes. We have received no satisfaction. I ask you now, as one whom I believe will heed me, to give me redress for your city's crimes."

This was the question she had been dreading. Gathering her courage, Traedis said, "What redress do you desire?" She put a hand on Rose as if the harp were a touchstone.

"I do not ask for the heads of all the assassins," he said, somewhat wryly. "That would be unreasonable." Traedis' mind flicked to Vandeyr, and tempered relief flowed through her. "Still, there have been some assassinations that were so heinous and so bold, that I must ask you for the perpetrators, that I may bring the justice of Telardur to bear upon them."

Carefully choosing her words, Traedis responded, "I will hear your requests, and take them under advisement." She had no intention of committing herself to any action until she knew what — and who — was involved. Extradition was not unreasonable, given the circumstances. "Please tell me for which actions you desire reparation."

Kenrydh drew his brows together and Traedis noticed that the muscles of one hand knotted slightly. "First among them is the poisoning of the Duke of Mirrei with an oyster made of *dragonsilver*," he said. There was gravel in his voice. "There is also the murder of my seneschal two years ago." He continued with a list of significant assassinations which Tolin had carried out in Telardur in the recent past. Traedis recognized many of them; her family had discussed some over the dinner table.

She swiftly took a piece of paper and uncapped her ink bottle; carefully she noted each victim, the details of the crimes, and the actors involved. This was not strictly necessary; the City's records were still intact, though the Council Chambers had been completely destroyed by Toledru. Copies were always carefully preserved in different locations so they could not be lost.

As Kenrydh's litany came to an end, Traedis swallowed, hoping that he would accept what she offered, since his requests were both reasonable and few. "I intend to examine the records and make my own decisions," she told him, her voice steadier than her pulse. "First, I will give you names of your subjects who contracted with us. I will determine whom among my people I consider to be truly responsible for each crime, and will deliver them over to you. I will also give you a list of those whom I cannot reach – many fled Tolin during Toledru's rising."

What she did not say, but which lay between them, unspoken, were the words, *"Many fled because they feared me."* And justly: her offer of redress to Kenrydh was real.

Kenrydh frowned, but thoughtfully, rather than in irritation. "Thank you, King Traedis. I am indebted to your goodwill."

"And I to yours." Traedis was genuinely grateful; Telardur could crush Tolin if Kenrydh chose. He would have done so many years ago if it the City had not been an immutable tradition. She did not want his confidence in her to be misplaced.

Memory of another matter teased at her. Kenrydh was to be wed at the turning of the year. "I trust your betrothed is well?" she asked. "How go the plans for your wedding?"

Kenrydh's eyebrows relaxed. "They go well. Duinedh is having a wonderful time with them. On my own account, I will be happier when it is over." He gave her a boyish grin before becoming the grave king again. "You will, of course, receive an invitation."

Traedis smiled. "I am most honored, but would be impolitic for me to attend – many will be suspicious of Tolin for far longer than it takes to settle on terms of peace."

"I expected you to say that," Kenrydh said, "but the offer is real. If you desire to come, you are welcome."

Warmed throughout by his words, Traedis nodded. "Thank you," she said. "I wish the both of you a long and happy marriage."

"Thank you." The faldro adjusted his crown. "I will speak with you later about other terms. May your reign continue as propitiously as it has begun."

"I sincerely hope so." Traedis felt simultaneously anxious and relieved; the narrow path might be negotiated after all. "Farewell, Your Majesty."

"Farewell, King Traedis." The red haze dissipated, leaving Traedis blinking at the green afterimage in her vision.

She stowed the ruby carefully in the safe where she kept it. Sitting down, she put her head in her hands, shaking as the import of Kenrydh's words struck home. She would have to turn over every person she determined to be at fault for those assassinations if she could. Some of them had fled the City.

Some of them were certain to be from her family.

Traedis looked out of the tall window which allowed light into the reception chamber. Costly glass made up all the palace windows, heavily spelled against breakage. It was too cold to open them, and the early edge of winter had rimed the surface with a lacy tracing of frost.

She could still see into the garden outside. Draped with climbing roses, now browned with winter, the garden wore a veil of white through which she could see leafless brambles, thorned with wicked needles. Bushes and bare stalks, thumb-deep in mulch, flanked carefully laid paths which gardeners had cleared for the season. To Traedis, it was more restful than dreary, a reminder that life could subsist beneath the soil, returning when the World Hare brought the sun back to warm the earth.

The massing clouds above suggested more snow would fall soon. It tumbled frequently from the sky at this elevation, often hiding the peaks of the Dragon Mountains in sheets so white it was hard to tell earth from sky. Traedis let her thoughts rest briefly on the Heart of Winter, the land ruled by winter's lord, Harfast. She had become a part of it, and some of her remained there, no matter where else she might be; her connection to winter was as strong in its way as her tie to the City. She loved Winter's Heart, but it was not a place she could stay without her own heart growing colder than the lances of ice which now hung from the palace eaves.

She shook her head and focused her attention inside, where she waited for the first ambassadors to Tolin. It was a little surprising those were from the n'korreld, a people known for their clannishness and distrust of outsiders. Traedis had chosen to receive them in the Brocade Room, so named for the heavy, gold-threaded cloth that covered all the furnishings and hung from the windows. Now she sat, strategically dressed in a brocade gown that complemented the room's décor. She had braided her hair into a crown and wore a simple gold circlet, intended to give the impression that she was a powerful, competent ruler.

Behind her, she could hear Vandeyr shift her weight, though the sound was barely audible in the silent chamber. A moment later, the door opened, letting in pages, servants, and Traedis' steward, followed by the karreldish ambassador and his people. Vandeyr's guards brought up the rear, wearing new livery both similar and distinct from that worn by old Tolin's guard. The gray Storm Eagle still soared against the surcoat, but he had taken on a silvery cast and flew against a background of Atenel blue.

The visiting party numbered fifteen. Karreldish guards came first, bowing to Traedis. These were all men, but the rest were a mix of men and women. They were very short, half the height of most humans; they had wiry builds and thick hair, and their skin varied between the colors of sand and rich loam. They wore long, brightly patterned tunics embroidered in complex figures and made of a shiny fabric Traedis could not identify.

In the center was a young man, tall for a karreld, perhaps chest-height to Traedis. His skin was the rich red brown of sandstone, his hair and eyes the surprisingly pleasant hue of fresh mud. The tunic he wore hung to his knees and was embroidered with gold threads, iridescent shells, and tiny but perfect pearls that were sewn into the shiny material with stitches almost too small to see. This was obviously a man of rank.

"King Traedis," her steward said as the door snicked shut. "I present to you Prince Atchûk, son of Thane Bi'ia of the n'korreld. Prince Atchûk, King Traedis of Tolin."

Prince Atchûk bowed respectfully as Traedis rose to greet him. She motioned him to a small, elegant chair, sized for the comfort of the diminutive frames of the n'korreld people. Delicacies, both human and karreldish, had been set on low tables for the convenience of the guests.

"Prince Atchûk," said Traedis. "I did not expect one of your rank to be chosen as ambassador to Tolin. You are most welcome, as are your people, now that Tolin is newly opened to the world."

The young karreld laughed. "Please, King Traedis, don't hold my rank against me. As a second son I'm more of a spare than anything, and I have a younger brother, so I'm not even the only leftover. My elder brother Darg is my father's successor; I have to find other things to occupy me than statecraft. When Darg suggested sending someone, I begged for the opportunity. Travel *and* duty? How can that be dull?" He grinned at her, and Traedis found herself smiling back. She liked this brash prince with his blunt manner of speaking. She did not, however, miss his sharp gaze, which traveled around the room, seeming to assess everything around him.

"Please, take some refreshment." She gestured to the table. "What would you like to drink? And would you care for some mushrooms-and-grubs?"

"Oh, that sounds delightful." A servant supplied him with a plate, and the young man spooned out some of the mushroom-and-grub mixture. He followed it with a pair of blueberry cakes sprinkled with rare nutmeg imported from Shaori lands far to the south. "That looks wonderful. Thank you." He took a forkful of cake, his expression blissful. "Ah, this is good." He ate several mouthfuls before putting his dish down.

A few pleasantries later, Atchûk's expression grew serious. "I will admit to you, King Traedis, that my father and brother wish me to watch you and determine if you are indeed sincere in the changes you are making in Tolin. I agreed to their request on the condition that I did not have to lie about what I was doing here. The City of Assassins has cost us many, and should you prove deceitful, we will exact our own retribution." He took a swallow of ale. "I'm personally hopeful. I think the catastrophe that has upended your city truly does spell the end of the old regime."

A warmth rose in Traedis' chest. "Thank you, Prince Atchûk."

"Given what I've told you, I don't expect you to quarter us in the palace." The young karreld flashed a brilliant smile. "If we must stay for long, we're prepared to pay our way."

"Don't be foolish," Traedis responded. "Hospitality demands better. And I doubt I will find your presence burdensome."

"You don't know how much I eat," Atchûk said, taking another cake.

"I will be honest with you in return." Traedis met the karreld's deep brown eyes. "Many of my people are unhappy with my rule, and those who are not outright hostile are wary of my judgement."

"That means you're doing it right." Licking crumbs from his finger, Atchûk gave her a wry look. "Do you think my father's rulings are always popular? Or King Kenrydh's? I can promise that if everyone is happy with you, they simply don't know what you're up to."

Traedis found herself giving an amused snort. Atchûk was likely to keep the palace lively. But now there was the question of reparations. Abandoning all humor, she fixed a steady gaze on the karreld. "Are there demands your father has for me? I know that Tolin has been anathema in every decent country for centuries, and though Haven and Telardur have been generous with me, many will be loath to trust us."

Atchûk nodded. "You are as direct as one of us – I find that particularly refreshing, considering how many sabers of twisted meanings your people fence with. We were treated to a sample while your royal guard was making sure I wasn't here to assassinate, subvert, or marry you."

Traedis felt heat in her face, though she kept her expression calm.

"I'm most sorry if I embarrassed you!" Atchûk took another forkful of mushrooms-and-grubs before pointedly turning the conversation. "Your cook makes this better than most humans." He frowned. "King Traedis, if you have not had suitors beating down the palace door, you are in for a surprise. King's Consort is one of the most prized positions to those who want power."

"I have only been king for a few days," Traedis said weakly. She did not like the thought of an influx of suitors who wanted her position.

He smiled. "It will come. But if I'm any judge, and if my father's intelligence is correct, you aren't the sort of person to succumb to a pretty face with a tiger's mind."

It was alarming to think that other countries were studying her, but Traedis knew enough about intelligence work to understand it was the first thing any potential allies would do. After hiding in Kaelennar and being buried in a City cell, she was unaccustomed to being the focus of attention.

She was king of Tolin. She must adapt.

Traedis sat a little straighter, bracing her spine against the chair's back. "I am afraid you're right." She sighed. Then she squared her shoulders. "Now, what are your father's demands of Tolin?"

Chapter Four
Family

Traedis spent half the night going through the records before retiring to a restless sleep in the large, ornately carved bed that dominated her sleeping chamber. Dreams of striking wyverns and inky shadows that crawled from beneath Tolin's stone foundation assailed her. Beneath the night's visions, she felt a creeping uneasiness, as if something were *wrong*: as if the world itself had been knocked askew. The strings of Tolin were out of tune.

She awoke to a gray dawn, greasy tendrils of the images still clinging to her. Shaking off the night's malaise, she reminded herself that the visions were no more than phantoms born from her unsettled mind. Nightmares had invaded her sleep for as long as she could remember.

She had not yet finished her examinations of the records as she tried to meet the demands of both Kenrydh and Bi'ia. She was encouraged by her oldest brother Lang's lack of involvement in the more sordid assassinations the City had undertaken. In recent years he had taken a more strictly ethical stance, urging Tolin to accept fewer contracts that entangled them with the esch people to the south, whose culture and morals were abhorrent to more civilized people. He had also spoken forcefully against dealings with the Nightdance, the circle of the most powerful and evil demons in the world. He had not challenged Tolin's way of life, but that was hardly a strike against him; changing a system that had endured for almost two thousand years required the *falmyros*.

Traedis needed a break from the taxing search. If she could regain her old combat skills, it would keep her from being entirely dependent on others to protect her. Ruth might not always be there, and Vandeyr's motives were murky. Besides, the exertion would clear her mind and make it easier to resume her task later. Dressing in sturdy leathers, she ate a stale roll left from last night's dinner, snatched up her harp case, and headed out of her apartments.

She was joined by both Ruth and Vandeyr, who had obviously been waiting outside her rooms. Vandeyr wore her livery as smartly as noble finery; her boots were immaculately polished and her hair in perfect array. Traedis looked down at herself to see if she were presentable, feeling grubby and unkempt next to her sister. Self-consciously, she pulled a long copper hair from her sleeve and flicked it to the floor. Ruth gave her a quick grin.

"Practice yard?" Vandeyr asked, indicating the leathers.

Traedis nodded. "I need to get my form back."

"I'll spar with you and see what I need to drill you on." Vandeyr's boots clicked evenly on the floor as they headed for the main staircase that divided the upper and lower house. "You need to train with someone who knows what she's doing."

Halfway down the stairs, Vandeyr asked, "How many Atenels are on that list of yours?"

Traedis stopped in mid-step. A surge of fear crackled through her veins, and her vision sharpened as her body prepared for danger.

Ruth whipped around, her head turning toward Vandeyr.

"What?" Traedis said, as soon as she could manage a word.

"I'm not stupid, Traedis." Vandeyr's words sliced the air like daggers. "How many of us are you going to give to Kenrydh? One, two, three, or four?"

If Vandeyr were using Traedis' full name it meant that she was very angry indeed. The pulse in her throat beat like a kettledrum; her wrists ached with the force of her heartbeat. She did not believe that Vandeyr meant to harm her, but she could not be sure. Some kinds of betrayal might be beyond her sister's ability to forgive.

She bit at her lower lip. "I haven't decided yet."

"*How many*?" Vandeyr's anger was almost tangible. So was the threat implicit in her tone.

Ruth moved between Traedis and her sister, angling her body to take the brunt of an attack. Traedis laid a restraining hand on her shoulder. She would not let the brunaidh pay for her own lack of courage.

"No more than two," she said. "And one of those I'm not sure of."

"Gods." Vandeyr slapped the railing; Traedis started. "Uncle Cordelayne at the least. Is the other one me, Lang, or Daymet?"

"You wouldn't be here if it were you." Traedis blessed the control over her voice she had learned as a bard; it did not tremble at all.

"Lang or Daymet?" Vandeyr's expression was grim. She glowered at Traedis, her gaze intent and searching. Then Vandeyr gave a small nod. "Daymet," she confirmed.

"I don't know yet." Traedis was more afraid than she had been when her sister burst into her office. That Vandeyr she knew. This was a new Vandeyr: the assassin, not the confidante and unreachable paragon of her childhood.

"How could you?" Vandeyr's voice was cold. "How could you give over your own kin to that insufferably self-righteous faldro? Does family matter so little to you? What happened in those two years you spent in Telardur?"

Guilt coursed through her blood, but Traedis also felt the slow burn of real anger start in her belly. She welcomed it; Vandeyr's icy words were untrue and unfair. "Perhaps," she said hotly, "you should ask what happened to me during those four years in prison." Her family had not given her quarter then, but wished her to cede it to them now.

For one of the few times in her life, Traedis saw her words strike home in her sister's expression. Vandeyr dropped her gaze, and her entire frame drooped just enough that she seemed suddenly less threatening. "That was justified," she said, her words softer. "But revenging yourself on us isn't going to return those years to you."

"It's not a matter of revenge." Traedis doubted that Vandeyr would agree with her, but she would not allow herself to be intimidated into backing down. She was not the same girl Vandeyr had known either; she had reached maturity in Kaelennar, and had survived prison's solitary four-year trial. Most importantly, in that time she had gained faith in principles that had not been laid down by the City. "My other choices are worse."

Vandeyr grabbed onto the railing, the veins knotting in the back of her hand. "You say it's not a matter of revenge, but I think otherwise." She glowered. "I can see the situation at least as well as you. Probably better. Kenrydh isn't going to attack even if you refuse to grant his every whim. He's just happy that he's got the City in his pocket without having to spend his own resources on it."

Traedis set her chin and glared back at Vandeyr, determined to hold her position. "I am not 'in Kenrydh's pocket.' And I wouldn't underestimate him. I told you – he won't continue to allow us to continue as assassins. And he's not likely to sign a treaty unless we give him concessions."

"Fine," Vandeyr snapped back. "Grant him concessions. But don't treat your own uncle and brother as nothing more than bargaining points. They're your flesh and blood, Traedis! Doesn't that mean anything to you?"

Ruth held her position on the steps, her body taut and still.

Traedis clenched her hands together tightly, allowing the pain to help suppress a heated response; she must not let herself be baited. Vandeyr had no way of knowing how much Traedis still cared about her family – especially Cordelayne. She was thankful beyond belief that her uncle had fled Tolin so that she could not actually hand him over. And she loved Daymet, though she could not say why, except that he was her brother.

"It means more to me than I can express," Traedis finally

responded, in a measured, quiet tone. "But kin or no, they are responsible for crimes in Telardur, and I cannot exonerate them simply because they are family. That would not be justice, and I refuse to use my power to protect our family when I am not willing to grant the same to those of equal guilt."

"Your conscience again," Vandeyr said bitterly. "I hope your conscience comforts you if it gets either of them killed."

"Are you sure it's safe to spar with her?" Ruth asked quietly as Traedis headed into the long, narrow outbuilding where weapons were stored. Traedis allowed her eyes to adjust to the dim lighting while trying to think of how to respond to Ruth.

"She could hurt or kill me any time," Traedis finally said. "She's had ample opportunity. At this point, I think she'd rather defend my back and harangue me to my face than to harm me." She cocked a half-smile at her friend. "I don't intend to spar with live steel, either."

Racks of weapons occupied both sides of the room, working ones to the right, practice ones to the left. Approaching the latter, Traedis eyed the swords keenly as she decided which to try. She had once been well-trained in combat, as was every citizen of Tolin, but four years in prison had dulled her skills.

"Your sister could probably beat you to death with a blunted sword," Ruth responded. "But I see your point. Still, I don't trust her not to give you a few broken bones out of spite."

Traedis shook her head. "No. I expect her to give me a number of welts, but if she says she's going to train with me, she means just that. She's neither a liar, nor is she vindictive."

Ruth shrugged a little. "I'm still going to watch the two of you. I'll stay out of the way, but I want to be close by. Just in case."

"Thank you," Traedis said, warmed to the core.

She quickly selected a short sword off the rack, testing its heft and balance. The grip was good, but it was heavier than she thought it should be, probably because she had not been able to keep those muscles in training while in prison. She considered taking another, then reconsidered; working with a sword too light would not retrain her in the way she needed.

The prison guards had taken her on short daily walks inside to keep her healthy; she had also exercised as best she could within her cell, as a form of defiance against the sentence of life imprisonment that had entombed her in the City's bowels. Such activity had given her action against the crushing knowledge that her days would never change and that she would never again feel a lungful of cold winter wind, or see a bird cross the sky. She had filled her mind with music and her body with activity, refusing her fate in the only ways she could.

Now, in such a vulnerable position, she needed to regain her skills. She could not be sure that Ruth, or Vandeyr, or any of Vandeyr's newly recruited guards would be there when she most needed them. She must be prepared to defend herself. She hefted the blade and went out to the training ground.

The practice field was flat, covered with sand to cushion those who fell. Vandeyr was already there, carrying a blunted short sword of comparable length and weight to the one Traedis now wielded.

As Traedis clambered over the fence, she was surprised to see Atchûk perched atop it, surrounded by three karreldish guards with sour expressions. He waved to Traedis with boyish enthusiasm, his dark hair fanning back from a stiff mountain wind. Traedis suddenly felt lighter.

"Just a moment," she shouted at Vandeyr. She planted her sword blade first in the sand and gestured for Ruth to follow her.

"Prince Atchûk," she said when they were within speaking range. "Greetings. I hope you had a restful night." She ignored the bristling of his guards; they must have a difficult time trying to protect someone who was clearly willing to take risks in an unfamiliar country.

"I slept pleasantly," he said. "I don't know what geese you breed, but their down is delightful. I may end up taking home a goose or two when I return."

Traedis grinned. "I am happy to supply your geese needs, if it's feathers you're looking for, Your Highness." She stretched a hand toward the brunaidh. "I'd like you to meet Mistress Ruth, one of my oldest and best friends. Ruth, Prince Atchûk is here as the n'korreld ambassador. He will be staying at the palace for some time, and, I am glad to see, is already making a home for himself." She found herself comparing the two – the brunaidhi woman was the only person on the field smaller than the karrelds, and Atchûk had a slender solidity compared to Ruth's delicacy of form.

"I am honored to meet you," said the brunaidh. "I'm just Ruth. Don't bother with a title – I'm common born and bred, and not ashamed of it."

Atchûk's eyes gleamed with mischief. "Then you both can call me by my given name, as I may be royal, but I am also – you might say 'common as dirt.'"

Traedis raised an eyebrow, but he did not seem ready to elaborate on his cryptic statement. Shrugging, she said, "If I am to dispense with your title, it seems only right that you should call me Trae, which is how I am known to my friends." She felt a surprising kinship with him, given that they had only just met. It was an odd sensation, as if she spoke to a distant cousin for the first time.

"That suits me," the karreld said, ignoring the scowls of his entourage. "Ruth, would you like to scramble up here? I think this is the best vantage for those of our size."

Ruth climbed onto the fence and sat beside him, watching.

Traedis retrieved her weapon on the way to the field's center. There she stood, stance wide and at the ready.

"Let me see what you can do." Vandeyr beckoned her with one hand. "I want to get an idea of what we need to accomplish. Show me." She stood on the balls of her feet, sword carried lightly.

Traedis held her weapon with both hands. Her thighs and calves ached as she walked in a wary arc around her sister.

Vandeyr turned with her, showing no hint of difficulty.

Traedis made a complete circle before realizing that her sister wanted her to attack first. Trying to catch her off-guard, Traedis swung her sword in a quick upward cut designed to catch her opponent's exposed side. Without any apparent effort, Vandeyr blocked her sword, knocking Traedis' arm sideways. Vandeyr followed through with her sword's weight, swinging it skyward, then back down to give Traedis a hard thump on the hip. Traedis grunted in pain and tried not to lose her balance.

"That would have been enough to cripple you with live steel," Vandeyr told her in an even tone. "You lost focus. You should know how to counter better than that."

In fact, Traedis did; it was simply that she was too out of practice to do it properly. She stifled her reaction to the pain, forcing herself through it. She would have a bad bruise later, but that would not stop her from working as hard as she could to regain old skills.

She brought her sword overhand in a smooth strike at Vandeyr's shoulder. Vandeyr ducked, danced to the left, and slapped Traedis' midriff with the flat of her sword. An explosion of pain erupted from Traedis' side.

Vandeyr stopped and lowered her sword, pointing it toward the ground.

"You aren't ready for this." Vandeyr shook her head. "I shouldn't have started you out with a full-on match." She pursed her lips and looked Traedis up and down. "Your arm muscles are far too weak, and you don't have good tone in the muscles of your left leg." For a moment she tapped her fingers on her sword hilt. "Still, it's not as bad as I would expect from someone who was just released from prison."

"I did exercises." Traedis did not want to talk about any part of her experience with her sister, but Vandeyr needed to know what might be relevant. She surreptitiously patted her hip, trying to ascertain precisely how bad the damage was.

"That would explain it." Vandeyr stepped forward. "At the moment we don't have an armsmaster, and I'm not going to trust just anyone to get close to you with any kind of steel. I'm going to need to drill you before you're ready to spar. I need to get you used to falling again, and also give you sword exercises that will strengthen both your arms and legs. I don't think I want you practicing without me there, either – it's easy to overstrain when you're trying to get your skills back." Vandeyr glared at Traedis as if she had weakened herself purposefully in order be irritating. "We may as well start now. Just don't think you can get away with slacking like you're used to. This could mean life or death for you."

The unfairness of her comment nearly choked Traedis as words of protest crowded, unspoken, in her throat. She had never been lax in her arms lessons, and always performed well for Master Ylom. It had been years since she had even dodged even her academic tutor, who *had* often accused her of slacking; he had possessed a vicious temper and the full support of her father in disciplining Traedis however he saw fit.

Like plunging into an icy river, Traedis lost vision of the present as the past surged around her. Absolute darkness drowned her, and the rough walls of the hall closet hedged her round, a closing trap. The old panic rose up, its icy fingers grasping her by the throat, clutching at her heart, squeezing her stomach. She felt a cry rise to, but not exit from, her suddenly dry mouth.

"Though I suppose," Vandeyr said, unexpectedly next to her ear, "that you may have learned a thing or two in Kaelennar."

Traedis started. The world returned around her in a visual cacophony of light, form, and color. Atop the fence, Ruth gave her a long, searching look. Traedis stretched her mouth into a responding smile, trying to feign confidence. It did not work; she remained weak and shaken.

It had been years since she had studied under Master Celdon. Why was she so susceptible to those memories now? Was it because of Vandeyr, or was it because she had been home so recently? She did not know the answers, but she could not allow herself to be that vulnerable. If she did not know how to control such memories, the predators in the City would take full advantage of her weakness.

Stepping in front of Traedis, Vandeyr turned sideways and feinted at the air. "Ten of these," she said. "Then we'll do swings and slices, and practice footwork. You can't possibly defend yourself when you're both out of practice and out of shape. And I'd just as soon not have to be a suit of chain as well as a personal bodyguard. I don't care how tired you get, you're going to practice until your muscles won't hold you anymore." She paused to frown at Traedis. "I sleep occasionally. So does your miniature guard dog."

"My name is Ruth," the brunaidhi woman called out testily from her seat on the fence.

Vandeyr ignored her. "So practice!" She barked the words like an order. In fact, Traedis thought wryly, it probably was.

Traedis followed her sister's directions, determined to prove herself. Vandeyr matched her move for move, seeming not to even breathe hard; after a few lunges, Traedis wanted to slap her sister in the face. Still, she did not complain even when sweat matted her hair, leaving her neck and face chilled from the wind that blew down from the mountain peaks. Before long she could feel her muscles quiver and cramp, unused to working so hard. She forced herself through both pain and weakness, her determination unflagging.

Traedis was wondering if her legs would continue to hold her when a tall, lean woman dressed in the new livery emerged from the armory shed. "Captain Atenel!" the woman called when she came within voice range.

Vandeyr motioned for Traedis to stop before turning. "What is it, Lieutenant Tethyn?"

As soon as she stopped, Traedis found herself shaking from the exertions which her sister had put her through. The sword sank in her grasp as her arms refused to hold it any longer. She dropped it on the sand and bent forward to stretch her trembling calves and thighs so they would not cramp.

"Captain," Tethyn said, "Lord Daymet is here to see King Traedis. I had him shown to the Silk Room, and the servants are bringing him refreshments, but he insists upon seeing the King right now."

Vandeyr made a colorful oath under her breath before turning to Traedis. "Your choice," she said. "I'd advise talking with him. Then you can at least try to figure out what's going through his head." She stuck her own practice sword point first in the sand. "That is, if you think like a hedge maze, all spiky branches and hidden paths."

If she had possessed the breath to laugh, Traedis would have; as it was, a faint smile twisted the very edges of her mouth. It was an apt description of the man whom the City had considered one of their best contract lawyers. The early feeling that she could not compete for anything in a house full of Atenels suffused her. The amusement lapsed into a sense of dread as she tried to figure out what sort of attack Daymet intended this time.

"I'll see him," she said, panting. Vandeyr was right; better to confront him directly and hope to glean some sense of his intent. Traedis straightened and stretched, though she felt like pulled taffy. "I can't afford not to."

Ruth hopped down from the fence with a quick nod to Atchûk. "I will be at your back."

"As will I," Vandeyr said stiffly.

Setting as brisk a pace as she could to loosen her tightening muscles, Traedis headed back to the palace. Delay would only prolong it, and she wanted to get through this ordeal as quickly as possible. Because an ordeal it would be. Her sister was not the only one who would guess what sort of concessions Traedis offered to Kenrydh. Daymet was shrewd, and had long experience in the practice of negotiation. He would know that his life was balanced on the precarious edge of Traedis' decisions.

A shadow passed over the sun; Traedis looked up, but saw no clouds. Even so, the hair on the back of her neck prickled, and gooseflesh rose on her arms. Something did not feel right, something that was unconnected with her fear of Daymet. She felt a shudder go through the *falmyros*, but she could detect nothing wrong through her other senses.

Stopping, she tried to perceive what caused the disturbance, rooting her senses in Tolin's soil and Tolin's rock. Her consciousness delved into the deep crevices of the earth, joined with the taproots of trees, and arced back out into the sky, where tall pines soared, and the clear air blew down from Dragon Mountains. A solitary raven flapped in the still air.

There was nothing she could perceive; everything was as it should be. Yet the threat still shivered in the air, like faraway thunder.

Traedis shook her head. She would have to track down the source of this new uneasiness later. Right now, she must speak with her brother. Whatever hung in the air did not feel like an immediate danger.

Daymet was. She resumed her pace and strode with determination toward the palace.

Chapter Five
Daymet

Before meeting with Daymet, Traedis returned to her rooms, sponged off the sweat from the practice bout, and hastily dressed in a high-collared, unornamented gown. Brushing her hair mercilessly, she twisted it into a knot at the back of her head and secured it with a pair of long, jeweled hairpins. She could feel curls of hair wisping around her face, and smoothed them down furiously, though it did little good. She would have to face her brother with unkempt hair.

Vandeyr waited by the door, looking neater after the practice bout than Traedis thought she herself did after changing. Falling into line behind Traedis, Vandeyr's boot heels clicked against the stone floor, trailed by a hollow echo of the centuries of high-family guards who had once walked these halls. Ruth followed also, her hand at the hilt of her white-bladed dagger.

Daymet was waiting in the Silk Room, another of the three large reception rooms at the front of the palace. Here, the furniture was upholstered in tasteful pastel silks, and intimate groupings of seats gave the impression that the room was smaller than it actually was. Daymet sipped wine from a long-stemmed goblet, ignoring the cakes that sat on a low table. He seemed calm and unruffled, which merely made Traedis more nervous. Her brother was like a great cat, his movements contained until he struck.

He rose as Traedis approached, holding out a hand in mock gallantry; Traedis found her jaw locking with suspicion. She took his hand, allowing him to seat her on the chair next to and at an angle to his own. Vandeyr took a stance against the wall, her rigid posture suggesting that she was a weapon waiting to be used. Ruth leaned casually against the wall beside her, though Traedis was not fooled. Her friend was as alert as was her sister.

Ignoring Vandeyr and Ruth completely, Daymet put down his goblet and gestured at the decanter of wine which sat before him. "May I pour for you?" he asked with exquisite politeness.

Traedis nodded, feeling herself shrinking, becoming the mouse that Daymet hunted. She was not sure when the attack would come, though she was certain it would. She simply watched as her brother filled their glasses.

"It is not too late, Traedis," Daymet added in tones of sable and velvet. "You haven't given any names to Kenrydh. You can still make peace with Uncle Cordelayne, ask for his wisdom in guiding the City. Mistakes have been made, but they can be amended."

A small shock prickled through Traedis' body; though she knew her brother had followed the same logic as Vandeyr, she wondered if anything she did as king could be kept secret. It was certainly possible that someone was spying on her.

"Which 'mistake' was it that sent me to prison for all those years?" Memory stirred the buried anger which had kept her company when even her harp had been denied her. She fought the suffocating weight of the dark by projecting confidence and power into her voice; Daymet would not find her easy prey. Not now. She refused to collapse under the threat she knew lay beyond his apparent gentleness.

Daymet shook his head. "No, Traedis – I'm not going to admit that was wrong. It was the only thing to do at the time, and you know it. You don't realize how much Uncle Cordelayne had you protected."

Traedis inhaled sharply. *"Protected?* Burying me in that cell *protected* me?"* The rage which flooded her was like a swollen river; it could drown her if she let it. "What sort of protection is it that kept me in darkness, without companionship or even diversion of any sort? How was I *protected?"* Her hands began to shake with fury.

Daymet sat for a long moment, his green gaze intent and serious. After a long hesitation, he said, "Do you realize how much danger you were in? You came back with strange abilities, a magic harp, and a sword given to you personally by the King of Telardur. Do you think that passed unnoticed? Some on the Council wanted to kill you out of hand. Some of them wanted to take you apart and find out what you had learned during your time away. " His gaze bored into hers. "That they neither killed you nor broke you is due to Uncle Cordelayne's willingness to speak for you. He dissuaded them from taking precipitous action, and kept you safe from summary execution and the possibility of torture. To give him to Kenrydh would be to betray that debt."

His words were like blows from a trained fighter; they hit home where they were clearly intended. Guilt stabbed her with its often-honed knife, the cuts deeper than dagger wounds.

From her place against the wall, Vandeyr cleared her throat. "That's a half-truth," she said, her face expressionless. "Uncle Cordelayne protected you, it's true, but he wanted your secrets as well. He was just willing to break you slowly."

Daymet's eyes narrowed; he deliberately turned his back on Vandeyr. To Traedis, he said, "I don't speak with traitors."

That was interesting and unexpected. Daymet and Vandeyr had always gotten along well, and though they clearly had differing ideas about how to handle Traedis' acquisition of the *falmyros*, she had not realized that they had quarreled over her. Gladness spread through her; Vandeyr's loyalty was deep as bone.

The import of her sister's words sank into Traedis' mind a moment later. It was not a surprise that Uncle Cordelayne had pursued a longer game; it was one of the things he was best at. It was still hard. Her uncle had been more a father to Traedis than Linden had. He had been the one who first taught her to play the harp. She had once known him very well, and understood that his loyalties were to the City first; he would sacrifice even himself if he thought the City needed him to do so.

"Vandeyr speaks the truth," she said, a put her goblet down firmly on the table. "Do you think I've forgotten what Uncle Cordelayne is like?"

Daymet gave a measured pause before answering in a softer tone. "I think you have forgotten how much he cares about you. Not every action is about expedience, Traedis. We've always tried to teach you the most important things: loyalty, obedience, cooperation. You're talented, but you need vision and guidance, and you continue to deny that. What can we do to help you if you won't listen?" Each word was a mallet struck on hanging bells, hammering different notes within the same song into Traedis' bones. Doubt shivered through her, its vibration dissolving what surety she had. Perhaps Daymet really meant to mend their rift. Perhaps he really was in the right.

Ruth winked at her.

The effect of Daymet's speech immediately shredded, blowing away like curls of mist. The spell he wove, not with magic but with words, could not stand up to the steadying effect Ruth had on Traedis, even when the brunaidhi woman did not speak. Traedis shook her head to rid herself of self-doubt, an effect her middle brother always caused. He did not know her as well as he might think.

"I can't shirk my duty," she said, projecting strength into her voice. "I must give Uncle Cordelayne's name to Kenrydh. I cannot exempt a Council member because he is my kin." That was the bald truth, and Daymet must accept that he could not change her direction. "I do it for the good of Tolin, and for no other reason."

"The reason doesn't matter." Daymet stared at her fiercely, perhaps attempting to force her own gaze down. Traedis met the stare stoically, unwilling to show any more weakness before her brother. Daymet might want to control her actions as ruler of Tolin, but that did not mean she would let him. If she allowed him to influence her once against her better judgment, it would be easier the next time, eventually leading to complete submission.

"I think the reason does matter," she told him. She felt her back stiffen with resentment, and the knowledge that she was taking an ethical stance.

Daymet shook his head. "You don't realize what you are doing, Traedis. You can't be allowed to destroy what the City has built over the course of millennia. I won't let you, and neither will Uncle Cordelayne."

Traedis jutted her chin forward. "It's not a matter of letting me or not letting me, Daymet." Her words came out with clipped precision. "The gods gave me Tolin, and I will do for it what I must. I do not recognize your right to rule me, and I certainly do not recognize your right to rule Tolin."

Daymet remained silent for several long moments, as if evaluating her sincerity. He ran a thoughtful finger along the rim of his goblet. Traedis continued to meet his stare, her natural discomfort overridden by the anger sparking through her veins.

Finally he said, "I see you mean what you say." His tone was completely level, expressionless. "Very well. I am sorry, Traedis. I had hoped that you would listen to reason, but it seems you cannot. Your actions will have consequences." He set down the goblet and rose smoothly, inclining his head toward her in farewell.

Traedis watched him, her stomach tightening. Daymet exited without another word, leaving Traedis to sit in silence as she sorted through the implications.

Later that day, Traedis sat playing her harp, plucking the strings with hands that were badly out of practice. She had tried to keep them strong and calloused during her four years in prison, but there was no substitute for holding an actual instrument. It was still a marvel; she had given up all hope of ever being offered a harp again. Keeping her fingers limber had been an act of defiance, not of hope.

Vandeyr entered without preliminary, sweeping in the door like an organized whirlwind. "Daymet is gone," she said baldly.

Traedis stared at her in shock. "What?"

"Daymet is gone," Vandeyr repeated, irritation sharpening her voice. "Will you listen when I tell you things?"

Traedis put Rose down on the floor, the aftertones quivering in the air between them. "What do you mean, Daymet is gone?"

"Gone," said Vandeyr crossly. "Left. Abandoned. Fled. Whatever you want to call it, Daymet is gone. He's left the City. Said goodbye to Mother and went. You know where he went, don't you?" She spat out a blistering oath. "I should have had him followed."

Traedis put a hand to her forehead. "He's gone to join Uncle Cordelayne." She squeezed her eyes shut, then opened them again. "Why didn't I think of that? Of course Daymet knows where he is." Whose idea it had been to try to talk Traedis around was an open question, but Daymet would not have stayed behind otherwise. There was too much risk that Traedis might give him over to

Kenrydh.

Vandeyr dropped into a chair opposite Traedis and leaned back, her hands cradling the back of her head. "Mother didn't tell me until he was out of our reach. I suppose she didn't want to take the chance that I'd try to stop him. I don't know if I would have. I'd probably have tried to talk to him first." She rolled her eyes at the ceiling. "How you've managed to create such a mess in such a short time is beyond me. Why do you always have to make things so complicated?"

"He wants to direct what I do as king of Tolin," Traedis retorted, ice riming her words. "What am I supposed to do?"

"You are supposed to smile, nod, and pretend you agree." Vandeyr scowled. "Why can't you ever understand the most basic things about getting along in this family? If you didn't want to comply, you should have let him think you did. Why do you have to be so blunt?"

Traedis realized that her mouth was hanging open with confusion and the injustice of Vandeyr's attack; she shut it quickly. "I couldn't agree... I mean, he would have known... I couldn't manage to hide what I was doing..."

"Always excuses," grumbled Vandeyr. "You're going to excuse yourself into an early grave and I really don't want that to happen, no matter how stupid you are. Daymet's gone to Uncle Cordelayne. That means you've got two of the sharpest minds of the City working against you. You'll be lucky to last through the next year."

Traedis realized that, despite her phrasing, her sister was partly right; Uncle Cordelayne and Daymet would make a formidable combination. Her limbs suddenly felt as heavy as if she had spent the last hour running. Was she completely unable to handle her family? How could she rule the City if even they did not respect her? All she knew was that she could not have convincingly lied to Daymet, and would not have wanted to even if she could.

"You're right," she told Vandeyr. "I didn't think to do it your way." Vandeyr's eyes widened. "But I think matters would have ended up the same, nonetheless. I could not have fooled Daymet with less than a complete capitulation. I couldn't let him think he could lead me like a dog on a leash." Bitterness accompanied her words.

"No one's ever been able to lead you." Vandeyr stood and brushed a disobedient strand of hair from her face with an angry gesture. "If you get yourself killed because of this I'm not going to forgive you. Don't think Uncle Cordelayne won't assassinate you. He'll do what he believes he has to do for the sake of the City."

Sweat broke out suddenly on Traedis' forehead; she felt cold and hot simultaneously. "I know."

"Don't say no one warned you." Vandeyr strode to the door and exited, slamming it after her.

Traedis listened, unmoving, to the echoes of her sister's passage until long after her footsteps faded down the corridor.

Chapter Six
The Elders

Traedis had been up only a short time and was breakfasting when she was summoned to attend the Elder Priests of Coran and Selyn. She hastily quit the table, changed into a blue-gray woolen dress, donned a pair of doeskin boots and a cloak, and prepared to head out into the cold late-winter air. She would attend them, rather than the reverse; her rule was too new for her to give offense to the one faction that had backed her instantly.

Traedis had met both when she was young, but remembered very little about them. Her father had referred to each as a 'stubborn old fool.' General opinion agreed that their minds were blunted with age. Even so, each servant of the divine must be treated respectfully, and the gods themselves did not abandon the most aged of their priests.

Leaving a note for Ruth, she headed out the door.

Vandeyr fell in step in the hallway, looking like she had swallowed an anthill. The carriage was already pulled up and waiting outside, surrounded by a number of guards who Traedis did not recognize. Vandeyr had been busy; Traedis reminded herself to learn the names of the new people as well as their capacities. It was not mistrust of her sister; Traedis cared about those who were guarding her life with their own.

They drew up in one of Tolin's less populated sectors, in front of a large house which housed the City's only observatory. A boy of about ten, dressed in the red of a Selyn acolyte, rushed out to usher them inside. The three guards dismounted and formed a vee around the carriage. Vandeyr put out a hand and climbed out first, looking around suspiciously before beckoning Traedis to join her.

The house was built in a single story, and the ceilings rose extremely high; the reason for this was that the elder of Selyn was a centaur. A smoky-gray stallion of great age, he walked with a pronounced limp. His surroundings were pleasantly chaotic, littered with mounds of functional debris that seemed to fill most of the room. Black-marked leaves of parchment sat in untidy stacks on several scattered tables, and unrecognizable mechanical instruments tilted at crazy angles amid the snowfall drift of papers. The room had not been dusted in some time; Traedis felt her nose twitch in a barely suppressed sneeze.

Some chairs had been dragged into the room and arranged hastily in an off-kilter circle. Seated in one of these was the elder of the church of Coran, a dark-skinned old woman who resembled a dried-up apple. Traedis bowed her head politely to both elders and took a seat facing them, but Vandeyr remained standing beside Traedis, her back unbending.

"King Traedis," said the Coran elder. Known in Tolin as 'the goat woman,' she tended Coran's sacred goats, and was considered, at best, eccentric. "You are courteous. I was afraid you wouldn't come."

Traedis folded her hands in her lap. "I would not ignore a summons from such venerable priests as yourselves. You called for me and I am here. I am most eager to hear what you have to say."

The goat woman laughed. "One test passed. You are polite. After all this time, a leader who listens to us – or at least, pretends to." She glanced toward the centaur. "My colleague and I have important words for your ears, dear. The sacred goats seem to think highly of you. Three curly goats were born at midwinter, which is almost unheard of, and a hairless kid was born dead."

Traedis tried not to show confusion on her face. She had no idea what curly and hairless goats meant, and the entire conversation seemed somehow ludicrous, serious though the goat woman appeared to be. But she clung to her resolution to treat the two elder priests respectfully, and kept the corners of her mouth from quirking.

Apparently, she was not entirely successful, or perhaps her long silence told the Elder that Traedis did not understand her words. The goat woman said, "It's quite simple, dear. The curly goats represent good influences on the City, and they were born strong and healthy. The hairless kid is the City under the influence of that demon, and its stillbirth tells me that those influences are dead and gone. What's more, the goats are giving extra milk. They haven't done that for quite a while, which means your rule is starting out fruitfully and constructively. The signs are quite auspicious, and the goats seem to look upon you favorably."

Traedis caught herself before she said a word about the animals' accuracy at predicting her behavior. If the god of Earth chose to use goats to communicate, he would use goats. It was hubris to assume that she knew all there was to know of them.

"Thank you," she said to the goat woman. "It is most kind of you to inform me." She smiled at the old woman; the irony that the Elder might have been speaking clearly all along pleased her.

The old woman smiled back, and the corners of her eyes crinkled. "You are the King of Tolin, and the goats have told me the measure of your rule. Informing you is simply my duty." She patted some loose hair into her gray bun. "The goats would be very angry with me if I did not pass their auguries along."

Behind her, Traedis heard Vandeyr snort so quietly that she doubted anyone else could hear. Traedis frowned. The fact that Vandeyr thought the Coran elder foolish made Traedis more willing to believe the old woman, contrary though the impulse was

"Even so, I am indebted to you," she said sincerely.

The Coran Elder nodded in return. "I will tell you more as the goats inform me."

Traedis turned to the Elder of the church of Selyn. "You also have words for my ears?"

"I do," said the centaur. He shuffled his legs uncomfortably. "Pardon me, my king. My rheumatism pains me of late, and there is nothing that can be done about it." He reached out to a nearby table and took from it a piece of parchment inked with cramped writing and strange symbols. "As you may know, I am a student of the stars, though this art has fallen out of favor in the City, and I am the only one with enough knowledge to read them these days. I would like to teach the great cosmology to one who could learn it properly, but no one is interested enough to take the years of study it requires to learn. Patience is something of which the younger priests have no concept. They want everything at once, even the auguries of the gods." He looked down at the parchment. "Pardon an old man's rambling, Your Majesty. The stars have been particularly revealing, and their knowledge is vast and encompassing."

Traedis waited with her own hard-learned patience. The centaur did ramble, but this did not necessarily mean she could dismiss him. He might have a great store of wisdom to impart, despite his method of divulging it.

Vandeyr shifted her feet, and Traedis could almost feel her sister's frustration.

"There is a perfect trine of three favorable planets, all of the element of air, in the heavens," said the elder of the church of Selyn. He pointed to one of the symbols on the parchment, but Traedis could make no sense of it. "These planets are precisely oriented to the east, signifying strong favorable influences over the world at present. At the midpoint between them, during the hour of the Eagle, is the constellation of the Eagle, suggesting that strongly favorable conditions currently apply to Tolin. I will overlook the question of the Dragon constellation's positioning in the sky during the midnight hour, as this seems to refer to two other warring states, and has little to do with the City." He paused and drew a breath, studying the parchment intently.

Traedis did not interrupt; she had learned in Kaelennar that people worked better when allowed to follow their own paths. She was quite sure the Selyn Elder was no fool; despite his circuitous way of speaking, he seemed quite sure of his knowledge.

"Now here," continued the old centaur, pointing to a series of concentric circles, intersecting lines, and odd symbols, "is where the problem lies. Though the conditions in the City are currently favorable, there is a danger period ahead of you, signified by the eclipsing by a small comet of this trio of stars which make up the Eagle's left eye. I take this to mean that the danger period ahead of you will last for three years, beyond which I cannot forecast accurately with what the stars have as of yet shown me." He pointed to a symbol that reminded Traedis of a circle bisected by a fish. "This planet, Aluria, representing leadership, opposes the planet Diuk which represents home and family, within the constellation of the Wyvern. That is an oversimplification of course, but its meaning is clear; positioned as they are, the two planets warn you to beware of family, and given the fact that the planets now ride in the head and heart of the wyvern – Aluria in the heart, Diuk in the head – I believe that your siblings are not the main danger, though there is no indication that you may trust them either." Vandeyr stirred beside Traedis, but said nothing.

"My last observation," said the centaur, "is one which I do not fully understand, though I can interpret it clearly." He stamped nervously. "I might say that it translates as 'beware the tailor with the silver needle.' Put concisely, the Needle's Eye is what we call the space in the midst of the cluster of stars which follow and occasionally transition through the Wyvern in its dance. The cluster itself is 'the Needle.' This has an odd property in that sometimes it darts back and forth across a small area of sky within the space of a few days. When it does this, we call it 'stitching the cloth,' and it always has great import of some sort, though the meanings vary widely depending upon the season, the quadrant of the sky, wandering planets, and other phenomena which I will not now describe." Traedis heard Vandeyr breathe a small sigh, quiet enough to avoid rudeness, but obviously weary of the long and overly elaborate explanation.

"The Needle has recently stitched a pattern in the sky which, though complex, indicates danger and betrayal. I take this to refer to you and your situation, as the stars of the Needle are transitioning through the Wyvern, coming into close conjunction with Aluria, and thence moving into yet another constellation. This constellation is usually referred to as 'the Tailor,' or occasionally 'the Weaver,' and its meaning is one of a powerful figure creating a pattern or 'garment' if you will, to influence a situation. Given the opposition between Aluria and Diuk and the pattern stitched by the needle, I interpret this as a negative influence." He glanced, brow furrowed, at his parchment. "What else? Oh yes. The needle is silver – the stars are quite clear on this point – because of the unusual silvery cast taken on by the needle due to a disturbance in the upper air every time the Wyvern is uppermost in the sky. Hence 'Beware the tailor with the silver needle'." He paused. "I do not understand what the warning refers to, however."

Traedis looked at him thoughtfully. "A strongly positive

influence lies upon Tolin at the moment, but there will be a danger period of three years ahead of me, is that correct? I should not trust family, but my siblings are not the danger..." She refrained from telling him that she could have predicted that herself. Apparently, the warning referred to Uncle Cordelayne, or possibly, her mother. The second possibility distressed her the most, but she could not be sure of Mitheira's goodwill, especially if Traedis' aims conflicted with those of Daymet. "And I should beware the tailor with the silver needle."

"Exactly, Your Majesty." The Selyn elder bowed slightly from the waist. "Excellently summarized."

"I thank you for your auguries and warnings." Traedis gathered her skirt and prepared to stand. "I will consider them seriously, I promise." She hesitated and regarded the goat woman for a long moment. "And I do mean what I say. It's not just empty politeness." She rose to her feet.

"I've had too many people try to charm me into believing them to take your word for it," the goat woman grumbled. "Your uncle, for instance. He always was more interested in people liking him than in the sincerity of his words." Vandeyr frowned in disapproval, and the goat woman laughed shortly. "Oh, don't tell me how sincere he is. I've known him since he was in the cradle. He always means what he says when he says it, but he's a master of convincing himself otherwise if the need arises." She regarded Traedis with glittering dark eyes which held both humor and a spark of challenge. "Show me you mean it, don't tell me. That's what will convince me, Your Majesty." She grinned wryly at Traedis' expression. "No point in looking at me that way. You know I'm right about him."

Traedis felt an uncomfortable and unexpected urge to defend Uncle Cordelayne; she pushed it down into the depths of her consciousness and nodded to the goat woman, who she rather liked for her brusque honesty. Those were unusual qualities in the City, and she valued them. Had she not herself been accused of speaking too freely?

"One more thing," the goat woman said. "I'll speak bluntly, Your Majesty, because there isn't a good way of asking questions like this, but – are you under a curse?"

Around Traedis, the world seemed to stop for an interminable length of time. "I…yes. I have a curse on me."

The goat woman nodded. "That explains the orphaned kid that won't leave the yard. It has something to do with a loss of – safety? Not quite right. Affection? Not exactly." She frowned, the wrinkles in her face more prominent than before.

A flurry of memories spun up in Traedis' mind. Wingblade, the massive, winged warrior who followed Kyaan and fought for his cherished cause of freedom. Wingblade, who had befriended many of Kyaan's creatures, as well as a small band of friends from Kaelennar.

Wingblade, who, lost in madness, had cursed her.

He had posed Traedis and her friends questions, and each question slid a deadly curse around them like a noose. To Traedis, he had asked, "*Who will lose her love to the storm?*"

"Loss of love," she said to the goat woman. "Or freedom. In this case, they mean the same thing."

"Oh!" The centaur elder picked up one of his pieces of parchment and examined it carefully. "That would explain the patch of darkness near the edge of the Harp. Yes, it fits nicely!" He took his pen and scratched something onto his map.

"My dear girl." The old woman clucked her tongue as she looked at Traedis, compassion in her eyes. "So young for the burdens you carry. Well, I suppose there's nothing to be done now – you've been cursed, it's a strong one, and that's that. What may come from it later we must wait to find out."

Traedis was not anxious to discuss the matter further. Instead, she nodded her head respectfully. "I understand that you must see how I behave before you fully trust me." Traedis looked intently at both of the elder priests. "I cannot prove myself here and now, but I hope to in the future. I thank you both for your counsel."

"I will wait and see," the goat woman told her. Her face creased into an impish expression. "I even look forward to it."

Traedis sat musing on the encounter during the trip back to the palace. Images of wandering planets and curly goats filled her mind as she wrestled with the question of what it all meant. The elders were most definitely odd, but they seemed true of heart.

They were passing old buildings and nearing the Council square, when a troop of short, brightly garbed n'korreld crossed the road in front of her; Atchûk was among them. Traedis called for her driver to stop and got out, follow ed by a sour faced Vandeyr. Waving her arm, Traedis hailed the karreldish prince.

Atchûk came to a halt, his guards moving in to form a circle around them. He said something Traedis could not hear, then gave her a cheerful nod and a wave. He joined her moments later, eyes sparkling.

"King Traedis! You are out early!"

The morning sun glanced through tattered clouds, warming the cobbles of the street that were grimy with old snow. Traedis pushed back her hood, enjoying the sunshine the day promised. "Prince Atchûk," she replied. "What brings you out here in the cold?"

Atchûk seemed to be enjoying himself; his high spirits cheered Traedis almost immediately. "Exploring," he told her. "And I'm not afraid of cold." He wore a goat-hair hat and matching coat over his tunic – this one embroidered with colorful fish and decorated with tiny but intricately carven gold beads – and his boots were of heavy leather tooled in wave patterns. As the n'korreld's land bordered the northern ocean, where the wind sliced into the shore with icy vengeance, it was not surprising that he knew how to dress for the frigid mountain climate.

"It's all so *square!*" he added, his eyes alight with interest. "And tall! And – is that a line of beetles on the edge of that stonework?"

"Yes," Traedis responded. She gazed at the top edge of the estate they were passing, three stories with a pitched slate roof.

Carven stone beetles crept around the roofline and marched along the sills. "They're everywhere in Tolin – I haven't noticed them in years. I don't really know why the architects of the City favored them."

"Tell me if you find out," the karreld said. "It's an unusual motif for a human city." He held onto his cap as a swirling gust of wind swept down to catch at their clothes and hair.

"Would you like to walk with me to the Council Spring?" Traedis asked. "It's not far. It's a place every visitor should see." She wanted to remain with the young prince; somehow, she felt a kinship with him, as if he were a distant cousin she had only just met.

"I'd be honored." The karreld beckoned to his people, who formed a cordon around the three of them.

Vandeyr made a noise of protest.

Traedis gave her a reassuring nod. "It will be fine. We're with good soldiers, even if they're not yours. I'm not worried."

Vandeyr stiffened. "I don't want to see another mob without anyone else to protect you. And you can't count on someone else's troops to defend you instead of their lord."

"It's all right." Traedis let an edge of annoyance slide into her voice. "I'll pull my hood up if you want." Smiling at the karreld, she pointed toward their destination. "It's around the corner, a block ahead."

The horses and carts they met in the streets gave the armed group a wide berth. It was cold, but the City was used to icy weather, and many citizens were about, not simply laborers cleaning and rebuilding, but also those bent on ordinary errands. They passed at least three workers shoveling compacted snow from the streets, their exertion keeping them as warm as their coats, mittens, and scarves.

They reached the heart of town, where the Council Hall had once stood before Toledru erupted from beneath it to take Traedis' mind and demand the death he craved. Here rose a hill of stone, granite and slate fractured into pieces no larger than a man's head, mute testament to the violence of the demon's emergence. The cracked foundations could still be seen ringing the place where the earth had collapsed. A spring welled joyously from its center, bubbling up into a stream that flowed enthusiastically through the city's heart and down the mountain.

Traedis shivered, though her cloak and gloves were warm. She had frozen as the demon invaded her thoughts and reshaped a tiny piece of her mind. Here the Storm Eagle had showed her how to peel Toledru from each stone and stalk of Tolin's lands. Here she had received the *falmyros* in trade for the death of the City's one-time lord.

"This is the Council Spring," she said brightly, hiding her discomfort. "We take it as a sign that the City will flourish despite adversity. The water is purer than any other, even the streams and the river that flow from the mountains."

Atchûk remained silent for a moment, regarding the stream, turned toward the hall's remains, then moved to face Traedis.

"Trae, what you have done is something no one has been able to accomplish in almost two millennia. If you do nothing else in your reign, this will stand as a crowning achievement." His brow puckered. "Though my joke is unintentional."

Traedis snickered. Stripping off a glove, she leaned over to sift a handful of water through her hand. Though no ice had formed on the swift-flowing stream, it was cold enough to numb her fingers almost immediately. She quickly put her glove back on, feeling Rose thrum a warming tune even through her lined case.

Atchûk examined the water with the delight of a child. Then he spun in a circle, his eyes seeming to drink in his surroundings. "The sky seems so much closer here. I'm used to it stretching forever over the sea, arching so high that you could fly up forever and never reach it. But here I get the feeling that I could climb a tall tree and touch the clouds." He laughed, a free, open sound. "Or am I being too poetic? My big brother Darg says I'm a dreamer. My little brother Bekk claims I'm pretentious. I don't require a consensus, though."

Traedis grinned back at him, her spirits raised by his sheer exuberance. "I think the sky looks closer here because it is – the sky dome sits half a mountain nearer. The stars are brighter, too. At this time of year, when it's so cold that the air won't even hold breath, they blaze in all the colors of light. The clouds hug the peaks some days, and when it rains, they drop almost down to Tolin's height. You really could touch the clouds if you went up mountain far enough." She was surprised to find herself speaking so passionately of the City; occasionally she remembered her few happy times here.

Atchûk nodded thoughtfully and inclined his head to Traedis. "What was it like, growing up here?" The karreld swept his arm in a half-circle. "Everyone always wondered about Tolin. Not just about the assassins, but about what it looked like, what the people were like, everything. I imagined it as a dark place, roofed over with stone, with people who wore nothing but gray and looked like a combination of esch and for some reason aelenin." He shook his head. "I guess I'm being rude, though I don't intend to be."

"I like your honesty," Traedis told him. She considered how to answer his question. "I do see why you thought of Tolin that way. It could feel like that, growing up." She gave Vandeyr a nervous look from the corner of her eye, but her sister did not react to her words; hopefully, she had not heard them. "If someone didn't fit in, it was oppressive, like living under that slate roof and never seeing the sky. As if the weight of the mountain pinned the City down, crushed it under the weight of expectation..." She stopped, surprised at how much she had confided in a man she barely knew. "I don't think you're rude."

"And then the demon." Atchûk became suddenly serious. "That must have been hard."

"I survived." Traedis said. "And I want no more dealings with demons."

Chapter Seven
A Visitor

A few weeks later, Traedis sat in her court, administering justice for the day. She had only recently taken on this task, and it had already become a burden. Not only were her decisions often unpopular, she had to decide carefully on matters of which she lacked knowledge. Though she consulted those who understood the complexity of tradition, she had made new laws and changed old ones. Secretly, she felt as if she merely pretended at statecraft, and that others would think she made her decisions based on whim or the quality of her breakfast that morning.

The court chamber had once been the house's great hall, its ceiling exceptionally high with massive beams arching over a chamber a third the length of the palace. Solid stone construction rose sturdily through the space of the second story, and stout oaken beams held the third floor firmly in place. The gray stone floor was worn with the centuries-old traffic of feet, and a perpetual chill filled the vast open space, despite warm tapestry hangings that covered the walls.

A dais had been erected some time later than the original construction, and here Traedis sat on a massive carved wooden chair which she had co-opted to serve the role of throne. Fine craftwork adorned it with woodland plants and creatures: oak leaves hid gamboling foxes; tiny owls perched on thistle heads; and mice scrabbled up the back legs. The seat needed no cushion, smoothed as it was with many years of use as the head seat of a formal dining table.

Some of Vandeyr's new guard stood sentry near the entrance of the hall as well as near the throne; Vandeyr herself hovered watchfully just behind the throne's left arm. A herald stood off to one side, announcing those who approached the throne. Ruth maintained a position to the right, her quiet support helping Traedis maintain the presence of mind she needed to deal with the potentially devious and treacherous people of Tolin.

Spread throughout the hall, the main bulk of the court was crowded with flocks of highborn followers, sycophants, and dissenters, both subtle and overt. Traedis watched the ebb and flow nervously; she knew the basics of politics in Tolin, but she had never been good at the games played with words and lives rather than pieces on a board. The bright colors of velvet and brocade that swirled through the room made her dizzy; like exotic birds, the plumage could fan out to attract mates or intimidate predators. Some of these folk were themselves predators in disguise, but she was not sure which.

A blond man a few years older than she approached; he wore a well-tailored suit of gray silk and carried a small box little bigger than his palm. He looked familiar, but Traedis could not place him. The herald called out, "Kaal Shefferie!" That was enough: Traedis remembered Kaal from her childhood. A younger son of a Council family, he had always been strictly disapproving in Traedis' presence. Now he smiled, bowing with a perfect precision that indicated nothing but admiration.

"Lord Kaal," Traedis said, scanning him for a hidden weapon. The Shefferies had made little secret of their dislike of her policies, and she did not trust any of them. "Speak your petition, please."

Kaal held out the package, being careful to show his hands. He smiled at her, but did not move, clearly understanding that Vandeyr would insist on verifying that he and everything he carried was harmless. Vandeyr nodded to one of her guard, who took the box and opened it carefully, examining it carefully before handing its contents over to Traedis. It was a necklace, with tiny sapphires worked into a mesh of fine, braided gold. "King Traedis, my petition is that you accept this gift and my suit as well."

Gods, he was another of her suitors. They had descended in hordes, flattering, cajoling, insisting that her inexperience required assistance. Everyone with pretensions to royalty had swarmed from their nests when the *falmyros* had fallen on her head, but none so persistently as those from the nine Council families. Those who decided they had little chance with Traedis pressed suits on Vandeyr and Gavaya, neither of whom was interested in marrying Traedis' leftover swains. Vandeyr had been known to challenge potential suitors to knife-throwing matches; Gavaya's quieter approach was to engage them in scholarly conversation until they became intimidated by her brilliance.

Traedis had neither of these luxuries. She must be politic with suitors, especially those with influence, no matter how little she wanted their attentions. She would have to marry and produce heirs at some point, but could not see how to accept a husband she did not trust. And she did not trust anyone from Tolin.

Diplomacy, however, was in order. "I cannot accept such a generous gift," she said politely. "As to your suit, I will neither accept nor reject it. I am still in the early days of my reign, and I am not yet ready to wed." She smiled, though she had less interest in marrying anyone from the Shefferie family than she did in marrying a three-legged pig.

"I understand," Kaal said smoothly. He declined to take back the necklace, however. Waving it away, he said, "Please keep it in token of my admiration for you. I consider it a gift, with no need of repayment in any kind."

Traedis felt anger stir beneath her breastbone. Despite his words, Kaal had obligated her indeed; to refuse the gift under these circumstances would be to publicly insult the Shefferies, giving them an excuse to undermine her power. She had been neatly outmaneuvered, and those in court today would see the obligation. A glint that shone in his lowered eyes told her that he had intended exactly this effect.

"Thank you," she told him. The best she could do would be to tuck the necklace away in her jewel chest and never wear it even once. "I am honored, then, to accept your gift." Moving her gaze carefully past him, she indicated that the next in line should approach.

Behind Kaal were supplicants and seekers of justice. Many, though not all, were common folk, their clothing less fine, their bearing less proud than their highborn neighbors. Traedis had thought at first that she would prefer the complaints of the common folk to the pretensions of the nobility, but after judging cases involving such things as cattle, fish, and minor property disputes, she decided that she despised all of the cases equally.

She had just finished pronouncing judgment on a breach of marriage contract when movement at the main door caught her attention. A figure, cloaked and hooded, entered slowly, bowed as if with age. The guards did not challenge the newcomer, who made a slow way across the length of the room and toward the throne. For some reason, Traedis was quite sure the figure was female, though she could see no features under the cloak.

Traedis gave a quick glance at Ruth, curious to see what the brunaidh thought. But Ruth stood unmoving except for the steady rise and fall of her chest. Alarmed, Traedis turned toward Vandeyr, who seemed also to be fixed in place. A growing awareness filtered into Traedis' consciousness that no one in the room had moved or spoken since the cloaked woman entered. The hush, now that she noticed it, was a smothering blanket.

As the figure approached the throne, Traedis felt the hairs stand up on her arms and prickle the back of her neck. Not certain what she was facing, she spoke firmly but politely. "Greetings, stranger. What brings you to my court?" Her voice, better trained than her nerves, held steady.

"I have come about my contract." The voice was that of an old woman, but its rasp of bone on bone sent an added chill down Traedis' spine. "It has been far too long, and it has not been fulfilled."

Whatever the woman was, she was no simple mortal. Traedis swallowed, not sure how to answer. She had believed that recalling the assassins was sufficient to break all the City's contracts, but clearly, she had not thought the situation through. Carefully picking her way, as if through a hedge of thorns, she said, "I do not know of this contract."

The woman opened her cloak wide; a blast of chilling *demonfear* spilled out, permeating the air with otherness so complete that Traedis' body rebelled against it. She gagged on terror. Nothing showed inside but a putrid darkness which surged and ebbed unnaturally. Similar memories poured into her mind: the sensory assault of Winter's demon consort; the overwhelming presence of the demonlands' guardian; the horror of Toledru in his rocky tomb. Her consciousness thinned as her mortal mind tried to reject her experience.

The woman closed her cloak, and the *demonfear* cut off as suddenly as it had started. Though Traedis' mind and body were glad of the relief, she also feared the implications; only the strongest of demons had the ability to mask their presence so thoroughly.

The woman said, "Contracts with the Nightdance are seldom written down."

Traedis inhaled sharply. Most people were afraid to even speak the name, lest they call the Dance's attention to themselves. She knew the City had trafficked with them, but had never considered that one of them might come to demand a contract's enforcement.

She thought she could put a name to the demon who stood before her. Known variously as 'The Old Woman Who Knocks at the Door,' 'The Mistress of Ravens,' and 'The Mother of Curses,' she was not only a demon, but was also one of the great Powers of the world. The curse that constrained Traedis' freedom brought even more danger should she thwart this demon's intentions.

"Madam Mardra." Traedis' every sense was alert to danger; tales abounded in all lands of the grim consequences should the Mother of Curses be turned away without hospitality. "As I have no knowledge of this contract, I beg you to inform me of its conditions." Though she still maintained control over her tone, Traedis' voice was huskier than usual. She had the unnerving thought that a purple eye was looking at her through the darkness that swirled within the hood, but she could see nothing.

"Seventeen months ago," Mardra said, the chill in her tone increasing, "a poorly executed assassination caused a powerful death curse to be laid upon your city. Nothing would come to fruition within Tolin; crops in the field would fail, plans would go awry, children would sicken and die. Your Council − including your uncle − came to me and begged me to lift it. I assented, if Tolin would do a service for me. There is a troublesome scholar I would see dead. The Council agreed to my terms, and our contract was formed."

Traedis' mind scrabbled for purchase on this news. She could not accept the fulfillment of this or any contract if she were to maintain the support of Kenrydh and Emmen, king of Haven. Furthermore, before the gods, accepting even one contract was to accept that Tolin was still fundamentally the same city, meaning that every other sworn contract must also be honored.

Still maintaining her wary politeness, she said, "The Tolin I rule is no longer the same city that you bargained with. We cannot fulfill your terms."

Mardra's cloak swung open again, buffeting Traedis with the horror of her presence before she closed it. "If you cannot fulfill your end of the contract, I cannot honor mine. If you are not willing to pay me in the coin which I am owed, perhaps I should return your city to its former condition."

The demon's words struck Traedis where she was weakest. If the Council had beseeched Mardra for help, the curse must have been terrible indeed. But even if Traedis had any intention of allowing Tolin to fall back to its former profession, she could not afford to lose the support of her allies.

This was not about a single contract; this was an attempt to restore everything Traedis had changed about the City. The Dance wanted Tolin to continue as their tool: a knife in the ribs, poison in the cup.

If Traedis agreed, Tolin would either need to stand alone, or to ally with the esch, things she was equally unwilling to do. In truth, Traedis would give up the *falmyros* before she would honor those contracts. And even that would not be enough, should the *falmyros* then fall on someone who would reinstate the assassinations. She was neatly trapped.

A delaying tactic was all she could do. Carefully, she said, "Madam Mardra, I am new to the rule of Tolin, and I must consider the matter seriously. Please grant me time, that I may think over your words and decide my best course."

The cloak turned sideways without lessening the sense of watching eyes. It turned back, the malice inside the hood palpable, though the *demonfear* was contained. "Very well. I give you three weeks. At the end of that time, you will have an answer for me."

Traedis gave the barest of nods, her heart pounding. She still did not see a way out, but others might. Surely someone must know how to circumvent the Dance.

"And one more thing." The cloaked figure billowed menace, like a mass of clouds ready to explode into storm. "You may tell no one what I have tasked you with: not your friends, not your captain, not your fellow kings. You may not hint, you may not lead others to guess what I wish to hide. Should you speak of my prey, or if someone should guess through any action of your own, I will lay a curse on your head as dreadful as the one you already bear. Do you understand?"

Traedis felt a wrench in her chest; this removed any hope of expert counsel from those more knowledgeable than herself. She might flout such a curse, were it merely on her own head – but what affected her affected Tolin. As king, she could not take such a chance.

She nodded. "We have an understanding. And thank you, madam, for your forbearance."

She heard a whispery sound, like bones laughing. "You may thank me when I come to receive your answer." Then she was simply gone.

Traedis suddenly felt lighter. Her lungs drew in clearer air, and movement resumed around her. The chamber filled again with voices.

Three weeks. Then she must have an answer.

Ruth looked at Traedis sharply. "What's wrong?"

The court moved normally; Traedis felt a sense of dislocation that was so strong she was momentarily disoriented. Vandeyr turned to give her a penetrating look, which swiftly became sharp concern.

At first, so stunned that she could not find words, Traedis merely swayed. Finally, she managed, "Did you notice anything?" She clutched at the throne's arm; in the aftermath of *demonfear*, she was beginning to feel faint.

Vandeyr leaned in to prevent her voice from carrying. "Poison?" She took Traedis' arm and motioned to her guard.

Traedis shook her off a moment later. "No. Nothing like that. It's something else."

Vandeyr reached back toward her, then retracted her hands. "What did I miss? Aside from the fact that you look like you stumbled into a vat of whitewash?" Her eyes narrowed. "What do you want to do?"

Traedis nodded, thinking that three weeks did not seem so long when it came to thwarting a demon and a Power. "I want to get out of here and talk." She quietly gestured to her herald to halt the judgment, and rose to her feet, scooping Rose up and placing her into the harp case. Rose's strings twingled a few comforting notes before falling silent.

The herald dismissed the supplicants while Vandeyr and Ruth

accompanied Traedis upstairs to her office, two members of the guard falling in behind as they exited the throne room. Traedis walked more quickly than usual, trying to work out the fear that trembled in her limbs and lay sour in her stomach. She could not think what to do; her thoughts flew in circles like a hawk on a creance. She shuddered, feeling befouled by the demon's recent presence in her *falmyros*.

"What is it?" Vandeyr said immediately after shutting the door behind them. The guards stood outside in the hall. "One moment you looked as if you wanted to fling cow pies at the supplicants, the next you seemed about to faint. What did I miss?"

Rather than answering, Traedis posed her own question, as she dropped into the seat behind her desk. "What do you know of a badly botched contract?"

Her brow wrinkling, Vandeyr scowled. "There are occasionally some, much as we try to cover it up. I know of three since you left."

"Seventeen months ago." Realizing that she still held Rose's harp case, Traedis set it on the floor and slowly released her grip.

Vandeyr made a noise of frustration. "Then yes. I know which one you're talking about. A man contracted to have the brother of his betrothed killed; the sister came upon them as it happened, and the idiot assassin killed her as well. It was a professional embarrassment, and the assassin was executed for dereliction of duty. Why did this suddenly come up?"

Ruth's gaze was sharp as she looked from one to the other.

"What in the name of Coran's muddy footprints does this have to do with you nearly fainting in open court?"

"I had," Traedis said slowly, "a visitor."

"You had several," said Vandeyr in an irritated tone. "Which one in particular disturbed you?"

"The one you didn't see." Traedis heard her own voice shake. "The Old Woman Who Knocks at the Door."

Ruth's eyes widened; Vandeyr swore.

"What did she want?" asked Vandeyr, her voice as hard as steel.

Still tensed for a blow that had not yet come, Traedis swallowed hard. "I can't tell you." She gripped the desk's edge, her knuckles whitening, as Mardra's threats echoed in her ears.

Vandeyr started to speak, closed her mouth, began to speak again, and again closed her mouth. Traedis could see her thinking through the implications. Then she nodded. "Can't tell? Or won't?" Her gaze might have seared meat.

"Can't." Traedis straightened in the chair; she would not collapse. Somehow, she would find a way to oppose Mardra without bringing the City down or restoring its former purpose. She must discover a way. She had no other choice.

Vandeyr stared at her minutely as if she were trying to diagnose an illness or injury. "Why did she approach you at all? Can you explain that?"

Examining the conversation with Mardra through the glass of memory, Traedis considered what she could say and what she most certainly could not. Carefully, very carefully, she chose her words. "Someone cursed the City because of that assassination." She reached out to straighten the books and papers on her desk, finding some solace in ordering her work. "The Council asked Madam Mardra to remove the curse in exchange for their services." The desk was cold under her fingers.

Vandeyr's eyebrows knotted. "No excuse in the world for how badly that job was bungled. Foolish, incompetent, useless!" She slammed a fist on the wall.

Then her tone turned crisp and businesslike. "What *can* you tell us? I know nothing about any curse cast on the City .." She stopped suddenly and drew a sharp breath. "Yes I do. Only I didn't know that's what it was. For a while, everything just – went sour. If something could go wrong, it did. There were a lot of deaths, especially children, and a number of contracts went badly, though not as bad as the job by the fool who precipitated this. Of all the sheep-brained things to do!" She frowned. "Then everything seemed to go back to normal." She tapped her dagger hilt. "Because the Council went to the Mother of Curses, apparently."

Traedis nodded.

"Who cast the curse?" Ruth approached the side of the desk, where she could see Traedis without having to peer over the desk's wooden edge. Her lips were pursed, and she cocked her head to one side. "Is that another thing you can't say?" She looked worried as Traedis nodded.

Vandeyr's expression was also becoming more concerned than

angry.

Traedis did not tell answer the question or tell them what Mardra had asked; she did not want to cut too near to disclosing the target. She was glad that at least she did not know *precisely* whom Mardra wished dead: that would make her choices even harder. Like the hiss of a serpent, the demon's words rang again in Traedis' head, her whisper sounding more present than simple memory should have made it.

Thoughts swirled in her mind, as she desperately tried to find some way around the terrible dilemma. One idea floated forward, and she grasped it firmly. "I need – I must speak to the author of the curse," she told them. "Perhaps I can convince them to retract it." It was an inadequate plan, but one not entirely without hope.

"You can't tell us what the Matron wants." Vandeyr flicked an errant hair from her sleeve. "I'll find the man whose children were killed. I suspect he's not going to want to traffic with us, but that's your lookout." She shook her head. "I can make a few guesses of my own what the Matron wants – "

"Don't!" Traedis snapped out, with such vehemence that she barely recognized her own voice. "I can't tell you what they bargained for because she will curse me doubly if I do, and that will affect Tolin through the *falmyros*."

Vandeyr stopped, completely motionless; even her breath ceased for several moments. Then, speaking as if to a spooked animal, she said, "I won't. I don't need to know." Despite the hint of a question in her voice, she asked nothing more, though her posture was restless.

"Promise me," Traedis said. "This is too important."

Ruth cleared her throat. "I, at least, assume you know what you're doing."

"She never has before," Vandeyr grumbled, before nodding her head. Traedis had no time to protest before her sister let out a prolonged breath. "Very well. I promise, Trae. I won't try to find out what you're hiding, unless I'm convinced you're making a bigger mistake than usual."

Traedis felt heat rush into her cheeks; she banged a hand hard on her desk. "You don't know what mistakes I have or haven't made – " She stopped as she realized exactly what her sister had been doing. She no longer felt faint, which was almost certainly Vandeyr's intention in angering her. Instead, she made a choked little laugh, and felt almost normal again. "And I promise this," she said. "If there's anything else you can do, I will call on you straight away." She cut off a brief impulse to ask Vandeyr if she agreed; it was old force of habit, but she was the king, and the *falmyros* was hers. She could solicit opinions, but she could not hand over the responsibilities of her rule to another.

"Well, that's settled, then." Ruth crossed her arms. "What can *I* do?"

"Help me keep my head," Traedis told her. "Remind me that Tolin isn't the entire world." Living in Kaelennar had given her a better understanding of what lay beyond the City, but it was easy to fall back into the old patterns of reacting, rather than acting. "Tell me when I'm being a fool."

Ruth nodded. "I can do that." She retreated to her stool in the corner, but kept her attention on the other two.

Vandeyr stretched like a cat. "Are you going to let me do anything? Wrangle demons? Build a wall from the stones of the Dance?"

It was still hard to think; Traedis' thoughts flowed like molasses. But there was one person who was responsible for knowing about demons. "I need to speak with King Emmen of Haven."

Like Tolin, Haven was a city-state, though very different in character: Haven boasted an order of knights committed to the pursuit of rectitude. It had not been until the Storm Eagle's death that the relationship between the two cities had been revealed. The Storm Eagle had been lord of both, and had given Haven's *falmyros* to Emmen at the same time Traedis received the *falmyros* of Tolin.

The two cities had not historically been friends. Vandeyr's brows lowered. "Is that necessary?"

Suddenly wearied, Traedis wanted nothing more than to head to the music room and play for an hour or two. Instead, she replied, "Haven's people are experts on demons and demon lore. It's part of their mission. And I would like Emmen's counsel." She shuffled two piles of paper into each other and anchored them with a stone paperweight shaped like a gyrfalcon.

"But *Haven*," Vandeyr said scathingly. "All those petty little saints riding out to song and glory." Traedis shot her a glare; she did not seem to notice. "I'd rather have you kissing up to Kenrydh than to Haven."

Ruth said pointedly, "You don't get to make the decision."

"It isn't 'kissing up' – " Traedis began, before realizing that she had taken Vandeyr's bait yet again. She pushed aside shame at her own lack of composure and met her sister's gaze squarely. "I need Emmen. I need her expertise, I need her common sense, and I need her support. Now, will you get her before I end up foaming mad all over my desk?"

Vandeyr blinked. "I wouldn't want to put a burden on the cleaning staff." She turned on her heel and strode out of the office without waiting for an answer.

Ruth stared after her. "She must wear out a lot of boots."

Emmen showed up in the palace three days later with a small honor guard, gating directly from the island of Haven to Tolin. Traedis welcomed her with pleasure; the older woman was one of the few people she trusted without reservation. Tall and strongly built, Emmen had the youthful appearance of mixed aelin and human heritage. She was dressed in court attire of a fine silk shirt, embroidered breeches, and calf-high kidskin boots which let her move easily and freely. Her blonde hair was cropped short.

Traedis had given orders that Emmen was to be shown up to her private sitting room, rather than a reception room. A servant brought in a plate of spiced sausages and cheese from the kitchen, as well as a hastily decanted bottle of fine, aged wine before leaving.

Emmen's guard waited in the hallway, and even Vandeyr was banished. This was to be a truly private meeting.

Emmen sat, hooked her thumbs into her belt, and fronted Traedis. "What's wrong?" she asked. "All I was told was that you needed me urgently. That it might be dire." She looked keenly at Traedis, then helped herself to a pair of sausages and a wedge of cheese.

Dire. The word was apt. Vandeyr's search had turned up the information that Lord Foli, the father of the two killed in the botched assassination attempt, was dead. Mardra had spoken of a death curse, but at first Traedis had not remembered, though she knew she should; the body's last breath gave a curse tremendous potency and power.

The news had come hard to Traedis, shattering her already faint hope of a simple resolution to the matter. She did not want to have to make either of the terrible decisions the Mistress of Ravens would force upon her. Perhaps Emmen could find a solution; she saw none herself.

Lifting a sheaf of papers which bore Vandeyr's report, Traedis quickly summarized what had happened in court, omitting only Mardra's request. Emmen did not speak but watched her minutely, her focus never leaving Traedis' face.

When Traedis finished, Emmen leaned forward on her elbows, a piece of cheese still in one hand. "This matter of the Dance is bad stuff, Trae. I trust the request she made of you is one you can't in conscience fulfill?"

Traedis nodded, glad for Emmen's quick grasp of the situation. "No." She licked her lips nervously. "If I only had something with which I could bargain, I would be in a better position. Which is what I want to discuss with you. How do I placate her without giving in to her demands?" In the previous days she had found time to contemplate the situation, and she hoped Emmen could find something innocuous that Mardra might still want more than she wanted an assassination.

Emmen nodded thoughtfully. "I see what you mean, but I'm concerned that you not pin your hopes too strongly on finding something tidy and precise to resolve everything. Sometimes neither choice is good, and all you can do is hold to your principles." She wrinkled her brow. "I don't know how to advise you, Trae. You are the best arbiter of what is right for your city."

Traedis felt her hopes sink even further. She had allowed herself to believe that Emmen would know the answer, that she would know how to defend Tolin. Her shoulders sagged, and she dropped the papers on the table.

"Trae," said Emmen. "Look at me."

Traedis looked up, her mind churning like a whirlpool. Ideas crowded her mind, welling into existence and flowing out just as quickly once she realized they were impractical. She set her shoulders and her chin, determined at least to present a brave front to her friend.

"I haven't said there is no solution," Emmen told her. "Just that there *may* not be one. We have by no means exhausted the possibilities." She drummed her fingers on the table for a moment, then snapped her fingers. "Here's an idea. It might be possible to help you call the spirit of Lord Foli. Some of my order have the gift, and as king, I am granted more than my measure. I don't know what this lord can do from beyond the grave, but if he still lingers in the world, he may have some power even now to alter the curse."

A spark of possibility ignited in Traedis' mind. She felt her thoughts slow enough to focus on a single facet of the report. Picking it up, she leafed through to find the piece of information she remembered reading.

"Lord Foli's brother said – " Stopping on the third page, Traedis underlined the words with her finger. "That he has dreamed repeatedly of his brother wandering an unfamiliar graveyard by the light of the full moon." She stopped and looked up again, excitement thrumming through her chest. "Listen to this. 'The graveyard lay in a slash of rock on a steep mountain face. Many of its teeth were broken or crumbling, and new graves lay close together, their stones small and unmarked. By the full moon's light, I could see that one edge rose sharply to a heavy granite wall; the other sloped gently downhill in a screen of trees, while the murmur of running water could be heard beyond. It was here my brother paced the boundaries, his gaze fixed and sad.'" She gave a quick bark of laughter. "The man should be a bard, and I thank

Kyaan for his eloquence."

"You know where this is." Emmen's words were a statement, not a question.

"I think it's the pauper's graveyard, just outside Tolin's walls." Perhaps hope was not yet lost. "What is the moon's phase?"

Emmen raised her brows. "Wandering *Tolin's* graveyard? Interesting." She took another sausage and poured a glass of wine. "The phase is waxing gibbous. Are you thinking to call him at the full?"

Traedis nodded. "Though it's odd he should haunt Tolin, if he hated it so much."

"Such hatred occasionally creates a bond." Emmen sipped from her glass. "And curses are odd anyway. They can recoil on their caster easily, posing as much danger as they do to the one on whom they are cast." Setting her glass down, she reached over and took Traedis' hands in hers. "Don't despair, Trae. Don't give up."

"I won't give up. I promise." Traedis said nothing about despair.

Chapter Nine
Visions

The moon bleached the countryside in a wash of pale light. Traedis, Emmen, Vandeyr, and Ruth walked tensely through the hollow shadows, which transformed ordinary features into fantastical shapes, and hid the daylight world in a patchwork of stark divisions. Traedis did not fear the night, and her unity with the land informed her of her surroundings, but so much depended on finding the author of the curse that her nerves started at every night noise and the rustle of every breeze through the dead leaves that still clung to the oak branches.

The graveyard was tucked beneath a wide cleft in the mountain below Tolin; the 'slash of rock' described by Lord Foli's brother. His description had lacked snow, however, and the gravestones could be seen only as humps under freshly fallen drifts. One new grave was visible, clods of earth and trampled slush scabbing over the clean purity in frozen brown splatters. A few footprints showed in the ankle-deep cover, but very few; a bitter cold had blown through from the Dragon Mountains only the day before. Traedis pulled her cloak tightly around herself and shivered. She might be known to the Lord of Winter, but Harfast's realm was still one to respect.

Emmen absently brushed off one of the humps to expose a crumbling stone which listed at a slight angle. "Let me concentrate," she told Traedis. "With luck I may find him right away; it depends on how restless his spirit is." She closed her eyes, her breath even as if she meditated.

Traedis nodded and waited with the stillness of winter itself for Emmen to call forth the spirit of the dead lord. An owl hooted softly from the trees, and Traedis planted her feet deeply in the crusty snow, concentrating on breathing evenly. Vandeyr began to walk the cemetery's perimeter, sword at the ready; Ruth rooted herself firmly next to Traedis.

As the stars inched through the sky, the air seemed to grow thicker and heavier, making it harder to breathe. Traedis felt a cold deeper than the air's chill settle over the graveyard. Near Emmen's form a patch of moon and snowlight coalesced into a shimmering shape of purest white. Traedis drew a sharp breath which tasted of dust and decay despite the cold of the winter night. She made a noise of surprise in her throat.

"What is it?" asked Ruth, pulling her white-bladed dagger.

"Do you see?" Traedis asked in a whisper.

"See what?" Ruth looked around from side to side as if expecting to view someone approaching from around the corner.

Traedis watched Ruth carefully, realizing that the brunaidh did not perceive the figure taking shape under the moonlight. Emmen stirred, but did not open her eyes.

Fascinated, Traedis looked at the glowing form. Rather than moongleam, it shone with the luminosity of cave moss or deep-sea fish, a cold dead light reminiscent of something long buried. The shape was transparent, and she could see the graveyard through him, but the figure seemed distorted somehow, as if seen through a pane of rippled glass. Gradually Traedis made out the features; a man of middle years, his face lined with joy and care. He stared straight ahead, as if he saw something very far away.

From the far side, Vandeyr's head went up; she immediately made her way back over to where Traedis stood. She glanced back and forth, before sucking in her breath quickly, and focusing on the same place Traedis watched.

Traedis placed a careful hand on Vandeyr's arm. "Let me past." To the phantom, she said, "Lord Foli?" Approaching him, she felt her skin prickle in alarm. She recognized the sensation quickly; it was akin to *demonfear*, though not nearly as strong; a sense of dislocation which tilted the world sideways and made her skin shrink.

The figure turned his head to face her, but his eyes still focused on something distant. "King Traedis."

Ruth jerked as if startled. She looked back and forth, clearly unable to see the specter.

"You are he whom I seek?" Determinedly, Traedis kept her attention on the ghost, despite her strong desire to turn away. "You are Lord Foli?"

"I am." He grew more solid, as if his words anchored him to Tolin's earth. "What do you want of me?"

Traedis found that now, confronted with Lord Foli's ghostly and potentially hostile presence, she wished herself elsewhere. She breathed in and out deeply, then lifted her chin. "You are the author of the curse which was placed upon the City of Assassins."

"I am." Lord Foli's voice rang hollow, as if it echoed through a long cold tunnel.

Ruth shivered. "I can hear something, but I can't see a thing. Only moonlight on snow."

"Right there," Traedis told her. "Two stones away from Emmen, to the left."

"There's a human shape," Vandeyr told Ruth. "Hard to make anything out."

Traedis thought of what Lord Foli had suffered through the City's doing, and felt a sudden compassion for him, though she still felt as if rime ice stung her skin. "I am sorry the City took so much from you," she told him gently. "I do not blame you for what you did. I am here to ask for your aid, though perhaps I have no right."

Lord Foli stared ahead with blank eyes, ignoring the others. "You have every right to ask for my assistance. But how can I aid you? I am powerless."

Traedis looked at him again. Were he living, she might have liked this man very much. She wondered again at the fate which had set him against the City and its clumsiest assassin.

"You called down a curse." The tips of her fingers were growing icier. "Were it to return, might you lift it from my lands?"

The ghost startled, his distant gaze turning to focus on Traedis. "The curse is already lifted. You say it might return?"

Traedis nodded, disquiet growing in her belly. "The Mother of Curses removed the curse in exchange for the City's aid in fulfilling a contract. But the contract was never completed, and now she threatens to restore the curse. I cannot do what she wants, but that means the City will suffer." She swallowed. "You have no reason to love us, but I am trying to turn the City from its long-mapped course. Will you help me?"

Lord Foli's mouth firmed into a line of pain. "I would help you if I could, King Traedis. But I am truly powerless." He sighed in a way Traedis recognized from her own long imprisonment: a sigh of hopeless patience and endurance. "If there were anything I could change about my life, it would be the calling of that curse. But I cannot."

"Why do you say so?" asked Traedis, her throat aching in sympathy. "It was your right, and I cannot blame you." His pain was unimaginable, and she hoped she would never experience the like.

"I blame myself!" Lord Foli's eyes sparkled with pale luminescence. "I had no right. I thought when I found the bodies of my children that my curse would damn those who had caused me such pain, but I never thought of the innocents I would destroy." He closed his eyes, but his expression suggested that he was still watching something terrible behind his lids. "I took the blood of my son in one hand and the blood of my daughter in the other and I called down the vengeance of the gods. It came like lightning through my body, and destroyed me from within, but I no longer wanted to live. I thought then that my action would be that of a hero." He paused. "The children of vipers are vipers still, but for the free-willed peoples, the children are innocents. By my curse, I caused death and pain to those who did not merit it, just as was done to me. I had no right. The gods have punished me for it."

"How?" asked Traedis softly, sure that his punishment had something to do with the reason he would haunt Tolin's graveyard.

Lord Foli opened his eyes and looked about himself, his lids never blinking. "I must walk these lands," he said, gesturing about him, "until everyone who lost something through my curse has passed away." He sighed again. "Do you know how long that will be? Two aelin families lost unborn children; that alone could bind me to this earth for generations. One event influences another, like a single stone tumbling down a field of scree. And I *know*." The agony in his gaze was hard for Traedis to bear. "I must see much of what passes in your City, and I cannot affect it. Especially I see the children – what harms them that I cannot alter. King Traedis, I would give anything that I have done to change my actions that day, but I am unable. The gods grant that you find a way to turn aside my curse without further harm to those you rule."

Traedis' eyes ached, both with sympathy and disappointment, laced with the acid fear that she would find no solution to her quandary. Curses, she thought, had long reaches, and their consequences did not always land only on the victim. Wingblade had died to cast his.

But even though Foli was powerless, she was not. It was a strange twist of fate that brought her to console him, but her impulse of compassion ran deep. If she could not find a solution, at least she could give some comfort to this one man who had suffered so much. "I am sorry, Lord Foli. I still do not blame you. I do not know what I would have done if I had found the bodies of my children murdered. Is there any way in which I can aid you?"

"I fear not," Lord Foli answered in his hollow, distant fashion. Then he shook his head, causing an illusion that the graves beyond him quivered and shimmered. "Perhaps – " He closed his dead eyes. "I have little right to ask anything of you, but perhaps you might come here sometimes during the full moon." His voice began to fade, echoing as if emanating down a long tunnel. "It has been long since I have spoken with another soul, and I crave company."

"You may be sure of it," Traedis told him, her eyes misting.

Lord Foli's form thinned like fog dissipated by a breeze, vanishing gradually into the night air. Traedis felt the icy sensation fade with him, leaving her drained, as if she had dug through the earth with her bare hands.

Vandeyr shook herself like a dog shedding rain. "That was – very odd. I feel like I was listening to something talking underwater. I could hear it, but it was very distorted." She stamped snow off her boots. "I can tell that being captain of your guard is going to lead to some interesting experiences."

Traedis looked first at Ruth, then at Emmen. "Emmen?"

Emmen turned slowly to face Traedis. "I heard." She stretched slowly, like an arthritic woman. "You should be able to call him without my help now; once he came, I did little to keep him here. He is in your *falmyros* after all. That's why you could see him, and

I could not." She shook her head. "I'm sorry this avenue proved fruitless. I hope that my people can find out something that helps." She frowned and took Traedis' hands in her own. "We won't give up, Trae, I promise you that."

Traedis found herself echoing Lord Foli's deep sigh. The fact was that she still could not depend on another to solve her problem for her. She, not Emmen, was king of Tolin, and it was time that she acted as such. Somehow, she must use the knowledge and abilities she had to find a solution.

Her fingers ached with cold, despite her thick gloves. Traedis' mind flickered to the silver trees and crystalline splendor of Winter's deepest heart. Its lord had given gifts to her friends and herself when they had aided him in finding his beloved wife. She wished now that instead of receiving the gift of speaking with snow, she had acquired the ability to ignore cold altogether. Though even Ruth's gift of scrying in ice would have been more useful just now.

Ruth's scrying. Traedis felt the heat rise to her face, feeling extremely foolish. There were other ways to hunt for answers. Between her own abilities as a bard, and Ruth's scrying, she might well have all the tools she needed in those same cold fingers.

"I think," she said slowly, "it is time to use my own skills to find an answer. Or, I should say, my own skills and Ruth's." She turned her head toward the brunaidhi woman. "Ruth, will you lend me your scrying?"

Ruth blinked up at Traedis. "Of course." She snorted. "I

should have thought of that myself. I'm a little embarrassed that I didn't."

Traedis felt her throat tighten. "Thank you. You're a good friend."

"Don't worry," Ruth said. "We'll figure things out."

It was midmorning of the next day before Traedis was ready to try tapping Ruth's winter gift. They had chosen to use her sitting room for the purpose; it was defended, not only by Vandeyr's capable sword, but by magic woven throughout the apartments, set there by the previous owners.

Emmen had gone back to Haven by gate spell, but she had told Traedis that she would return at a moment's notice should she be needed. Traedis felt tremendously grateful for the support. Friends were supporting her when most of her family would not.

Ruth hopped up on a divan along the same wall as the table which held Traedis' books and papers and lay down with her head pillowed by a powder-blue cushion. The divan, upholstered in pale plum silk with graceful dark wooden legs that curved into eagle's claws, was not a piece Traedis would have picked out, but it had come with the house, and she was determined not to waste funds by replacing perfectly serviceable furniture. It was comfortable, and that was more important than whether or not the shade matched her hair or her latest dress.

It also backed up to the windows, keeping the morning sunshine out of Ruth's eyes. Traedis squinted, then rose to pull the curtain. She did not want to be blinded by winter's brilliant glory when she was trying to concentrate on her music and her spellwork.

As a bard, Traedis knew that her greatest talents lay in her ability to improvise and to harmonize disparate elements, both of music and magic. Part of her studies in Kaelennar had involved both learning and creating bardic spellwork, and she had been an apt pupil. Inspired by the way her friends had helped and supported each other, Traedis had created a weavework of magic which took different spells and laced them into a single one with a sole purpose.

Even in Kaelennar, others had difficulty in learning her spell chording. But during her four years in prison, she had kept what sanity she could through concentrating on her music, though she had lacked even a harp to play. She had forced herself to pluck without strings; had kept her callouses by scraping her fingers along the rough stone walls of her cell; and had sung every song that she knew so many times she could invent multiple harmonies against the melody in her voice. When that had not proven enough, she had forced herself to focus on every scrap of musical and magical theory she had ever learned, turning both over in her mind, adding, changing, and inventing new twists on the songs and spells she had learned.

The work she had spent on her spell chording had borne fruit; she had considered how to add magical abilities or objects to the spell, and how to strip elements from other spells before adding their essences to the chording. Once freed, she had discovered that she could indeed play them. Whether others could learn the refinements would be tested at another time. This spell would tap into Ruth's scrying ability.

She played a few scales to warm and limber her hands, every touch of the strings a hard-won joy, the smooth soundboard alongside her cheek a delight. Rose sang like bells, sweet as honey and twice as golden. The harp would play even if Traedis did not touch the strings, but she wanted to use her own hands, both for the exhilaration of making music and for the important grounding it gave to her music and her spellwork. She did not want her art to outstrip her craft.

She placed her hands against the double rows of strings which gave her harp a wide range of notes. Her long, strong fingers pulling melody from metal, she let a lullaby flow out, her voice melding into the complex tension of harmonies. Calling the magic to her, she began to sing Ruth to sleep.

It was the only way to reach Ruth's magic. The brunaidhi woman had been a mage once, but she had buried all magic deeply. The City had taken her, years ago, and tried to turn her into an assassin; renouncing her magic had been the only way to keep them from using her power and abilities. Her white-bladed dagger was a quiet but absolute denial of the City's right over her.

Ruth's scrying talent was easy for Traedis to call, for it was another of Harfast's winter gifts. It created a link between the two women that provided a conduit for the spell.

Ruth's breath deepened as she fell under the enchantment; she gave a small snore. Traedis felt her lips curve upward as she finished the last notes and regarded her friend. Ruth would sleep for an hour or two if no one disturbed her. Now came the difficult part: the chording. Traedis forced down fear that rose from her stomach to her chest to her throat. She must relax, or her notes would be forced, and the magic diluted.

She had spent four years learning how to put everything aside except for her music; it was how she had survived. She straightened her back and lifted her chest before coming in on a high, clear note that vibrated and buzzed against the window glass. She had no melody fixed ahead in her mind – it was the pattern, the friction with her harpsong, the harmonies and the grace notes that created the magic; this, and how they interacted with the other enchantments the music encompassed. The notes spilled out, liquid and fluent, pouring out melody and countermelody as Traedis laid the foundation for the chording.

This was the hardest part, for though there was a logic and a pattern to the magic, it was enough of an art that Traedis could never be sure which chords and rhythms she would need until she integrated the blended magics. Her fingers plucked the strings with knowledge of their own, ringing with eerie clarity on the gold-coated *sagathas*. Her soaring voice twined with the instrument, a duet of power and skill that had always been the one thing on which Traedis could rely.

A twist of magic held by the dancing notes of the harp caught

Ruth's scrying in an invisible grip, thin and strong as a spider's thread. Now, twining her own magic into the chording, Traedis began to find the harmonies for spells to understand and interpret what Ruth's vision would show. Teasing the brunaidhi woman's gift out of her sleeping mind, she used discordant notes to highlight the chording rather than to disrupt it. The unison of their winter gifts beat as one in a slow, dreaming tempo rimed in hoarfrost and moonlight.

From here it would be a delicate balance. If she lost a part of the pattern, the entire spell could dissipate. Closing her eyes, Traedis pulled Ruth's harmony closer, letting herself fall into the music and the magic she and Rose wove together.

Slowly the dark behind her lids became color and image. Traedis saw the Mother of Curses within her cloak, and pulled back sharply to avoid the flood of *demonfear* even a remote picture might convey. Mardra's presence sucked her in like an impossibly powerful lodestone, and Traedis was not sure that she was strong enough to struggle against the demon. In a moment, the Matron would notice her. Traedis felt her pulse throb in her throat; she struggled against the feeling that she would fall into the well of the demon's attraction, barely keeping the spell matrix intact.

In a terrible effort like ripping off a layer of skin, she summoned the power gathered from the chording and forced it to her will, bending Ruth's scrying to focus on the bargain rather than the bargainer.

Something broke free. Traedis felt the rush of magic and her throat opened once again. She played a quick scatter of ascending notes, casting her voice into the middle of the song like an arrow shot from the bow. *Who can aid me?* she pleaded through the magic. *From whom shall I find an answer?*

Emerging from smoke and memory, a picture formed: a giant bird the size of a small house, lifting slate gray wings through a clouded sky. The Storm Eagle.

Traedis started, and her fingers dropped from the strings. The spell unraveled in a cacophony of jangling strings and ragged breath.

The Storm Eagle was dead these last three months, killed by one of the Nightdance. How she could speak to him she did not know, nor how he could help her when he had not possessed the power to help himself. But she had already spoken with one ghost to protect Tolin. Perhaps there was some way to reach the Storm Eagle as well. She knew where he was; she had dreamed of him. Instead of the final home of his people, he rested on the Isle of Ymre, the far land of flowers that most thought mythical.

Traedis knew it was no fable: she had been there. Rose Goldsong had been re-strung with *sagathas* by a great magic-smith of Ymre. The land was named after its lord, Ymre the Wise Hound, a star who no longer shone in mortal skies. If he were to consent, Traedis might have some hope.

Rose whispered a quiet susurrus of affirmation, ghosts of air pulling sounds from its strings like speech.

Ruth gave another snore. Traedis rose and went to shake her

friend's shoulder. "Wake up," she said. "I think I know what to do next."

Ruth roused slowly. "What?" She sat up and ran a hand through hair already tousled by her nap. "You know how to bake a mouse?" She knuckled her eyes and blinked ferociously. "No. That can't be what you said."

Traedis' lips twitched. "I said I know what to do next."

"Oh." Ruth waited for several moments. When Traedis did not respond, she said, "What should we do next?"

A thrill of fear screeched through Traedis' bones. "We must speak to the Storm Eagle. And quickly."

Vandeyr and Emmen entered Traedis' sitting room, both of them taut as strung bows. Emmen dropped into a chair opposite Traedis, her mouth a grim line.

"You need to speak to the Storm Eagle," she said. It was no question.

Traedis nodded. "I do. At least according to Ruth's scrying gift."

Ruth sat on the windowsill, kicking her legs and squinting into the noonday sun. Then she moved back through the room, and though Traedis had a proper brunaidhi seat for her, she instead chose to perch on a conveniently low footstool. It was obvious that Ruth was also anxious, despite maintaining a cheerful demeanor. Her friend did not fear adventure, but she also knew what was at stake.

Emmen shook her head. "It's one thing to call up a wandering ghost, it's another to call back an aelin spirit from his home. I don't see how this can be done."

Traedis cast her memory back to her dreams of the Storm Eagle. Ever since the *falmyros* had come to her, he had spoken in her sleep, his smoky form perched on the edge of a great tree limb above a field of lavender. He spoke to her of small things; of Tolin's woods; of nests that enshrouded songbirds in the icy winter; of the river that leapt playfully down from the Dragon Mountains and cut through the wilds. A spring sky above him cast a sourceless pale light that intensified colors and emitted a sense of profound peace.

"He's in Ymre," she told Emmen. "I've dreamed of him there. What I don't know is how to reach him of my own accord when I'm not in the grip of sleep."

Vandeyr shifted slightly beside her; Traedis knew her sister was uncomfortable with the extent to which magic had touched Traedis' life.

"Ymre?" Emmen scratched her thigh. "Some of the aelin dead do go there, whether to rest before their final journey, or to abide out of time." She pursed her mouth. "That's another matter. Not an easy one, but it might be possible." She turned to Vandeyr. "I can call Lord Ymre from here – whatever magical wards you have on the palace won't block a connection to his land."

Vandeyr scowled at her. "That's supposed to be comforting? Are you aware of any other holes in my security?"

Ruth shook her head and repositioned herself on the stool.

"Enough," Traedis said with a sense of daring in contradicting Vandeyr. It would take a great deal of time to be comfortable with the idea, but she could at least put on the appearance of bravery. "We don't have time to spare. Emmen, what can you do?"

Emmen nodded at her. "I think I can establish a connection with Lord Ymre, but whether he chooses to respond or not isn't up to me. Still, he has helped us before, and I think he won't ignore a petition from two kings."

Emmen had been with Traedis and her friends when, in fleeing the City in the days before Traedis had gained the *falmyros*, they had gone to Ymre seeking help for the Storm Eagle. There they had learned of the true nature of the relationship between Tolin and Haven, and the Wise Hound had given them aid and counsel. Traedis fervently hoped that he would assist them again.

Vandeyr's scowl had turned into a glowering sulk. She turned on her heel and exited the room, letting the latch close behind her. Moments later, she returned and shot the bolt. "I've told the guard not to disturb us for an hour. Is that enough time?"

"I don't know." A thoughtful line grooved Emmen's forehead. "If it's not, you can speak to them again."

She straightened and stared ahead, her eyes gazing at something Traedis could not see. Her lips moved silently, and the noon light's beams seemed to gather and pool around her as if funneled into an unseen whirlpool. Sweat broke out on her forehead and her brow furrowed with effort.

Traedis breathed shallowly, fearing to move in case it might interfere with the other king's concentration. Her chest hurt.

The glow around Emmen began to brighten, shimmering like starlight without a moon. "King Emmen," said Ymre's voice. Traedis had expected it to ring in a hollow or sepulchral way, as if spoken by a phantom; she was surprised that, instead, it sounded as if he stood in the room. "Why do you seek me?"

"King Traedis is in trouble," Emmen said without preliminary. "The Mother of Curses wishes her to complete a contract made with Tolin before King Traedis' rule. To this end, the Matron threatens to restore a curse on the city of Tolin if this contract is not fulfilled."

"I know this," Ymre stated. "What do you wish of me?"

Traedis recalled the kindness the Wise Hound had shown her, and did her best to summon enough courage to speak. "My Lord," she said a little breathlessly, "I cast a spell to find who could help me – my spell showed me the Storm Eagle. Am I right that he is in your land? If so, I must petition you to allow me to speak with him so that I may care for the city of Tolin."

Ymre's voice sounded thoughtful. "Under ordinary circumstances I find it best not to allow mortals to speak with the aelin dead. But your cause is just, and is not for yourself. I am minded to grant your request." A small growl escaped him. "I do not care for Mardra, and if I may thwart her by means within my power and right, I will do so. I will send my son Rana to bring you to Ymre, where you may speak with Eldasaan – the Storm Eagle – if he chooses."

A sigh blew through Traedis; her legs felt boneless. Though she knew the Storm Eagle might not aid her, at least one hurdle was past. She owed Ymre more than she could be sure of repaying. "Thank you, my lord," she said, trying to convey the depth of her gratitude through her voice alone.

"He's gone," Emmen said in a thoroughly exhausted tone. "I don't know how long it will take for him to send Rana, but given his response I doubt he will waste time. Do you want me to come with you if he will permit it?"

"Yes!" Traedis said, grateful for the offer.

"If anyone goes with her, it should be me." Vandeyr's tone was implacable.

Emmen's expression softened to compassion. "Your loyalty to your sister is commendable, but the Storm Eagle has a connection to the both of us in a way he does not with you. It is perilous enough for a mortal to speak with the dead, but it is more perilous for you than for Trae and myself." Ruth stirred as if she wanted to speak, then subsided again.

"Facing danger is part of my job." Vandeyr stilled, reminding Traedis of a hunting cat. "It's not for you to tell me what I may or may not do – "

"No," Traedis cut in, earning her one of Vandeyr's scowls. "That's for me to do. And I think Emmen is right. She needs to come with me, and you don't."

The argument was interrupted by a wavering in the air like heat haze, which shimmered into golden light before becoming a tall figure that entered the room as if it had stepped from a dream into the waking world. *Which in some sense, it has*, thought Traedis. White hair, pulled into a tail at the nape of his neck, framed youthful features with the long, delicate bones of an aelin countenance, set with extraordinarily vivid green-blue eyes. He smiled and bowed gracefully from the waist.

Emmen rose to embrace him. "Rana," she said with affection.

Traedis also rose and gave him the bow of a king to a great prince; though as a king, she outranked him, his father was so much greater than she that there was no true comparison. "I am glad to finally meet you, Prince Rana." She liked the lines of kindness and determination that etched his face.

Vandeyr kept her back rigid, standing to attention like the soldier she was. Ruth rose and bowed, then resettled herself, watching all of them with the appearance of keen interest.

Rana bowed and nodded to each of them in turn. "Follow me, King Traedis, and I'll take you to Ymre and to the Storm Eagle."

Vandeyr cleared her throat.

"May I accompany her?" asked Emmen. "I want to hear what Eldasaan has to say – it might be material to Haven as well."

Rana looked at her thoughtfully, then nodded. "Yes. You may also speak with him." He shot a glance at Vandeyr, who Traedis thought looked as if she might bite, though others would see only an alert guard captain. "I cannot take anyone else. I agreed to bring King Emmen only because she is also in a unique position in regard to Eldasaan. I'm sorry, Captain."

"I suppose that goes for me as well," Ruth said, wry resignation informing her voice. "I would like to have a chance to visit again, but I suppose this isn't my task. Let me know if there's anything else I can do, though. I'm not going anywhere."

Traedis could see from the minute bracing of her sister's spine that Vandeyr was angry. In order to turn the anger on herself rather than her friends, she said, "Thank you, Prince Rana. I know that I need not fear while I am under your father's watchful eyes." She was rewarded with the quick flicking of Vandeyr's eyes in her direction. "I am ready."

Rana nodded. "Then follow in my steps. Don't worry if I seem to be taking you through the wall – we won't actually reach it, though it may be disconcerting." He turned and began to walk toward the north end of the room.

Traedis shouldered Rose's case and followed, Emmen close behind her. The memory of the other time she had been to the strange, timeless land of Ymre rose in her heart like a treasure. She yearned for its peace and beauty, the antithesis of the nightmare her rule of Tolin had become. In Ymre she would not need to guide a people who hated her, nor would she be expected to rebuild a city heavily damaged by Toledru. In Ymre, she could be herself: the bard, and not the king.

Phantom trees swelled between them and the wall, stone replaced with wooden boles that soon branched into living birches, aspens, and willows. Green-and-golden leaves shivered in her vision, defining a path that was most certainly not part of Traedis' apartments. A layer of mist drifted in, its spectral fingers teasing their ankles. The trees, delicate as children, cast strange shadows of light and darkness over their faces like trailing moss.

As the path grew more defined, Traedis felt a lightening of spirits which told her that she walked now on the soil of Ymre, the land more distant than an ancient tale. Around them, boughs and branches thickened into oak and beech without crowding out their more fragile cousins. Emerging completely into Ymre was like the first sight of morning.

Soft piles of cloud hung over the sun, marked with purple and blue linings which promised later rain. The three of them stood on a slope swaying with ancient trees that arched protectively over the ground. A riot of blooms, blue, white, silver and purple, covered the ground and the bushes, their growth echoing different seasons. Lilacs grew profusely in every natural color. Mingled perfumes of flowers twined with the spicier scent of grass and leaf mold, but the odor neither cloyed nor overpowered. Above them birds sang, and butterflies fluttered in the lower air alongside bees and iridescent dragonflies.

Traedis stopped and gazed, her eyes full of wonder. The air tasted cleaner than was possible in the mortal world. It reminded her of the peace of Winter's Heart, but in many ways the two were each other's inverse: Ymre teemed with life, not the still cold sleep which Harfast imposed upon his land.

Movement caught her attention: a white figure streaking toward them on four legs. Moments later, they were joined by an enormous white hound. Its shaggy hair hung low, and its narrow, delicate head held eyes of the same deep green blue as Rana's. This was Lord Ymre, the Wise Hound, Rana's father. She curtsied deeply to him; as a star, he was as far above her station as she was to an ant. Emmen swept him a low bow.

Ymre nipped at something on his flank, then sat up and cocked his head. "You needn't be so formal, Traedis, Emmen. You are my guests here, not my servants. I am who I am, and I don't require obeisance to remind myself." He spoke clearly, though his mouth was not made for words.

Rana's brow rose. "I was just about to take them to Eldasaan. Should I wait?"

"I would like to borrow Traedis for the space of an hour." Ymre's tongue lolled from his mouth. "There is something I would like to teach her."

That was strange, but Ymre was renowned for his knowledge and wisdom. If he wanted to teach Traedis, she would learn. "Very well," she told him. "Though time is short, I know you would not delay me for something unimportant." She cursed herself silently the moment the words were out of her mouth; she sounded arrogant and rude. Deciding that trying to explain would only make her sound worse, she shut her mouth.

Ymre did not seem to be offended. "You forget," he said, and wagged his tail. "I am master of time here. If I desire that your time claims no hours in the mortal world, it will not. And I do so desire."

Traedis had forgotten. This time she did not speak, but only nodded.

"Come this way, Traedis." Ymre shook his fur, then angled off in a different direction than Rana had taken. Traedis followed.

They arrived at a white marble pavilion, one of many that dotted the landscape like columned growths. Pink veined the stone; cushioned chairs and benches were artfully arranged, and purple honeysuckle climbed the pillars with joyful determination. In the center rose a plinth, though Traedis could see nothing atop it.

Ymre stretched himself out between two benches, and thoughtfully licked his paws. "Please sit." He thumped his tail as Traedis took one of the cushioned chairs. "There is a discipline I would like you to learn, one which I think will serve you well. Tell me, have you ever heard of bardic runes?"

Traedis cast her mind back to her lessons in Kaelennar. They had studied a variety of topics, including those which the teachers wanted students to avoid. "I understand they're terribly dangerous because they give power for a cheap cost. As such, they're often misused, and my teachers thought none of us should ever try them."

Ymre turned his head to sniff at something Traedis could not see. "True enough, but not comprehensive. All words have power. For those who want to exert power over others, runes are dangerous, though 'cheap' is perhaps not quite the word, since it can take many years to master the art. You, however, are not a woman who desires power, and any magic can be dangerous." He chuckled. "I confess that when I invented writing, I had no real idea of using it in such a way, but the world changes, and others have built on my foundation. Let me show you something."

He rose and padded to the plinth. Traedis followed, and saw that it was engraved with a single symbol: the perfect circle of a serpent swallowing its own tail.

"I am the *quixil;* it is my first rune, and that on which all writing is based."

Traedis examined the symbol minutely. Simple yet evocative,

it made her think of spirals and helixes spinning off into infinite distances.

"Take time," Ymre added, his tail wagging back and forth so enthusiastically Traedis was afraid he would sprain it. "Study it. Try to let its meaning soak into your bones. Only if you can understand this will you be able to see the meaning and the pattern behind all runes and symbols."

"What *does* it mean?" she asked. The *quixil* remained tantalizingly distant, like words spoken in another tongue.

Ymre shook himself thoroughly. "It is the beginning and the ending, and the new beginning beyond that. It is eternity, the circle of the gods and the way in which they encompass the world."

Traedis stared harder at the rune before her. She could see how the meaning fit, but it did not seep into her understanding the way she wished it would. Her eyes unfocused. Still she stared, determined to absorb its mystical significance.

Lord Ymre walked slowly to her side, his nails clipping the floor loudly. He nosed in front of her, pointing as if alerting a hunter to prey. "You make this too difficult. Look first at its shape, and no further. Then think of its overt symbolism, fitting meaning to form. After you have done that, consider how endings and beginnings are related. Soon you will begin to see spirals where there were only circles to begin with."

Traedis looked at him, startled. "That was my first reaction. Spirals and helixes. I thought I was being fanciful."

Laughing, Ymre stepped back from the pillar. "Your instincts are good. Try not to talk yourself out of what you already know." He sounded very much like one of Traedis' teachers in the bardic college.

"Why spirals?" she asked, and the answer came quickly to mind. "Oh. Because, like circles, they have no beginning and no end, but they rise out of the closed loop and spin into a sort of eternity." She reached out to trace the figure in the stone. It felt cool and smooth beneath her hand.

Ymre nodded. "You understand quickly. Now, if I tell you that the *quixil* is related to other runes both the ordinary and magical, what does that tell you?"

Traedis closed her eyes to sort the random ideas spinning in her mind. "All other runes are encircled by this? All meanings are gathered within the *quixil*?"

"Which do you think?" asked Ymre patiently.

"Both," she answered promptly. Drawing her brows together in thought, she opened her eyes to look again at the rune. For a brief moment she saw it shine with an elusive brilliance before it returned to its graven form. She opened her eyes wide and turned to face the Hound.

Ymre gave a bark of laughter. "You are beginning to see. The *quixil* must be understood with the heart as well as the mind: language expresses both, and so writing must follow." An opalescent dragonfly flew by his head; he snapped at it, then turned his attention back to Traedis. "Runes are a distillation of language; they gain their power from the word's written form, but they compress meaning. By holding in the power of those meanings until they are released as a rune, they gain force. Look at the rune again," he said, pointing upward with his nose. "Envision the *quixil's* meaning, rather than its form. Try to avoid expectations or suppositions, and simply *see*."

"I'll try," Traedis said. She stared at the rune, trying to remain mindful of its many nuances. At first, she saw only its chiseled shape. Gradually, it seemed to protrude from the plinth, shining brightly. As Traedis looked in amazement, the rune lifted into the air and expanded before her astonished gaze into a great circle of flame. She could not turn her eyes aside as apprehension of the circle's eternity and renewal blazed in her mind.

"Close your eyes," Ymre said softly.

She shut her eyes tightly. Nothing shone behind her lids but ordinary darkness.

"Now look," the Hound continued.

She cracked her lids cautiously. Over the image on the pillar hung a ghostly duplicate which radiated a significance her mind could not fully assimilate.

"And that," Lord Ymre said in the same soft tone, "is how to see all runes. You will never be blind to them."

"That's all? Just that? Shouldn't it be more complex?"

Lord Ymre's voice was full of humor. "It would be – if I myself were not teaching you how to see such things within the land of Ymre. Here much may be learned which is normally beyond mortal ken."

Traedis bit her lip, feeling foolish for asking such a question of the Wise Hound.

"You have a good mind," Ymre added, "and the senses for a wide range of spellwork. Your spellchording has sensitized you to what most mortals never perceive. That makes it easier to teach you this sort of sight. Were you not a bard of extraordinary skill, we would not have been so successful. So be assured that your question was not as foolish as you believe it."

"What do I do with it?" she asked slowly.

"When you are home, I will send you a pair of books which will teach you the beginnings of runework. I would like you to take time – and I do know you have little – to study it, to learn its parameters, to teach yourself what you can. You must learn it yourself, however. I am not allowed to teach you, but only to point you toward it."

"Why?" Ymre was concealing something. "What am I going to need this for?"

Ymre turned, his nails clicking on the floor. "Rana and Emmen are waiting for you. Let me return you to them."

That was obviously the only response Traedis would get. She scooped up Rose and followed Lord Ymre back up the hill.

"It's not far," Rana told them. "He's waiting for you just over the ridge. This way."

Fewer trees grew on the ridge, leaving room for a carpet of emerald grass. Sourceless light flooded down in gentle beams that shone whiter than the sunlight of the mortal world, but did not dazzle or burn. On the other side lay a field of lavender, whose blossoms stretched cheerfully before her, nodding their slender heads.

The Storm Eagle perched near the edge of the trees. His pinions gleamed with a silver edge, though most of him still wore the smoky gray of storm and thunder which Traedis remembered. Her gaze had difficulty containing him, as if she and he did not truly exist together even in the space of this self-contained world. As she watched, his form flickered and shrank to the naked form of an aelin boy, then again expanded to the awesome shape of the City's former king.

Traedis walked down the slope reverently, aware that she now confronted the one she still considered her lord. Though Eldasaan was dead, he was of the high aelin race, and power surrounded him like an incipient cloudburst.

The Storm Eagle looked up as she arrived and his form partially solidified, though he still transformed back and forth between the two shapes. Traedis blinked and felt the beginnings of a headache. She massaged her temples and tried not to focus too hard on the details of his body. This was something mortals were not meant to see, and she trespassed on dangerous territory.

"Greetings," the Storm Eagle said, his voice edged with the low growl of thunder. "I'm glad you are taking care of the City for me. How is it? I rather miss the place." He fluffed his feathers and preened them with his beak.

Traedis curtsied deeply, a sense of awe suffusing her. "Lord Eldasaan, the City is in danger, and I am in need of your aid. The Mother of Curses has threatened to restore the curse which once stunted Tolin, if I do not fulfill her contract. And that I cannot do without destroying everything I am trying to change about the City. But what can I do if she chooses to reinstate it?"

The Storm Eagle looked into the air beyond as if searching the breeze. "I remember that curse." Darkness swirled around him as he once more shrank into the aelin boy. "I was powerless to affect it when it was laid, but it burned beneath my feathers." His voice was smaller now, but clear and strong. "I was unable to exercise my rule over the land, but you are not. Did I forget to teach you how to lift a curse with your power?"

Traedis simply stared at him. "You taught me no such thing."

He shifted back into his eagle form, the transformation obscuring Traedis' sight as his boundaries blurred. "There was much I could have shown you, but I had so little time." A mournful note suffused his voice. "It is something you need to know, however, and so it remains my responsibility." His form unexpectedly billowed to even greater proportions, and Traedis flinched involuntarily. Cocking his head, he looked at her piercingly with his golden eagle eyes. "This is how to break a curse with your power over the land."

A great force settled into Traedis' skull, then expanded, pressing outward with such violence that she felt her head might burst. She cried out and clapped her hands to her head. The world around her dimmed and disappeared.

A concerned voice spoke to her quietly; Traedis listened, but did not recognize it. Gradually she realized that she lay on the ground, her face to the sky. Grass and flowers tickled her cheeks. She wondered where she was.

"Traedis?" Emmen's voice awakened little memory of what had happened. "Can you hear me?" A few muffled notes rang out: Rose's call of alarm from within her case.

An unfamiliar voice repeated, "Traedis?" then continued in a tense tone, "It can be dangerous for the living to speak with the dead, and he forgot with whom he dealt. She's lucky to be alive."

"She knew there were risks, Rana," Emmen said quickly. Traedis felt returning circulation in her legs and arms like the bites of thousands of tiny ants. "Considering that she's still breathing, she'll probably count the price worth the danger."

"I expect she will," Rana answered. Traedis finally put a face to the second voice. Memory flooded back as she identified Rana Ymril and recalled what the Storm Eagle had done. He had spoken to her mind to mind, and such communication was not meant for the living. She wanted to shudder, but her body would not cooperate.

The revelation crashed around her like a resolved chord: she did indeed know how to remove a curse from the land. The *falmyros* should be sufficient. Despite his mistake, the Storm Eagle had given her what she asked. Relief cascaded through her like a freshet in spring.

Tentatively she tried to move an arm; it twitched, which was a good sign, but did not change position. Traedis groaned and her eyelids flickered of their own accord.

"Eh?" she managed around lips which tingled and did not want to move.

"She's waking up," Rana said. A gentle hand brushed her forehead. "King Traedis, you should be all right in a short time. Don't try to move yet."

"The Storm Eagle is terribly sorry," Emmen added. "He says he forgot himself."

"S'fine," Traedis struggled to say. Though her lips now burned as well as tingled, they moved more easily. The ant bites on her limbs had also turned into a fierce burning, but she welcomed it; at least she was still alive. She fought to lift her lids and was rewarded by a faint sliver of light, and by the sight of Emmen and Rana kneeling over her anxiously.

"Do your arms and legs hurt?" asked Rana worriedly.

"Yes," croaked Traedis, pleased that she was managing to make herself understood. "Much."

Rana took her right arm and began to massage it up and down its length. Traedis felt a wash of excruciating pain flow through it, then drain away into an exhausted state of rest. She moaned softly.

"Take her legs," Rana told Emmen. "I'll get the other arm."

As they massaged her limbs, a brief period of exquisite pain drained into a heavy languor, and she found that she could move more easily. She opened her eyes wider, pleased that they too seemed to be under better control.

"Can you talk?" asked Emmen, a deep line marring the skin of her forehead.

Traedis reached a hand to her throat. "I think so," she told Emmen, surprised that the words came so smoothly. "It's better."

"Do you want to sit up?" Rana hovered over her, waiting for her reply.

"I – yes." Traedis put weight on her right arm and pushed. She did not get far off the ground before Rana joined in supporting her to a sitting position. For a moment, the world tilted in a disjointed spiral, then the dizziness passed, and she was able to see clearly. Her head felt less like a melon, and more like a part of her body.

"He did tell me what I needed to know," she said in relief. Tolin was in her keeping; the Storm Eagle had given her the ability to protect it.

"I know he did." Rana shook his pale head. "He just didn't choose the best way of telling you. He wants a few more words with you if you're feeling up to talking with him." He stopped and considered. *"Safely* talking with him."

Traedis examined herself mentally. Though she still felt shaken, she did not seem to be injured; the blow had been to her mind and her integrity as a living woman, not to her body.

"I'm willing." She looked around. She still lay along the tree line, but the Storm Eagle had moved farther off, to a great oak which jutted above the canopy. Traedis could see him continuing his change from eagle to aelin and from aelin to eagle.

"Are you up to walking yet?" asked Emmen. "I'll help you to your feet."

"Thank you." Traedis took her hand and let Emmen's strong grip pull her up. For a moment, her legs did not want to work, and her knees nearly buckled. Then they straightened, and the earth steadied under her. This time there was no dizziness. She let go of Emmen, stretched her back until it cracked, then shouldered Rose's case. Emmen and Rana trailed behind her, their support both warming and heartening.

Approaching the Storm Eagle, she found herself reluctant to face him, despite her own brave words. He had been her childhood terror, and though she understood him now, his mistake had brought back much of her instinctive dread. She stopped in front of his tree and forced herself to look him directly in the eyes, fierce and golden now with the nature of the predator.

"You are better?" The Storm Eagle stirred restlessly, feathers rustling in the slight breeze. "I did not mean to hurt you. I forgot myself."

"I know that." Traedis quivered but did not look away. "I don't blame you. I'm the one who came to you for help. You wanted to speak with me further?"

"Yes. There is something about you that might cause difficulty in removing the City's curse." The Storm Eagle shrank back into the aelin boy, but his eyes were still those of the bird.

This time Traedis looked at him slantwise instead of directly; somehow it was harder to face him in this form. "What difficulty?" she asked, her voice subdued.

"The curse you bear." The boy's expression was sad. "It is a mighty curse and gives Mardra great power over you. It may prove harder to remove the curse on Tolin because of your own."

Traedis felt a spurt of anger; Wingblade's curse poisoned her future, just as it had her past. Though no longer confined to the City's prisons, her rule of Tolin was a chain she could not break without offending the gods. All she had wanted for her life was to define herself, to wrench herself from Tolin's stifling grasp and to become the bard that she had longed to be. Though she was a bard now, she must play the king and protect those who would be happy to see her deposed or dead. But duty was duty, and as an Azenel she understood that.

"What can I do?" she asked truculently, though her anger was not at him. It was not Eldasaan's fault that she hated the kingship and wished to be free of its shackles. His own imprisonment had been immeasurably longer than hers. "How can I fight the Mother of Curses if she already has a hold on me?"

"You cannot, on your own." The aelin shape solidified,

dispersed, expanded, and became again the great bird of prey. "I know what might help you, though." He scratched at the bark with a talon the size of Traedis' head. "Beneath the City library, in a seldom-used storeroom, is a long-neglected treasure. The storeroom is a natural cavern."

His words surprised her. Her father had overseen the City library, and she had spent a great deal of time in it as a child; she had thought she knew its secrets better than anyone. From the covert listening niche behind one of the bookcases to the secret cache of records kept in a safe room, she had hidden and spied out its every handspan: or so she had thought. She could not remember such a storeroom.

Without warning, the Storm Eagle sprang from the tree and fluttered down next to her among the lavender flowers. Traedis flinched and reached for her dagger before her mind understood that he meant no harm. It seemed that even in Ymre, her fears could overtake her reason.

"Down the lower staircase?" she asked, wrinkling her brow.

"Yes." The Storm Eagle hopped back from her, as if just now seeing her nervousness. "It goes very deep, you know."

Traedis nodded, mollified to know that she had not totally forgotten what she should have remembered. "There are two hundred steps at least. And it was closed in – " She suddenly remembered it. Her fear of enclosed spaces had not been as bad then.

"At the bottom is the cavern, where a door opens onto a deep chamber. Now it is filled with rags and buckets, broken mops, and old crates, but once it was a holy place of the n'korreld race." He fluffed his wing feathers. "On the ceiling, they painted five constellations, whose own light may be awakened by starshine. They have not been tended since before the City's founding, and are buried under nearly two thousand years of soot. If you uncover them, they may aid you – particularly the constellation of the Southern Dragon."

Traedis tried to remember if she had ever entered that room. Memory supplied her with images: a dark cold chamber of rock which held broken odds and ends that the library could no longer use. Now that a crack had been opened in her recollection, she could see it, though she had been too afraid to explore it the way she had the library itself. She had always thought of it as an eerie place, for though it was of a fair size and the ceiling was high and domed, the rock pressed around her with the weight of a darkened tomb. "Even if we uncover the constellations, how are we to awaken them? If they are painted on the ceiling, how may we bring them outside to wake under the light of Tolin's stars?"

Rana stepped forward and smiled. "About that – I may be only half a star, but will I do?"

Chapter Twelve
Starlight

Rana led Traedis and Emmen back through the trees, their footsteps muffled. Whether this was because of the soft dirt under their feet, or because of some abstruse property of the space between worlds, Traedis could not tell. Certainly, the earth felt solid enough, but Ymre was no normal place.

As the trees faded around them, she could see gray mountain stone which formed walls, not of the palace, but of the City library. Rana was leading them as directly as he could to the cavern which lay beneath; the library had safeguards against magical entry that would be hard to circumvent. Traedis had not realized that Rana knew Tolin so well. Perhaps the Storm Eagle had given him directions.

Approaching the entrance and moving into the main hall, she felt memories seize her, immersing her into the cold water of the past. She knew every carving, every chink and scratch in the granite, every chip of mortar. As a child, she had taken refuge in its quiet, and in the knowledge that sat on its shelves, pinned between leather covers, and awaiting release into her mind. The only place that held painful memories was in her father's office, but that was where she needed to go.

Gavaya, Traedis' eldest sister, sat behind the library custodian's desk, her straw-colored hair shining pale in the light which seeped into the small window at her back. Ancient texts stood in neatly stacked piles, their spines aligned with military rigor. Gavaya had one volume open and was taking notes in writing as delicate and precise as a cobweb. Her gaze took the three of them in and her eyebrows rose to a peak; she nodded respectfully, but made no comment. Traedis was sure that she recognized both Emmen and Rana, but Gavaya had always possessed a high level of prudence, and spoke little when affairs of state were involved.

Traedis took a long moment, battling darker memories. *"Useless, willful girl!" her father shouted, his face red with rage. "Why the gods saw fit to inflict you on our family is beyond understanding!"* For a moment, Traedis felt like a child, helpless to turn aside her father's wrath, to convince him that she had tried to learn the many skills that an Atenel must have to uphold the family honor.

She had been younger then. Later, she had stopped trying.

Attempting to exorcise her father from her mind and heart, Traedis shook her head. Right now, Tolin's needs were preeminent. "We need to go to the lowest storeroom," she told Gavaya briefly. "Is there still a freestanding ladder anywhere along the way?"

Gavaya blinked. "A long one. It's in the same room." She blotted her pen and shut her book. "The cavern is high, but so is the ladder – it's almost as tall as the room."

Traedis studied her sister, and wondered if she should explain. Gavaya would not repeat king's business or do anything to impede their work. The fewer who knew what they intended, the fewer there were who could, even unknowingly, tell Mardra. Uncovering the Southern Dragon was too important to risk. She would keep her own counsel.

"We may be down there for a while," she told her sister.

Gavaya's pale blue gaze rested thoughtfully on Traedis. "Do you want anyone to know where you are?" She moved her book to the top of a stack and selected another.

Traedis considered the question. "If Ruth asks, tell her. If Vandeyr wants to know – you'd better tell her, too. Anyone else, no."

Then she remembered that this was a n'korreld holy place, or had been thousands of years before. If Rana was important to its restoration, perhaps a karreld would be as well. "Wait. Can you please ask Prince Atchûk to join us as well? In clothes he can wash. I'd prefer not to have his entire guard here, however – ask him to be discreet."

"Very well." Gavaya nodded and rose, her demeanor studiously disinterested. Traedis knew better. Gavaya might be the most intelligent of them all, and she had learned to mask her thoughts in the hard school of the Atenel household: something Traedis had never learned to do.

They left the office together, their paths diverging in the main room of the library. This was a tall, vaulted hall with skylights that allowed illumination to seep in at the height of day; high windows were set into both the east and the west walls. Massive shelves stretched almost two stories up, and shorter freestanding bookcases ran the length of the room. Traedis looked down the long row of volumes, half expecting to see her younger self tucked into a quiet corner escaping her family's expectations.

Across the hall from the entrance was the door leading to the stairs. The battered old lantern she remembered still hung on a nail outside; she lit it before starting down the steps, the others at her heels. Emmen placed a comforting hand on her shoulder as they passed into the closeness and shadow of the lower levels.

The steps were smooth as they began the descent, and paused at two landings studded with doors before winding all the way to the bottom. After the second landing, the stair narrowed and roughened, the smooth plastered wall giving way to cold mountain stone. Traedis felt her heart clench as she tried to push down the rising fear of being trapped. Focusing on the lamp, the sound of feet, the height of the stairwell, she forced herself to continue. Her legs ached by the time they reached bottom.

She glanced back at Emmen and Rana. Emmen's gaze was sharp, and her movements wary. They must not alert Mardra one moment earlier than necessary, and the demon was only one of Traedis' enemies. For that matter, if the City knew Emmen was here, they might be moved to violence.

The stairway ended at the opening of a small natural cavern with a low ceiling, about the width and depth of six broad men. A wooden door, badly in need of repair, opened on the far side, leading into the deepest storeroom. Traedis walked forward and tugged it open. It was not locked.

Beyond the lantern's circle of yellow light, shadows hovered as if waiting to engulf the intruders. This was a large cave, the ceiling high for an underground space. Brooms, crates, broken furniture, and all manner of odd items cluttered the space inside so thickly that it was difficult to walk without knocking into something. Traedis remembered having explored this room as a child, fascinated by the number of hiding places it offered for a small girl, but terrified of the close, smothering darkness which shrouded its corners. Her father had put a stop to that exploration by confining her to her room for three days on the premise that Traedis had trespassed where she had no right. She had not returned since.

She put Rose on the floor and looked around. The ladder she was expecting leaned at a crazy angle against the wall, shielding a pile of forgotten junk under its length. Traedis set the lantern down on a box and went to examine it. The wood was rickety, and wobbled when she shook it, but its rungs remained in place, and Traedis judged it safe enough. She set it upright and climbed cautiously to the top, hoping it would hold. Her heavy velvet skirts swung precariously around her ankles, threatening to throw her off-balance. Had it not been for the importance of uncovering the treasure hidden in the cavern, she would have gone back to the palace and changed.

At the top, she examined the ceiling minutely, noting the thick coating of soot which crusted its surface. She ran a finger along it, barely managing to scrape off even a flake, though it smeared her finger with oily blackness. Traedis looked around for something to wipe her hand clean, unwilling to deliberately stain her dress if there was something else available.

"Meda's pissing fish," she muttered, disgusted that she had not thought exactly how they were to scour the ceiling. "Emmen, look around, will you? There might be some rags somewhere, and perhaps a bucket or two. I wish I had an apron as well, though if I ruin my clothing, I suppose it will be in a good cause. We'll need to go back up to the library to get water, though."

Emmen's voice came from beyond the pool of lantern light. "It's hard to see, but I think I've found some things that will work. You might want to get additional supplies though, because these rags look like they'd be better burnt than used for scrubbing. They might end up making things dirtier rather than cleaner."

Traedis sighed. "I'll be right there." She clambered down, feeling one of the rungs bend under her slight weight. She winced, hoping she had not made a mistake in choosing to trust to the ancient ladder. She had no desire to fall from such a height. There would be no time to change to her wren form and spread her wings.

At the bottom, she inspected the rags Emmen had turned up. They were stained with something as black and oily as the ceiling, and Traedis wondered why they had not simply been discarded after use. She looked at Emmen and Rana. "We'll have to go back up and get supplies. Did you find any buckets?"

"One," said Rana. He held up a partly rusted bucket which had no apparent holes. "You certainly meant it when you said this place isn't used very often."

"There will be some things upstairs." Traedis sighed again.

"This is going to be messy work." Giving up on cleanliness altogether, she shrugged and wiped her hand on the velvet of her skirt. Her launderer would just have to be angry.

Retreating back up the steps, they stopped at the first landing to check the doors. These led to better-kept storerooms which contained more valuable items as well as finer supplies. One contained most of the items Traedis was looking for. A shorter ladder leaned against the back wall, which was lined with cabinets holding neatly labeled equipment. Emmen found two stacked buckets in fair condition, and Rana made the discovery of a large jug of old vinegar on the bottom shelf. A basin full of dirty but usable rags sat atop a closed crate, and a mop stood by itself in the corner beside the shelves.

As they returned to the landing, they met Atchûk coming down, followed by two of his honor guard. He was dressed in another of his brilliant tunics, though this one had nothing sewn to it.

"I'm intrigued," he said, a grin spreading over his face. "Being called out in secrecy to assist…" He stopped, scrutinizing Traedis' face, and his eyes widened. Turning to his men, he said, "Go back upstairs. Wait for me there. I may be some time."

"But sir," one of them began.

Atchûk shook his head. "No. I mean it. I will come to no harm here, and I think this is more important than a little extra safety. Do not tell anyone else where I am unless you are commanded by my father himself. Is that understood?"

The two nodded and headed back upstairs, their postures indicating discomfort with their orders, though they obeyed.

When the door upstairs shut, the karreld turned to Traedis. "Greetings, King Traedis, King Emmen, Prince Rana. King Traedis, I would love to know why you, the King of Haven, and the prince of Ymre are carting buckets around beneath the library looking like you've been investigating the back side of a fireplace. Can you assuage my curiosity?"

"Oh dear." Traedis looked at the tunic, a complex turquoise and green zigzag pattern which looked like it had taken weeks to weave. "I don't want you to ruin your clothing."

"Ruin my clothing?" Atchûk looked puzzled, then laughed outright. "You don't know what it's made of, do you?"

"I do." Emmen gestured toward him. "Mushroom fibers, aren't they?"

The young karreld nodded. "We dye them first, so the color doesn't come off. Dirt washes right out." He raised his brows. "But why am I here with such an illustrious cleaning staff? What is so important that it can't be touched by common hands?"

Feeling heat in her face, Traedis said, "It's not so much a question of who is touching it as who knows about it. This is something that needs to be tremendously secret, at least for a few days."

Atchûk put his hands on his hips. "Then why call me? Shouldn't you be trusting as few people as possible if you want to keep this – whatever it is – secret?"

Rana said, "If you would like to know, follow us. You'll understand when you see it."

Taking the cleaning items with them, they descended again to the lowest level. When the wall changed to carven stone, Atchûk gave a small cry, possibly of recognition, though Traedis could not be sure. When they reached the bottom, the karreld began to breathe heavily, as if the weight of his expectations was too much to carry.

"I know this place," he said softly. "I feel the stone in me and around me. It's a holy site of our people, though I have never heard of it."

"I thought it would take you this way," Rana responded. "This is indeed one of your holy sites, and one that has been neglected for thousands of years. We're here to remedy that."

Traedis gestured upward. "The ceiling needs to be cleaned, carefully. There are paintings beneath. We thought you'd want to be included."

Atchûk's breath caught. "I'm not sure what to say." He wiped his forehead with his sleeve. "Yes, I want to be part of this!" His voice was full of wonder. "What sort of paintings?"

"Stars," Emmen said. Her face was shaded in darkness. She knelt beside one of the buckets and poured the vinegar into it. "Constellations. That's soot on the roof."

"I care *nothing* if my clothes get dirty." Now the karreld's voice shook. "I'd sacrifice an entire wardrobe to be part of this. Any of my people would."

The four of them set to the business of cleaning the ceiling. Emmen stacked crates in a pyramid, which Rana scrambled up nimbly, rags and basin tucked easily under one arm. Emmen took the shorter ladder, and with the mop gently worked at the top layer of soot so that it could more easily be scrubbed down to its surface. Traedis and Atchûk alternated climbing the tall ladder, each painstakingly removing layer upon layer of ancient soot. Traedis was most concerned with making sure that they did not accidentally clean the paintings themselves from the roof, destroying her best chance to defy the Mother of Curses.

It proved exhausting work, and at first nothing showed beside the grain and the pitting of old stone. Then Traedis uncovered what seemed to be a painted curve and gently dabbed at it, attempting to clean it without further damage.

The stars were painted oddly, swirls and coils rather than familiar stylized points. Had the Storm Eagle not told her what lay beneath the grime of centuries, she would never have entered the cavern at all, and certainly would never have suspected the ancient wonder it contained. As it was, she found it hard to translate the whorls and spirals as stars against the cavern's rocky sky.

She also began to notice something else. The stars glowed, especially those closest to Rana. The glow was faint but noticeable in the extreme darkness of the room's upper half. Somehow, even this dim radiance seemed to make the cavern less close, the air less thick and choked with blackness. Each curve they uncovered not only lightened the gloom, but also lifted the fear Traedis carried of being entombed beneath the City. The shreds of Toledru's presence in her mind retreated, scuttling away into the edges of her consciousness like a spider before a broom.

Emmen seemed to see the brightness at the same time as Traedis, and a startled exclamation escaped her. Rana made a low noise of satisfaction and continued to work. He too, was glowing, more faintly than the swirling stars. Traedis smiled to herself, relieved that he had been right: his heritage was enough to wake the power in the n'korreld masterwork.

Soon, a glow infused the granite. Atchûk gave a small cry as a chill wind seemed to blow through the cavern. The air no longer tasted like vinegar, soot, and mold, but like pine resin and nights spent under the open sky.

Traedis' arms began to ache with the unfamiliar effort of reaching over her head and moving in that position. She set her jaw and forced them to keep working. It was no more difficult than hours spent playing harp, and she did that all the time. If she was to rule Tolin properly, she must do more difficult things. She continued to remind herself of that when aches became cramps and her muscles weakened. She had braved her fear of the Storm Eagle for this, and she would not falter.

A quiet rap on the door startled Traedis into swaying precariously. She clutched at the wood with one hand, her other palm steadying her against the ceiling; her breath came short and harsh. She told her heart to slow its sudden pace; there were few people likely to be knocking. She climbed down and went to open the door.

As she had suspected, it was Gavaya; she carried a covered tray. "I thought you might want these," she said, and set it down on a crate by the door. When Traedis twitched back the cloth, she uncovered a teapot, teacups, a plate of fine cakes, and wedges of yellow cheese. Beside them lay a large bowl of water, a piece of soap, and several linens.

Traedis looked down at herself and was horrified to discover that her entire front, as well as her arms up to her elbows, were black with soot, coating her dress so that the original blue had turned the hue of midnight. Then she shrugged, laughing a little. Her mother might find her appearance inexcusable, but she would not flog herself with Mitheira's imagined opinions. Emmen, Atchûk, and Rana were equally as dirty.

With the cramp in her arms lessened, she became suddenly aware of a sharp pain in her stomach. Hunger had crept up on her while her attention was turned, and her sister had guessed they would need something while laboring on the stars. "Gavaya, you're wonderful. How did you know we'd be wanting this?"

"Bless you, Lady Gavaya," Emmen said gravely. Her white shirt and clean breeches had been sorely dirtied by the work she had done. "Those cakes look wonderful – and solid. You had the sense to get us sugar *and* cheese. I, for one, can use both."

"And I," Rana added. He smiled. "It was both thoughtful of you and useful as well. Thank you."

The karreld swept Trae's sister a low bow, hand over his heart;

Traedis had already learned that his mannerisms were exuberance, not mockery. "Lady Gavaya, if it weren't for the fact that you've chased so many suitors away, I would be begging you to be my wife. That looks *so* good!" The chuckle in his voice made it clear that he was not serious about the proposal.

Gavaya answering smile was ghostly, but real. "I hope you enjoy the repast, King Emmen, Prince Rana, Prince Atchûk. I'll be upstairs if you need me." She turned to Traedis. "I told Ruth where you were, and Vandeyr. Vandeyr's angry."

Traedis was unsurprised; Vandeyr was likely to be furious by the time the star cavern was cleared. But Gavaya could be implacable as well, and Traedis knew that neither she nor Vandeyr had ever been able to sway their oldest sister. Even so, it was Traedis who would have to bear the brunt of Vandeyr's anger.

"Leave the tray when you're done, and I'll collect it later." Gavaya brushed a hair from her face and disappeared back up the steps.

Traedis dipped her hands into the water bowl and cleaned them off as well as she could with the soap and linens. What that meant in practical terms was that her fingers had regained a pink tinge, and that the water in the bowl was already turning black before Emmen, Atchûk, and Rana had a chance to clean their own hands.

"I'm sorry," she said. "I should have had you go first." Her face grew hot.

"Trae," Emmen told her, "I, at least, am not holding you to

Tolin's ideas of propriety. All I care is that I can scrape my hands off well enough that I'm not going to be eating soot. The water is still good enough for that." She briskly cleaned and dried her hands, then handed the water and soap to Atchûk.

"It's just soot." Atchûk shrugged and wiped his hands on the underside of his tunic. "Good, honest soot."

Rana climbed down off the pile of crates and looked appreciatively at the tray. "I'm not offended," he said. "Hungry, but not offended." He took the remaining linens and washed quickly.

Traedis offered them first pick of the cakes, which were of the hearty sort, designed for sustenance rather than the social niceties of an afternoon call. The cheese was good country cheese. The tea also smelled hearty, and Traedis recognized it as an invigorating variety which was a favored drink for the start of a journey. It was a refreshing break from the labor of their work on the ceiling, and Traedis felt restored after she had finished.

Afterward, they climbed back up to work. Traedis' arms and wrists screamed with the pain, but she continued to clean doggedly, determined that she would do whatever it took to protect Tolin from Mardra's malice. She *would* thread her way through this pass, no matter how narrow. Tolin's future depended on it.

The constellations were now beginning to show as whole patterns, five of them which clung to the ceiling in an intricate dance of painted luminosity. Their collective brightness was greater now that more stars shone, and Traedis thought that once they were all uncovered, they might softly illuminate the entire chamber without benefit of lantern or torch. That would certainly solve the problem of more soot collecting.

Some of the paint was worn and flaking, but it was in surprisingly good condition for having been painted some indeterminate time before the founding of the City. Gradually, Traedis began to feel a sensation like pinpoints of lightning on the surface of her skin. The patterns coalesced into wholeness, each completion burgeoning with meaning she did not understand with her mind, but knew with her heart and felt in her marrow. Though she had never seen two of the constellations in Tolin's sky, she recognized them in a half-forgotten way, like the tendrils of an ancient dream.

Instead of the cool of deep under stone, she began to feel heat, a surge that came not from without, but from within. Something instinctive bloomed in her mind, pulled at her blood like a lodestone tugging a piece of iron. The painted stars no longer seemed alien, but were a memory from a childhood that was not hers. She greeted the feeling gladly. She was meant, she knew, to be the one to wake these constellations from thousands of slumbering years. Bard as she was, she could not have explained what she experienced; it lay deeper than thought, housed in blood and bone.

Rana's gaze flicked across the chamber at her, but he said nothing. Traedis thought that he might sense something, but he did not ask, and she did not volunteer to tell him. She might have asked Ymre to help her understand her own feelings, but Rana was not his father, and did not have his father's powers.

As each constellation completed its pattern, she felt it flare to wholeness. She named them again as they emerged: the Southern Dragon; the Bowl; the Firebrand; the Twin Lions; the Great Road. There was a balance to them that she did not entirely comprehend, but that did not trouble her.

The Southern Dragon was the aid she needed; her human learning supplied the reason. The constellation was Anciliestes, one of the air dragons who had sacrificed themselves to give free will to the secondborn races. She needed that power to free Tolin from Mardra's curse.

Now she understood why the Storm Eagle had mentioned this particular one; the reflected constellations carried a connection to the real stars and some of their power, lending themselves to her use like a bridled horse. It was an unruly, fierce horse, however, and Traedis determined that she would use its strength with care. Even the images of stars and constellations carried more power than most mortals could channel.

The magic tingled in her skin and throughout her body, calling to her, imploring her to waken the constellations fully. She fought the urge and continued with her work, focusing solely on how to best uncover the paint. She could not afford distractions, and the potency sweeping into her *falmyros* was a distraction.

She gave a final swipe of cloth to the tip of the Southern Dragon's tail star, feeling the completion in her *falmyros*. Lowering her arms with a grimace, set let the cloth fall to the floor before climbing after it. Emmen quietly put out the lantern, and the four of them stood without speaking as they contemplated the astonishing sight above. Despite the stylized nature of the stars' depictions, somehow it felt exactly like standing at night under the true stars. Magic sparked in Traedis' hair, lifting a few strands. She could smell an almost-burnt odor, like the scent of a lightning storm. That was right – The Southern Dragon was a constellation of air. Rose hummed with its enchantment, sending a breathy *arpeggio* into the chamber.

Atchûk lay down on the ground and stared up at the ceiling, his eyes wide. "All this time, and none of us knew it was here," he whispered. "Some of the Reborn may, but it's a place I've never heard of. The gods have honored me, to have let me be one of those to reveal it." He lapsed into silence, which stretched out into apparent awe.

Finally Traedis spoke. "We'll need to empty the trash from this room, but that's the worst of the damage." She wiped her hands on her ruined skirt and clapped them against each other to remove excess soot. It did not help much.

Rana, several shades darker than he had started, climbed down. His hair seemed gray now, so thickly did oily black mingle with the white strands. Smudges patched his face with black and his clothes were as dirty as the ones Traedis wore. "There. That seems to have worked." He grinned. "I should get back now and clean up."

Despite looking more like a scullery girl than a king, Traedis still performed a formal curtsey. "You don't have to go, Prince Rana. You have given Tolin inestimable aid, and I thank you. You are welcome here, now and anytime."

Rana bowed in turn, graceful despite his general appearance, which currently resembled an aelin chimney sweep. "I am glad I could be of assistance. I hope it is enough."

Emmen lowered the mop and leaned against the ladder. "Please thank your father for us, Rana. This matter is of concern to Haven as well as Tolin, and your aid has been invaluable."

Traedis looked up at the ceiling; the painted swirls shone steadily. "Thank him for me as well," she said. "I hope this will prove to be what I need."

"I hope so as well," said Emmen. "Though time will speak the last word."

Traedis waited in her sitting room, her heart fluttering like a trapped bird. She prayed fervently that the power from the star cavern and the strength of the Southern Dragon would permit her to break the curse Mardra would lay when Traedis defied her. Traedis would need to bolster it with a spell chording in order to send the effects through her *falmyros*. Perhaps she could indeed brook the Mother of Curses, but the odds of such an attempt turning out badly was high.

She was alone – she had insisted upon that — though Ruth and Vandeyr waited outside in the hallway. She did not want Mardra to even notice the existence of those Traedis loved. *Who will lose their love to the storm?* rang Wingblade's voice in her memory. Only Rose sat beside her on the floor, her touchstone and sole companion.

Lanterns lit the room; there were no outside windows here, and skylights were not possible since there was a full floor above her head. Traedis was beginning to feel hemmed in, and the familiar unsettled feeling of panic quivered in her gut. She breathed a little faster, wanting both to see this through as soon as possible, and to stretch out the time before her so that it did not come so soon.

The room seemed to darken as if a shadow had overtaken it, and Rose, unbidden, sang out a single low note. The anxiety in Traedis' chest surged into a frantic beating of wings. She forced the feeling down, setting it aside so that she could focus on the things she must do. Her vision narrowed.

She did not see the moment Mardra arrived; first she was not there, and then she was. Her black cloak billowed around her like raven's wings, and the thunder of *demonfear* was evident but distant, like a storm massing in the mountains. Her face was still impossible to see.

Traedis shuddered; she could not keep the reality of the demon in her memory, and seeing her afresh rekindled the wave of dread and self-doubt that Mardra had evoked at her first appearance. Traedis' stomach knotted, and acid rose to the back of her throat. Even so, she kept her spine straight, and though she swallowed hard, she did not turn her head. She might not be able to banish fear, but she could banish the expression of fear. She was an Atenel; she must behave like one.

"I have returned for your answer," the Mother of Curses said in her hoarse voice. "Will you fulfill the contract to which your city was bound before you became its king? Or must I restore the curse to the land and its people?"

Traedis felt sick. Refusing Mardra would be perilous even for a member of the Nightdance. For Traedis, already trapped in her own prodigious curse, it was as good as asking the Matron to pull that curse tight, lacing her into a webwork from which she could never free herself.

She swallowed, feeling the movement as if it took twice as long as it should. She summoned her training to relax her muscles, to allow her voice to flow free from its constriction. "I am sorry, Madam Mardra," she said with clear, precise words. "I cannot do what you ask of me. We are no longer the City with which you bargained." Sweat beaded her forehead; she felt simultaneously cold, as if an icy wind blew on her face.

Mardra's cloak rippled of its own accord, as if agitated. Traedis glimpsed corpse-like flesh and a glint of purple before darkness overtook the image.

"Am I to receive no redress?" the Mother of Curses said, her voice sibilant as a snake. "I have freed this city from such a trial as you have never experienced in all your years in these mountains. Is my pay to be rejection and scorn?"

"I do not scorn you, madam." That was certainly true; Traedis feared her, but she also respected the Matron. "You have been wronged, though not through me. I cannot fulfill the terms of your contract, but I am not unwilling to bargain. Is there anything else that you would accept for payment?" She felt faint and took a slow, measured breath. This offer might be ill-advised, but if they could strike a bargain that Traedis could honorably fulfill, it would be better for both herself and the City.

The demon's voice softened. "There might be things we could do for each other." The empty place where her face should be seemed to burn with blackness.

Traedis tried not to recoil, though the beginnings of a headache set the air to swimming. Even if she were minded to deal further with the Nightdance, any dealings would jeopardize Tolin's position with both Telardur and Haven. She had no such intent. "I am willing, madam," she said slowly, "to bargain with you on this one matter only. I am not willing to extend that bargain to future acts."

The demon's tone sharpened with deadly malice. "Be very sure," she said in a voice colder than Harfast's heart. "This is the only chance I will give you to free yourself of the City's curse – or of the curse you yourself bear."

Traedis felt as if the world suspended itself for one long heartbeat. Free of Wingblade's curse? A chance to escape the suffocating rule of Tolin? True freedom to follow her own path without fear? Her breath rushed into her lungs with painful force, and Traedis realized that she had been holding it for several seconds.

"You think," said the Mother of Curses, "that you have the right to decide this City's path because you hold its *falmyros*." Her cloak swirled. "Do you think that you are fit for the rule? The gods chose you because you were the only citizen in the Council Square at the time. They might have chosen anyone else, had the circumstances been right. Most would govern it more wisely."

Traedis opened her mouth to speak, but no words came out. She tried a second time, with the same result. It was no magic of the demon's, but her own uncertainty which choked off her breath and forbade the words to rise to her lips.

Mardra continued in tones of quiet contempt. "If you abdicate your kingship to one more qualified, I will free you of the curse you carry. And I will do one more thing." She moved fractionally closer to Traedis, staring at her with an invisible eye. "The Nightdance has no cause to love you, but if you leave Tolin in better hands I will see to it that they never trouble you again. That is a great concession on my part, and you would be wise to consider my words."

Chaos stirred Traedis' mind like jangling strings. She knew what was right, but the cost was so high that she was unsure if she had a right to pay it.

She also knew that the City was the only weapon of its kind in this quarter of the world. The resources and knowledge it had amassed in the service of assassination was unparalleled, even by the esch or the twilight aelenin. Returned to its former path by Mardra, it would be wielded by the Nightdance, most likely against the high faldrim. And *that* she could not allow.

The words came out haltingly. "I have a responsibility to Tolin," she said, barely speaking above a whisper. "I cannot give that up no matter how much I may wish it."

"And why," asked the Mother of Curses, "do you have a responsibility to those you despise when you could follow your own heart? You owe nothing to the people of the City that tried to destroy you."

Traedis found that her mouth had gone dry. "Responsibility has little to do with liking."

"Does it not?" The Mother of Curses let a wave of *demonfear* run from her to Traedis. Traedis flinched from the horror of its cold and alien aspect.

The demon pressed on in contemptuous cadences that seemed familiar, though Traedis could not at first identify them. "You are an incompetent ruler, though you think yourself wise. You will only hurt your city by keeping it from the greatness for which it was founded." The air darkened around Traedis, smothering her in the suffocating odor of mothballs. "You were not born or raised to rule, and though you believe yourself chosen, you still have no ability to lead Tolin through the dangers ahead."

Traedis stared at her, panic clawing at her chest. The darkness and the smell brought back vividly the memory of the closet, filled with old furs, where her tutor would lock her as a punishment. That memory summoned others even more powerful: the four years of imprisonment in the dark, narrow cell where she had struggled against madness; the even narrower grave where Toledru had lain entombed while his sanity had drained from him like water through chinks in the stone.

Rose whispered a melody into the air, bringing Traedis back to mindfulness. She panted hard. Mardra knew weaknesses and was willing to exploit them. Traedis must not let the demon force her into betraying her principles.

And yet, there was sense in the Mother of Curses' words. Traedis was a strange choice for the City's king, for who would follow her? She did not love Tolin's people, nor they her; already there would be assassination plots against her, and she might not live long enough to make the changes that must be made.

She wanted to obey Mardra, to be free as she had felt when she had first escaped to Kaelennar. She had been happy during those two years: happier than she had been before or since. But Tolin was not only itself in danger, it was a danger to everyone outside its walls.

The thought flashed through her mind that the Mother of Curses was wrong on one count; though she had not been raised to rule, she was an Atenel, and the Atenels were born to leadership.

She could not cede the argument to the demon, for she knew where her duty lay. "Perhaps I cannot lead the City well, but it has been given to me and it is still my responsibility. I cannot abdicate that responsibility without the gods' permission." She managed to keep her voice strong this time: a small victory.

"You demean the City with your presence at its head!" The Mother of Curses gestured with a handless sleeve. "If you truly feel a responsibility to the City, you will allow someone to lead it who understands and appreciates its destiny. Someone other than a half-grown girl who has never been able to behave in a way proper to a daughter of Tolin." Her withering tone told Traedis what the demon thought of her: childish, petulant, selfish.

Traedis suddenly recognized the tones in which the demon spoke. They were echoes of her mother's voice. Mitheira's words over the years resonated in Traedis' memory. *"Contrary, willful child! Have you no concern for your family?"*

"I do not trust those who want the rule of Tolin," she said, anger rising at last. She knew now where the Mother of Curses had found her words, but they still hurt, exposing an old but still raw wound. The fear remained as well, a warning to contain herself no matter how angry she might become.

"And for this you would condemn your city?" The Mother of Curses nearly spat the words, precise, poisoned darts. "You hardly have the wit to understand what you are doing. Do you think yourself wise enough to overturn two thousand years of tradition?"

"I must do what I believe is right." Traedis tried to modulate the edge on her voice, but some of the acerbity remained. "I cannot accept your judgment when it conflicts with my own."

"You are a fool and will bring your city to ruin!" The Mother of Curses seemed to pull into herself, as if her invisible body had contracted to almost nothing. Traedis flinched.

The demon continued, "Traedis, I have offered to free you from your curse and from your obligations, and you have denied me. If you *ever* wish to be free of that curse, you will not cross me." Her voice lowered, and *demonfear* quaked in the air like thunder in the mountains, growing stronger as she spoke. "It will cling to you like your own skin, it will nestle in your bones, and when you are asleep it will creep through your dreams. It will wait for the times you have forgotten it, and will return endlessly. I have the time, Traedis, and I have the prerogative to impose this on you. I will offer once more – will you accept, as would any wise person, or will your stubbornness and obstinacy keep you from doing what it best for both yourself and your city?"

Traedis could feel her curse as if vines were snaking into her flesh and twining themselves around her bones. For a moment, she quailed; how could anyone expect her to defy one of the great Powers of the world?

Then, knowing what duty and rectitude required, she drew a deep breath and clenched her hands into fists. "I am sorry," she told the demon, dreading what might follow on her words. "I cannot."

Her cloak swirling, Mardra said, "I will ask you once more, and never again. Will you accept my offer?"

The force emanating from her stooped form battered Traedis like a gale. Traedis could barely move to shake her head.

"Then I leave you and your city to share a blighted future!" The Mother of Curses disappeared with a clap of thunder and an explosion of wind. As she vanished, Traedis felt the curse settle on the City in a detailed resolution that she suspected was enhanced from its original form. The plight of the City overwhelmed her momentarily, so strong was the curse; she felt it like a malignant disease. Grabbing for her harp, she sent up a quick prayer that she might succeed despite any cost to herself. Then she threw herself into a chording.

Creating the groundwork was simple. She first laid the chording: a sequence that progressed up the major scale so it would hold the magic she was about to pour into it. Then she began to add connections, weaving melody and countermelody together like a tapestry, ready to fit other spells into its matrix. She reached within herself for the braided cord of the *falmyros;* that would be the melodic thread around which the enchantment hung.

This was harder and more intricate than any magic she had ever tried. The land overwhelmed her senses and threaded details into her consciousness that normally lay below awareness: the rushing of the river, partly iced over in its channel; the long winter dreams of bees; a child's distress over her missing dog; and myriad other sensations which threatened to overwhelm her and shatter her fragile spell. Struggling with the tide of her *falmyros*, she coaxed it into the spell matrix with the essential aid of her harp and its *sagathas* strings.

A hail of chords burst from the harp, evoked both by a wild spurt of creative power and the steely discipline Traedis had taught herself in prison. Her fingers conjured a flurry of grace notes, moving with swiftness and precision against the strings. She leaned into her harp, conscious more of where she wanted to take the music than of her own movements; her mind led, and her fingers followed. Finally, she brought her voice into the song, laying it against the instrument so that Rose's strings hummed with harmonies whispered in the air.

The chording pulled taut, and Traedis prepared to add the final elements of the song. She teased out another countermelody, threading through it a spell that compelled any listener to hear and heed. Then, with a crash of dissonant chords, she stripped the heedsong's essential quality, resolving music and magic together by sending it into the main body of the spell and connecting it to the land itself.

Traedis sank deeply into the chording, holding Tolin in the space between her harpstrings. She had no eyes but what the land saw, no ears but what the land heard. She touched earth, felt wind across her skin, smelled mold and woodsmoke and the musk of rabbit warrens, tasted pine resin and honey.

Now everything in the land – living, dead, or without life at all – *listened.* Into the *falmyros* she sang an unbinding song, trying to sever the land from the curse which clung to it like a tarry shadow.

Finally, she called the Southern Dragon.

The constellation blew into the spell as if carried by the winds of the Dragon Mountains. Its power swelled into the chording, overwhelming her with more power than she had ever tried to channel, though thankfully softened by her connection with the Star Cavern and the rectitude of her summoning. It came with a clarity that opened minds and snapped tethers.

Traedis felt it tug at Wingblade's curse, trying to peel it from her like the rind of a fruit. A desperate hope seized her; could it sever her from that terrible legacy?

It could not. Traedis felt a heaviness as her curse settled back against her skin. For Tolin's sake, she set that aside and concentrated on her chording with the *falmyros* and the Southern Dragon.

Lifting the City's curse was not the same as unpicking the demon Toledru from his mooring in Tolin. This curse saturated every fiber of the City's life, aborting the growth of eggs and seeds, lambs and children. Even ideas were interrupted before they could reach fruition. It was devastatingly comprehensive and powerfully malignant.

Traedis directed the force of the Southern Dragon into everything she could touch with her *falmyros*, using the constellation's properties to loosen and shift the pieces of the curse so that she could blow them free of Tolin, a dandelion gone to seed. It was tremendously hard work, like scrubbing ink from her hands; each time she succeeded in freeing a piece of the curse it felt as if she shredded pieces of her own flesh. Nonetheless, she continued grimly in her task.

Time slipped away, its passage unimportant. Traedis was grass, tree and rock, dog and hare, falcon and child. She lost awareness of Rose, though the music continued like a heartbeat. She was the music, the patch of ice, the seedling which slept until the spring. As she and the melody interwove, she cleansed the land, her scrub brush the indomitable will of the Southern Dragon, shining radiantly from the dome of the Star Cavern.

Traedis opened her eyes. At first, so full of Tolin that she barely remembered herself, she could not understand what she saw. Then her mind came into focus, and she recognized the ceiling of her bedroom.

She lay in her own bed in the palace. Light slanted through the window, almost too bright after the darkness of sleep. Her limbs were weighty with fatigue.

"Trae?" Vandeyr's voice, surprisingly concerned, sounded distantly from somewhere in the room. Traedis had no need to answer; she still felt detached from herself, her body covered with trees, her breath the mountain gale.

"Trae?" said Vandeyr again, nearer.

A shadow fell over Traedis' face. She blinked impatiently, not wanting to stir.

"Trae? Are you awake?" Vandeyr bent over, her face obscuring Traedis' view of the ceiling.

"Mmm," Traedis responded, wishing Vandeyr would go so that she could enjoy her well-earned lethargy. "Mmm."

Vandeyr's lips narrowed. "You've been asleep for two days, Trae. Are you all right? Can you talk?"

"I can talk," Traedis mumbled from between numb lips. "Tired."

"I can't believe you succeeded, but the priests said you did." A trace of surprise tinged Vandeyr's voice. "I didn't notice a thing from outside the room."

Traedis wondered what she had done, to grow so exhausted. Then a shadow passed over the sun, and she remembered a black cloak, a purple eye. She had defied the Mother of Curses with the aid of the Southern Dragon. She opened her eyes wide. The land still overpowered her senses, more strongly than she had felt it before chording into the *falmyros*.

She inhaled sharply. Vaguely, she remembered patrolling the land with her power while scouring clean the last traces of Mardra's malevolence, though her recollection was so hazy it might as well have been the half-memory of an old tale.

Music had played through her dreams, comforting and strengthening her. Licking dry lips, she asked, "Rose?"

"Your harp?" Vandeyr made a brief gesture at the floor on the outside edge of the bed. "Down there. No one really wanted to touch it after what happened."

Her words made no sense to Traedis. "What?"

Vandeyr speared her on a sharp glance. "Everyone who passed by your door in the last two days could hear faint harp music. But whenever anyone entered, it was sitting right there on the floor, completely silent. None of the servants would touch it. Can you explain that?"

Traedis rolled over to look at the harp, taking in the contours of the rose carvings, the delicate leaves and tangled thorns on the cherrywood frame. She felt thick-headed and slow. Rose whispered a cadence very softly, and Traedis realized what might have happened. "She plays when I will it. Well, she also plays when she wills it sometimes. Not always."

Vandeyr blinked. "Trae, you talk about that harp as if it were a dog. It doesn't have a mind, does it?"

"I'm not sure." Traedis rolled back so that she could look up at the ceiling again. "She's certainly got a personality. But what the *sagathas* did to her... I can't tell you." She did not feel as if she had slept for two days. Her eyelids were gummy and sudden pain splintered the thoughts in her head. "I don't think Lord Ymre... all of her strings... reforged..." Her lids drifted closed as her consciousness floated.

"*Sagathas?*" Vandeyr asked, her tone incredulous. Then alarm rose in her voice. "Trae! Don't fade on me again! Stay awake!"

Red exploded through the black that dragged down Traedis' thoughts. Her eyes snapped open right before she felt the pain on her cheek. Vandeyr had slapped her.

Focus returned a moment later. "I'm still awake," she said, and flashed Vandeyr a brief smile. "No need to manhandle me. Can you help me sit up?"

Vandeyr frowned, but slipped a gentle hand beneath Traedis to support her. Waves of aching pain washed down Traedis' back; her spine popped. Her vision dissolved, then returned with more clarity. She would have sworn that slivers of glass were lodged in her skull. The light in her room was a blinding spear lancing into her eyes; she rubbed her scalp to lessen the discomfort. Surprisingly, it worked.

With her blood moving, her thoughts were not far behind. She was weak, certainly; two days of inaction would atrophy muscle. She would spend extra time in the practice yard in the coming few days. The more important question was whether or not the wasting curse still lay over Tolin, turning its future to ash and darkness.

Something had changed in her relationship to the *falmyros*. She had felt it strongly from the first, but now it seemed almost like another sense, as natural to her as sight and sound. Its imminence did not overwhelm her human faculties, but she knew it was there. Just as she could feel the rub of her foot against her shoe, she could tell that the squirrels were hungry; that a pine in the forest was dying of rot; that the rock beneath Tolin quivered once in response to a shudder far off in the Dragon Mountains. These things did not clamor for notice, but she was aware of them if she turned her attention in their direction.

Vandeyr was the only other person in Traedis' bedchamber, a fact that seemed strange, now that Traedis had woken. "Where is everyone?"

"You mean all the people who were hovering over your bed like mosquitoes over a bloody pig?" Vandeyr gave a short bark of a laugh. "If you'd woken up half an hour ago, I would have been at lunch, and Ruth would have been sitting like a carven saint on her little chair over there by the fire. Three hours ago, you had a visit from King Emmen, who examined you and said you'd wake in your own time, nevermind who's worried about whether you're going to be the same person as you were when you went to sleep.

And two hours before *that*, Master Shorarit was here – you remember her, don't you, Shorarit Greymont? About Gavaya's age? She became the head of the Kyaan church three years ago or so. She's been personally supervising your care, and she's not likely to knife you in the back when you're asleep, so you can count her as being on your side." She shook her head. "Unpopular as you are with the nobles, you seem to be the darling of the priests. They're terribly excited to have a ruler personally anointed by the gods."

"What about Mother?" Traedis asked softly.

Vandeyr's lack of expression told Traedis what she needed to know.

Traedis breathed in deeply, trying to steady herself against a wash of hurt and grief. The breath ended up as a cough, doubling her over. "This is – the other disadvantage of – lying in bed for two days." Momentary lightheadedness struck her, then let her go as her lungs began to clear.

Letting her eyes roam around the room, she inspected the familiar homey details like a touchstone. She sat on her wide bed, its headboard carved from oak in shapes of leaves and acorns. Two quilts patterned in blue and green covered her, still warm against an icy draft from the window. Traedis' bureau and nightstand sat beneath an enormous mirror with a frame polished from night-black wood. A carved screen which hid the chamber pot stood discretely in a corner; two small chairs upholstered in blue and green were marooned near the center of the floor. One of the wardrobe's doors had escaped its latch and hung ajar.

"King Emmen wants to speak with you," Vandeyr said, a growl in her tone. "When we found you, she said that you were deep in your *falmyros*, and that time would bring you out of it. And that I should make sure that you didn't stop breathing." Vandeyr stopped abruptly, and Traedis knew that bad temper cloaked genuine concern. "At first I thought you were dead."

Traedis had thought such an outcome likely herself. The power of the Mother of Curses was such that Traedis could almost hear the suggestion of a hoarse, breathy voice at the nape of her neck telling her that she could not succeed as Tolin's king. Mardra was not present, but she had stirred Traedis' simmering self-doubt and seasoned it with dread.

"Where is Emmen?" Traedis asked, trying to turn her attention away from such a dangerous path. She did not want to incite the demon's further anger; Mardra had enough power over her as it was.

"I didn't like this idea from the start." Vandeyr scowled, the expression marring her flawless countenance. "I don't like trusting the King of Haven, I don't like you playing with ancient magics you don't understand, and I particularly dislike having one of the pillars of the Dance paying social calls for the purpose of cursing the City." As Traedis began to respond, Vandeyr waved her quiet. "I have *always* hated the City's traffic with the Dance, and this is a fine example of why – you can call them up easily enough, but getting them to leave is trickier. Every dram of power you cede them lessens yours by a full bottle's worth. Why couldn't you let well enough alone, instead of deciding you had to change everything you didn't like about us in the course of a week?"

"I had to." Traedis shifted her weight and tried to sit straighter. "Vandeyr, I had to. I've told you why over and over again. Kenrydh and Emmen won't allow more assassinations, and we're a country surrounded." Her limbs trembled with the effort of sitting, and one of her feet had fallen asleep. "I *couldn't* accede to Mardra's demands – " She broke off, realizing that even now she could not tell anyone what the demon had wanted.

"She's got a lock on your tongue still." Vandeyr muttered an imprecation, though whether at Traedis or Mardra it was hard to tell. "Of course she would. She's no gambler, not like the Piper. She'll out-bargain you in a heartbeat, but she won't take chances." She shook her head, then leveled a direct but not hostile stare at Traedis.

"Trae, everyone in the City must have felt you doing *something* and most of us knew you were fighting for us. I don't expect you to tell me anything useful, even though I'm the one who's in charge of defending you, but I do know there was a reason."

Traedis raised her eyebrows. Apparently the heedsong she had threaded into the spell had worked on more than the *falmyros*. This might not improve her standing with many of the City's people, but at least Vandeyr had noticed and cared.

"Where is Ruth?" Traedis shifted position again, finding it

marginally easier this time.

Vandeyr flapped her hand in the direction of the door. "Sleeping. She spent every moment with you for the first day and a half, waiting for you to wake up. I finally sent her to bed since we couldn't tell when – or if – you would open your eyes."

Traedis nodded, warmed by Ruth's loyalty as well as by Vandeyr's. "Let her sleep. I do need to speak with Emmen, though."

"I'll send for her. She told me she'd be here as soon as you awoke." Vandeyr turned away, then back. "You'd better not keep sending me on stupid little errands like this. I've got a palace guard to run." She strode angrily out of the room, letting the door bang on her way out.

Traedis watched her go, not sure whether to be amused or annoyed at her sister's attempt to needle her. She decided on amused; Vandeyr did not take well to being afraid. Traedis realized that she understood her sister better now than she had as a child. Vandeyr had been the one expected to be perfect, the one who was to set an example for her younger sibling. It was not a surprise that such a burden had made her prickly and short-tempered.

Gingerly, Traedis swung her legs over the side of the bed, feeling small shocks through the lower half of her body. Her stomach muscles knotted with the effort, and her bladder felt painfully full. She managed to ignore the pain and the sudden discomfort as her feet hit the frigid stone floor. Panting, she forced herself to inhale deeply and evenly so that she would not faint upon standing. The weakness seemed to increase tenfold as her weight moved from the mattress to her legs; her vision spun. She quickly sat and lowered her head to gain clarity before attempting to stand again.

The second time, she found she could move more easily, though it was still an effort. She carefully walked over to the screen, relieved herself in the chamber pot beyond, and donned a velvet dressing gown she kept there for modesty. She wrapped it around herself, grabbing a comb from the dressing table and retreating to one of the chairs. By this time she was shaking with effort, and kept her back straight only by sheer stubbornness.

She was still trying to drag the comb through the mass of tangles in her hair when Emmen arrived, stepping quietly in doeskin boots; her simple riding leathers were stained with use. Vandeyr trailed behind her with politeness so icy she could have come from directly from Harfast's court.

"I need to talk to Emmen alone," Traedis told Vandeyr with a touch of trepidation. Her sister was not likely to appreciate being excluded.

"Of course," Vandeyr said. "Your Majesties." She bowed with exact precision and left. Traedis sighed and watched until the door had fully closed and latched.

"Captain Atenel still doesn't like me." Emmen smiled a little sadly and took the chair opposite Traedis. "I could hardly expect more, but she is quite expressive. Who is older, you or she?" She gave Traedis a rueful look. "Perhaps I should know, but I never learned about the junior members of Tolin's Council families."

Traedis shot Emmen a surprised glance. "She is. By eight years."

"That much?" Emmen's eyebrows rose. "She doesn't look a day older than you, and you could pass for fifteen. Do you have aelin blood in your family?"

"Not to my knowledge." Traedis shook her head. "I suppose it's possible, though there are few aelin families in the City. If so, no one has ever told me."

Emmen shrugged. "It's not important – it's only curiosity on my part. What *is* important is Tolin's welfare. I can tell you succeeded in lifting the curse. What I can't tell is if you suffered any ill removing it."

Traedis flexed muscles in her arms and legs. They ached, but the weakness was passing, and she no longer felt dizzy. "I think I'm all right. Yes."

Emmen regarded her seriously. "What happened?"

A sudden wave of nausea flowed over Traedis; she dropped the comb and doubled over until it passed. From the edge of her vision she saw Emmen begin to rise, then sit back down.

"Traedis?" said Emmen's concerned voice.

The force of Mardra's malice trailed through Traedis' mind like a slug dragging slime. The Matron's words echoed through Traedis' head; Traedis shook it from side to side, as if to empty her memory. Despite Mardra's obvious intent to terrify and shame Traedis, some of what she had said might be true.

Fury surged behind the fear. She would not allow the Mother of Curses to demean her in such a way. She was an Atenel, and would behave as one. She straightened her spine.

"Mardra came," she told Emmen brusquely. "I told her we could not fulfill the contract. She left and restored the curse. I removed it. That's all."

Emmen wrinkled her forehead. "That's all?" She did not sound accusatory, but Traedis felt a wash of heat through her cheeks.

"That's what I said." She felt unaccountably angry at Emmen; she did not want any of her struggle with the Mother of Curses to pass her tongue. It made her mouth feel filthy, like eating rotten meat.

Emmen frowned. "Ruth told me that you were quiet for a long time before she heard your harp. No one entered until it fell silent." Her concerned gaze flicked to Rose and back. "You must have spoken with the Matron."

Traedis looked down at her hands, avoiding Emmen's scrutiny. "A little. She tried to convince me. She didn't. It's not important."

"Traedis." Emmen's words were gentle, but there was the force of urgency behind them. "It may well be important. Few speak with a demon as powerful as the Mother of Curses and escape unscathed. You don't want to tell me something, and it might be vital. What exactly happened?"

"Nothing important," Traedis repeated with an edge in her voice. "Nothing worth all this concern." She did not want to aim the anger at her friend, but the shame that Mardra had evoked wanted to scuttle into the dark corners of her consciousness, not sit exposed in the light of a holy knight's attention. Traedis wanted that shame buried deeper than Toledru.

Emmen shook her head. "It would gain no reproach if you were daunted by her presence. She is a very powerful demon – "

"I'm not a fool!" Traedis snapped, stung as much by guilt toward Emmen as by her unwillingness to think of Mardra's crushing words. "I know what she is, and I'm not fool enough to succumb to her wishes."

"Nor am I a fool." Emmen's voice was rimmed with frost; Traedis flinched from the anger. "You spoke with a demon who ranks among the greatest Powers of the world – the Mistress of Ravens, the Mother of Curses. You refuse to tell me what passed between you. Is it any wonder that I question when you act so unlike yourself? I need to know because if you have been daunted it affects both Tolin and Haven. *What happened?*"

The words were like a blade to the heart, but Emmen was right. This was not simply a matter between Traedis and the demon; it was a matter between the two cities.

"I'm sorry, Emmen." She relaxed her muscles, trying to find the strength to admit to her weakness. "It is true that I would rather fight a rabid bear, but the reason is not what you fear."

"What, then?" Emmen's voice softened again. "What could she have said that must be kept so secret?"

"It's not that." Traedis clutched her comb for security, feeling the teeth bite into her palm. "But Madam Mardra – does a very good imitation of my own mother." She spoke the last part of the sentence almost in a whisper, and she could see Emmen nod. It was an added shame to know that the demon intended her to feel that humiliation.

"I begin to see." Emmen leaned forward, hands on her knees. "What were her precise words?"

Traedis closed her eyes, calling upon her trained memory to detail what had transpired. The demon's image formed behind her eyes almost immediately; she snapped her lids open, and fought against the sucking pull of despair.

"She asked me for my answer. I told her that we were no longer the city with which she had dealt. As politely as I could." Her breath rasped in her throat. "I suggested we might be able to bargain." The tears swam in her eyes again, making the room shimmer and quiver; her voice caught. "She told me that if I abdicated my position..." She swallowed around the tension in her throat. "...if I abdicated my position to one who would be more 'suitable' that I would be free to do as I chose – and that the Dance would never trouble me again."

The hardest part of recounting the exchange was her longing for that freedom: to be released from the burden of the kingship; to possess the liberty to return to Kaelennar, an unknown bard and not a member of a Council family.

Emmen asked softly, "What did you say to her?"

Traedis simply stared at her for a moment; Emmen should not

believe Traedis would have capitulated. "I couldn't. The gods gave me Tolin. I might abdicate, but the gods have not freed me of the responsibility."

Emmen nodded and reached out to put her hand over Traedis'. "It wouldn't have been that way, you know." She wrinkled her brow. "She would have kept her word, but you would not have been happy with it. Whoever replaced you would be subject to the wishes of the Dance and you would be tormented the rest of your life by knowledge that you could have prevented the City's actions."

Emmen's words beat against the cage in Traedis' mind that trapped her reason. Traedis could only repeat, "I couldn't accept her terms. What else was I to do?"

"Of course you could not." Emmen nodded. "What did she say to convince you?" Emmen tapped her foot. "How did she come to sound like your mother?"

"She said – " Traedis could barely stand to think about the words. They mingled in her mind with Mitheira's sharp criticisms of her younger self. "That I received the rule of Tolin not from merit, but because no one else was in the Council Square. That I would destroy Tolin by my incompetence or at the least, keep it from greatness. That I demeaned the City by my presence at its head, and that only my selfishness kept me clinging to the rule."

Emmen shook her head in disbelief. "You received the rule of Tolin because you were willing to sacrifice yourself for its lord and for its welfare, and because you are very well suited to make the necessary changes. Incompetence? You are one of the most supremely competent people I have ever met, though you seem to understand little about your own talents." She sighed. "I am relieved, however. I feared much worse. Very few people face a demon of her power and handle it as well as you have done. That her words stay with you is partly a measure of her power, not of your weakness."

Traedis clutched the comb tighter. Mardra had not written the notes of Traedis' self-doubt, but she had plucked them like a master harpist. "How do I know that? I was not raised as king. What do I know of ruling a city? What are my qualifications for such a position?"

"You might consider the gods' recommendation as a slight qualification," Emmen said dryly.

Traedis jerked back and lowered her gaze. "I'm sorry. I don't doubt the gods' will. It's myself I doubt."

"I know that," Emmen told her. She gently pried open Traedis' hand and looked down at the marks the comb had left in her flesh. "Some of us trust you more than you trust yourself."

"Thank you," Traedis said, still unconvinced. "I'm glad you're here. Without your support and aid I don't know what might already have happened to Tolin."

"You would have managed." Emmen smiled. "I have no doubt of that."

Chapter Fifteen
The Quo'at

One thing was obvious to Traedis; the Star Cavern needed to be repainted. Considering its significance and power, it was not a simple matter of retracing the lines with a brush. Traedis feared that any such attempt would destroy the work and its connection to the stars. Given that Tolin might not have survived without the aid of the Southern Dragon, and that it was an n'korreld holy place, she was determined that it should be repaired by the hand of a n'korreld master.

Sending a message to the Thane gained her an excited communique the same day from the Quo'at, the head of the n'korreld church of Coran and the spiritual leader of the entire n'korreld people. He requested permission to journey to Tolin and to see the Star Cavern for himself, permission which Traedis granted it at once. It was no small thing to restore a holy place to the people who had created it.

After dinner that evening, a small party of n'korreld arrived at the palace, including the Quo'at and an accompanying retinue of priests, acolytes, and soldiers. Traedis could only imagine how excited he was to receive news of an abandoned piece of karreldish heritage. For thousands of years they had been enslaved to the istronian people, and it had scarred their trust of any other peoples.

Traedis waited in the Brocade Room of the palace. Small, elegant furniture had been brought in, each sized for the comfort of the diminutive and wiry frame of a karreld, and covered in matching fabric. Delicacies, both human and n'korreld, sat on low tables for the convenience of the guests. Vandeyr and her guards stood like pieces of furniture themselves, fading into the surrounding walls.

Traedis had dressed in a rich brocade dress of blue and silver, the Atenel colors. Her hair was braided into a crown, and she wore a white gold circlet. The entire effect was more ornate than she preferred, but she needed to do honor to the supreme priest of the n'korreld people.

As her guests entered, she watched sharply to see which of them wore the ceremonial robes and pendant of office; she could not afford to offend the Quo'at by mistaking him for another. Even the City's usually extensive records had relatively little information about the n'korreld religious practices and leaders.

The party numbered fifteen. Seven ceremonial guards entered first; These were all men, but the others were a mix of men and women. Five of these were priests and wore the ram's horn symbol of Coran, and three were likely acolytes, much younger than the others. All had sinewy builds, thick hair, and sharp features; their skin ranged in hue from sand to rich loam. They wore long, brightly patterned tunics embroidered in complex figures and made of the soft, shiny mushroom fabric that the n'korreld wore.

Had she not been looking for the Quo'at's ceremonial garments, she would have thought he was one of his own acolytes. He appeared a boy no more than six or seven years, his peat-hued skin unlined, his tiny face unformed. He wore a robe very similar to the tunics of the others, but it was embroidered even more finely, with motifs of animals and birds as well as more abstract patterns. His chain of office was far too big, its links weighing his neck into a slight bend, though he bore it proudly. His eyes sparkled, and mischief tugged at the corners of his mouth.

Traedis rose to greet him. "Most Blessed Quo'at, welcome to my city and to my home. I am honored by your presence in Tolin, and I hope that you will find our hospitality sufficient. Please treat my house as your own."

He nodded politely to her, as befit a great religious leader to a king. "Thank you, King Traedis." His voice was high and reedy but not at all tentative, with cadences that Traedis associated with adults rather than children. Traedis kept her expression free from curiosity, though she wondered how one so young came to occupy such an exalted position.

The Quo'at seated himself on a small chair that was nonetheless a little too high for his legs, which kicked the air below his seat. He wore soft slippers embroidered as richly as the rest of his attire. His attendant priests settled beside him, though the acolytes and soldiers remained standing.

"Please refresh yourselves," Traedis said, and swept her hand out to indicate the food before them. "We have mushrooms, sweet rolls, pickled beets, cakes, sausages, and dove's eggs. If there is anything else you desire, let me know, and I will have my cooks make it for you." She reminded herself not to stare at the Quo'at, and added, "We have cider and sweet liquors, milk, tea, coffee, and wine. My servants will fetch anything else we have."

The Quo'at smiled, and an impish look overtook his face. "I would like some wi – "

One of the attendants, a middle-aged woman with a face like a squashed turnip, fixed a baleful eye on him.

Without more than a moment's hesitation, the Quo'at continued, "While all of the choices sound excellent, I find myself desiring a good draught of milk." His attendant gave a very small nod and settled back. the Quo'at gave her a wide, gap-toothed grin.

As the servants served the n'korreld party, the Quo'at spoke again. "I came as soon as I could manage. I understand this is an inconvenient hour, but King Traedis, I am most anxious to see the Star Cavern." His features lit with excitement. "If this chamber is what I believe it to be, it has been many lives since I have seen it." He swept his robe from the chair's arm and settled himself more firmly. "Many, many lives."

Traedis suppressed an urge to raise her brows. She knew little of the n'korreld, and this was something of a surprise. Still, there were many odd things in the world, and she had seen some of them. If this boy were older than he seemed, his position among the n'korreld made more sense.

She had heard of some people living more than one life, but she had never realized the n'korreld numbered among them. She had not expected to meet one who remembered many incarnations of the same spirit. It made her shudder, the thought of finding oneself in the body of a child, but possessing the mind of an adult:

a reversal of the natural order.

She looked at the Quo'at with keen fascination, wondering how he had adjusted to lifetimes of repeated experience. He smiled at her, not the innocent smile of a child, but a mature smile that radiated contentment and peace. His eyes met hers, and she could almost imagine that she saw ancient wisdom shining from them, ages of experience in both suffering and joy which was different from the patient wisdom of very old aelenin.

"I would be happy to show you tonight." Traedis found the Quo'at's excitement contagious; she wanted to see his face when he beheld the treasure uncovered on the cavern skies. "It's no difficulty. I can access the library at any hour." She guessed that Gavaya had a bed tucked away for the many nights when she worked late, but one of the under-librarians was usually available, even when Gavaya was not. "I myself will escort you there."

"My most gracious thanks, King Traedis." The Quo'at kicked his feet again. The incongruity struck Traedis anew; his poise and confidence had succeeded in reversing Traedis' initial impression.

"Do you wish to be shown your quarters first?" Traedis asked, guessing he would not. "You have traveled a long distance. Perhaps you wish to refresh yourself and rest?" She assumed he would not accept, but it would be poor hospitality not to offer him the opportunity.

"Pardon me, King Traedis, but I do not." The Quo'at smiled his brilliant ageless smile at Traedis. "You have found a sacred place which has been lost to us for longer than your city has existed. It was once one of the greatest holy places of our race, but was forgotten in one of our times of trial, and no one knew where in this range of mountains it stood. Many thought it destroyed in an earthquake, or by the hands of those who wished to erase our legacy. To find that it has survived into this time – " His voice grew thick. "It is impossible for me to express to you what this means to my people, and to me personally."

If nothing else, Mardra's malice had indirectly brought joy to someone; that was a comfort to Traedis. "Then I will take you there straight away." She stood and nodded to Vandeyr. The Quo'at and his people rose to follow.

Gavaya was still in her office, a single oil lamp illuminating the book over which she pored. Fresh moonlight spilled over the windowsill in squares on the floor, though not bright enough for reading. Gavaya's fingers bore smudges of ink, and a quill and parchment lay ready to hand. She lifted her head to regard the party of n'korreld before laying a scrap of parchment in the margin of her book and shutting it carefully. Rising, she nodded in the direction of the stairs.

"New lamps are ready," she told them. "They've been freshly filled, and need only to be lit. We've had some traffic by the curious, but I've made a point of discouraging those who have heard there's something valuable in the lower chambers."

Eventually the word would get out that the lowest storeroom harbored a great magical work, but Traedis was not anxious for that time. It would come with recriminations from the lords of Tolin, and many would try to stain her reputation by accusing her of hiding its power. Yet, Traedis would not have felt right if the Quo'at had not been among the first to enter its chamber and marvel at its beauty.

She thanked her sister and led the small party through the old wooden door; Vandeyr left two guardsmen at the entrance and followed at their backs. Though far smaller than Traedis, the Quo'at kept pace, excitement seeming to resonate through his step.

The descent was still close and stifling; Traedis again forced herself not to notice the nearness of the walls, the low hanging ceiling, the darkness outside their pools of lamplight.

As they reached the bottom, she said, "We haven't had time to clear much out, so there are old and broken items cluttering up the room. Watch where you step."

The smaller cavern at the bottom held a few items that Vandeyr's guard had moved out of the Star Cavern proper, but had not yet hauled upstairs to be tossed away or stored in some other location. Traedis eeled around a rotting wicker chair, three broken crates, and something that looked for all the world like a rusty pig trough. How that had found its way down here was a mystery.

Opening the door to the Star Cavern, she led them through.

The Star Cavern was wide and high, and now that the stars were uncovered, it felt more like standing in Tolin's velvety night rather than the terrifying storeroom of her childhood. Traedis could bear the long climb if the destination was not abhorrent.

The Quo'at stopped dead, an expression of exaltation and awe settling over his features.

"Please extinguish the lamps," he said softly.

A glow penetrated the darkness, starlight soft and white. The patterns were as faint as the palest stars on a cloudless mountain night, though the majesty of their dance still echoed the true dance within the heavens. The Quo'at sighed, the sound whispering in the chamber as if the space was larger than its actual dimensions. Soot still clung to most surfaces, coating the floor in a fine black powder; the contrast deepened the sense of standing under a moonless sky.

As she looked at the ceiling, Traedis could see that some of the stars were fainter than they should have been, given the relative brilliance of the constellations themselves. She wondered if those were the ones the Quo'at needed to repair first. It was astonishing that they had not been destroyed under the soot's two-thousand-year accretion.

"This is indeed the place." The Quo'at's craned his head back as far as he could manage; the muscles on his neck knotted as he strove to tilt it even farther. "This place has been lost to our people for more years than I can count. I barely remember it myself."

Traedis looked at his face, aglow with wonder. "It is lost to you no longer," she told him quietly. The Star Cavern inspired a hush of awe in her upon seeing the Quo'at's reaction. "If this place is holy to your people, they will be free to visit it. I will make arrangements that those of the n'korreld who wish to visit it may do so without regard to any other consideration."

In that instant, Traedis felt her bones thrum, as if they vibrated with some great, unseen harp. She shuddered, not with revulsion, but because the sensation overwhelmed her senses. Then, as quickly as it had come upon her, it seemed to sink *into* her bones, absorbed like water into a sponge. She shook her head, the deep reverberation still throbbing through her body.

The Quo'at's head lowered and he turned toward Traedis, though he did not remark on or seem to have noticed her experience. "King Traedis, free access is a gift which can scarcely be repaid. I will think upon this matter once I have repaired the damage to the stars upon this ceiling. That is, of course, my first priority, but I will not forget such a generous act of friendship." He looked back up at the painted sky as if he could not bear to lose it once again.

Traedis nodded, though the Quo'at was not watching her. "They need repair sorely, and I am sure you want to address that before anything else. They are most certainly powerful, but there is a weakness in them which I can feel. If you can restore them to what they once were, they will welcome that."

The Quo'at froze, then whipped his head around to pin Traedis with a stare that made her feel as if he looked into her marrow. "King Traedis? You can feel these stars? They are in your *falmyros*?" He sounded as startled as if she had claimed to have dragon blood.

She looked back at him in puzzlement. "Yes. They are a part

of my land, though not precisely subject to my rule. There is too much power in them to be subject to anyone."

"Then you are indeed a friend of the n'korreld." The Quo'at's brow creased in a very unboyish way. "I would not have thought such a thing was possible. I will give this matter thought as well."

Traedis nodded, still confused, but willing to let the matter pass. "I know that you are anxious to begin your work, but it will be easier for my people to find you the necessary supplies if you wait until morning." She would not prevent him if he insisted on beginning now, but if he had brought materials to repair the paintings, she had not seen them. Besides, as host, she should allow him a proper bath and bed after his travel.

The Quo'at hesitated, obviously weighing his own anxiousness to work with the stars against his need for sleep and the convenience of Traedis' people. He nodded. "Sleep will help me to restore them with a surer hand – and my nursemaids will be much happier if I give them what they want before I am allowed to have my own way." His infectious grin seemed aimed as much at his own people as at her. "It is simply that I have waited long enough, and it is hard to wait longer. One would think I might have cultivated more patience, but I feel very much the age that I look."

Traedis breathed out, a little relieved that he agreed with her. She did not want to keep the Quo'at working through the night, even if it were his choice.

"Very well," she told him. "If you will return with me to the palace, I will have the servants show you your quarters and provide you with everything needed for your comfort. How early co you wish them to awaken you?"

"Dawn," said the Quo'at, sounding for the first time like the small boy he appeared to be. "It will be hard enough to sleep as it is. I do not want to wait one more moment than necessary."

Chapter Sixteen
Two Offers

Exhausted, Traedis readied herself for bed, events running through her head like the lyrics of an old song. First Mardra, then the Quo'at – dissonant notes in a very odd chord. She had not yet allowed herself to think about the consequences of refusing Mardra's offer. But the truth was that she knew who would succeed her as king, should the Dance have its way: Uncle Cordelayne.

Donning a formal and modest nightdress, she climbed into her warm bed, sitting indecorously cross-legged for comfort. She unbraided her hair and began to brush it, finding the long curls already tangling despite hanging loose only for a short time. Other kings might have body servants to dress them and coif their hair, but that was not for her. She could attend to her own needs, and had done so since she was old enough to forego nursemaids. A cup of hot spiced wine sat on her night table, waiting until she was ready for sleep.

She wished heartily that the *falmyros* had fallen to Lang or Gavaya; either would have known how to pick their way through a political morass, or what to do when the Dance came calling. Despite how little she wanted to believe Mardra's words, she knew that she had not been the Storm Eagle's best choice for Tolin's ruler. Only through a coincidence of circumstances had she been chosen for the role. If she could have convinced the Mother of Curses to accept either of her eldest siblings, she might have stepped aside.

Uncle Cordelayne would also know what to do, but his choices would be opposed to hers. He would never have called off the assassins, would reinstate them if he were able. He would never have established relations with either Haven or Telardur, and if he had known of the Star Cavern, he would not have opened it to n'korreld pilgrims. And Traedis would have been imprisoned again, without her harp to keep her company.

As if it heard her, Rose played a breathy sequence of notes, which Traedis recognized belatedly as a melody she had herself written. She smiled sadly and stopped brushing her hair long enough to pat the harp's solid frame. Rose chimed happily before falling silent.

A knock at the door from Vandeyr's room startled her. "Yes?" she asked, her pulse slowing again. "What is it?"

The door cracked open. "Trae, may I come in?" Vandeyr sounded both annoyed and disgusted; Traedis hoped it was not at her.

"Yes," she answered tentatively. "I haven't gone to bed yet. What's wrong?"

Vandeyr entered, still dressed in her uniform, every hair precisely aligned. She stopped halfway across the room and raised her eyebrows, her expression thoughtful. "Traedis, I swear, when you're dressed like that you look all of sixteen. You'd just better hope you don't get any emergencies in the middle of the night – no one will believe you're the King of Tolin."

"I can't sleep in my clothes," Traedis said, somewhat

defensively. "Even aelin silk isn't meant for wear day and night." She glanced guiltily at her hairbrush, feeling like a child brought before her mother for some misdeed.

"I wasn't criticizing you," Vandeyr said, as if she were suggesting the opposite. She shook her head crossly. "Of course you can't. It's not your fault you look like a woman scarcely out of girlhood. It still won't help anyone take you seriously if you have to handle a crisis in linen and lace. I almost expect you to be holding a doll instead of that brush."

"What did you want?" Traedis asked wearily. She was not looking forward to sleep; she was afraid she would have more nightmares tonight. She often did, and recent days had been so fraught with the whiplash between terror and hope, that terrible dreams would almost certainly haunt her sleep. Vandeyr's interruption, however cross, was welcome.

"You have a letter." Her sister spoke the words as if she were saying that Traedis had received a gift of goat manure. She thrust a sealed missive forward, every movement conveying disapproval.

Traedis took it. The red wax seal was not one with which she was familiar, a stylized pair of trees with intertwined branches. She flipped the letter over to see who had sent it. In excellently calligraphed letters were the words:

To King Traedis Liori Eisel Atenel of Tolin, from Elben Tallforest, Haven Deputy Captain of King Kenrydh's royal guard in Faldrohaven.

That brought back a host of other memories, most of them

bad. Traedis had been hired out of Tolin's prisons by her well-meaning friends to carry out a covert mission against the City itself. The fiasco had necessitated seeking sanctuary in Faldrohaven. To protect Traedis from unintentional conflicting oaths, King Kenrydh had taken her prisoner, and assigned some of his guard to watch over her; this Elben Tallforest was presumably one of these.

That had been immediately before he Storm Eagle's death and before Traedis had received the *falmyros*. It had been before Toledru. Traedis hastily brushed away the thought.

Puzzled, she broke the seal and opened the letter. She was not sure why one of the Haven guard would write to her; the only one she particularly remembered was Arlen Longspear, Kenrydh's guard captain.

The letter read:

Greetings, King Traedis,

Perhaps you do not remember me; you were understandably preoccupied during your enforced stay in Faldrohaven. I am the Haven knight who chased you under chairs and tables in the form of a fox. It was one of the more unusual experiences I have had in a most varied career.

Memory rushed back in a flood; she could place him now. No wonder she had forgotten. She had been a fox most of that time, and in fox form her memories flowed oddly; the fox remembered scents and sounds, and experiences rushed past like a brisk wind. Elben was the red-bearded Haven warrior with the form of a fox, though red to her gray. Unlike many of his companions, he had been openly friendly to her, though she was a citizen of the City.

She remembered the chase of which he spoke, though her memory was clouded. Frightened to the point of panic, her instincts had overridden her human self; Elben had followed her as she fled, keeping pace while allowing her as much distance as he could. She equally appreciated his kindness and restraint.

Your rule of Tolin is much talked about. There are those who suppose it is merely another assassin's trick to quell the fears of the surrounding nations. Having met you myself, I know differently. I have no doubt that your honesty and honor will bring a new era to your city. I have found myself arguing this point frequently these days, as some are slower to accept change than others.

Should you find your way back to Faldrohaven, you will find at least one friend here; more than one, I suspect, though I can speak only for myself. I understand that you cannot leave Tolin in its current state of unrest, but in the future, I hope you will remember my words. You have not had a chance to see much of Faldrohaven, and presumptuous though this may sound, it would be my pleasure to escort you to visit its sights. I believe that many would be of great interest to one with such a lively mind as yourself.

I wish you the utmost good fortune as you begin your rule. Should you wish to write to me, you may do so through King Kenrydh's Haven bodyguard in Faldrohaven. I would be glad to hear from you.

It was signed, *Your Friend, Elben Tallforest.*

Traedis stared at the letter in complete bemusement; she could not discern why one of King Kenrydh's bodyguard would choose to write to her. The letter made her uncomfortable, though she was not sure why. Perhaps it was the unexpectedness that gave her an itchy feeling, like rough wool worn next to the skin.

"I should answer it, I suppose." She shook her head and stared back down at the page.

The capital letters of each paragraph were illuminated with stylized pictures in brilliant colors. Clearly it had taken a long time to craft.

"What does he want?" asked Vandeyr, disapproval etching lines around her mouth.

Traedis shook her head and handed the letter to her sister. Vandeyr read it quickly, her disapproval turning into a full-fledged scowl as she took in its contents. She snorted and handed it back. "I wouldn't," she grumbled. "You don't want to encourage this sort of thing."

What sort of thing? Traedis wanted to ask, but she was sufficiently annoyed at her sister that she was determined to remain silent. Instead, she took up her brush and pulled it through her curls, hoping that Vandeyr would take the hint.

Vandeyr glared at her. "I'd better go see to the change of door guards. If you need me, I'll be awake half the night." She stalked from the chamber, leaving Traedis gaping in her wake.

Alone at last, Traedis quickly braided her hair and leaned back to read the letter again. She would not feel right until she had answered. Sliding her feet into the fur slippers she kept at the bedside, she went quietly to her sitting room and sat at her desk, taking out a quill and parchment. Then she tried to compose a reply.

It proved surprisingly difficult. She was a bard; language was her profession. She had not found phrasing her thoughts so difficult since she had fled Tolin at the age of fourteen. The syllables would not come, try as she would to summon them in order to ink her response.

Deputy Captain Tallforest, she wrote.

Your words are most gracious, as befits one of your position. I confess that I do not understand your aim in sending this missive... "

She stared at the words, which sounded full of lofty disapproval. That would not do. She blotted her pen, moved the parchment into a pile to be scraped clean, and started another.

Good Deputy Captain Tallforest, I thank you warmly, both for your concern and for your defense of me. I am grateful for your attention to me during my time in Faldrohaven, and I remember you kindly.

That was almost worse; it reeked of condescension. Giving a sigh of frustration, she began a third. This time, she determined, she would write as she spoke, and say what she wished to say plainly.

The result was not perfect, but it was honest and from the heart.

Deputy Captain Tallforest, Greetings. I remember you and I am grateful for your avowal of friendship. I doubt, however, that I will be free to visit Faldrohaven in the foreseeable future, and I fear your offer to escort me will be wasted. Should you ever visit Tolin, I would like to tender a matching offer: I will escort you, and you may bring word back to your men of what sort of city Tolin has become. It is good to know that you speak in my defense, and I thank you. I hope that trust between Tolin and Faldrohaven may grow with time, and I am pleased that you will be part of that growth.

Your friend, Traedis Atenel, King of Tolin.

Afraid that any further attempt to re-write the letter would end in a much less satisfactory result, she folded the parchment and sealed it with wax, stamping it with the Storm Eagle signet. Then she laid it on her desk to be sent in the morning. The sense of discomfort had dissipated, leaving her ready for sleep. Relieved to have found a response, she retired to her bedchamber and to the welcoming cradle of slumber.

The Star Cavern had been transformed. Six days of the Quo'at's intensive work, and an equally intensive effort on the part of his priests and Traedis' servants, had changed day into night. Broken and useless items had been carried out of the chamber, freeing up enough space to add several low beds on which pilgrims could recline and look up at the constellations. The beds were large enough for humans or aelenin: the Quo'at had insisted upon it. "These stars have set themselves in your *falmyros*," he had told her, "and what they have chosen, I will not gainsay."

He had invited Traedis to see his work. She had immediately left a stack of petitions on her desk, taken Rose, and gone down the long stair to join him and his priests. Now they sat facing each other, the karreld's feet dangling above the floor.

Every trace of soot had been scoured from the stone. No lamps or torches were allowed in, but the brilliance of the painted stars obviated their use. It seemed like a moonless night with a radiance of starglow.

Traedis felt a breeze brush across her face, the scent of summer lightning in its wake. She knew that the chamber was ventilated, or no one would be able to breathe, but this was the first time she had felt the actual sensation of air moving in a mostly closed cave. She looked at the Quo'at and saw him grin.

"It's amazing, isn't it?" he asked, sounding as enthusiastic as any actual six-year-old. "With the restoration of the paint, the constellations have woken fully. They have moved this cavern into – well, I'll call it an *otherspace*. They are not truly what they seem, but there is a connection between what the stars appear to be and what they are." He scratched at a flake of paint on his nail; it did not glow, Traedis noticed.

She leaned back and looked up. The beauty caught at her heart, evoking wonder she had first experienced as child. "I had not imagined it would be like this," she said huskily. "I can feel their power and presence in my land as firmly as I can feel the Dragon Mountains edged up against the back side of Tolin. What *is* their connection with the dance of the heavens?"

The Quo'at's demeanor changed to that of a teacher instructing a student. "That is a thorny question to answer," he said. "You must understand that you do not hold the constellations themselves in your *falmyros*. No mortal power is great enough for that; even dragons do not command the stars. But the n'korreld have an affinity for the heavens, and we have trafficked with them since we first became a people by the sacrifice of the air dragons. This place holds a supplication for the intercession of those constellations, that they might heed us and aid us in need. They connect us to that reality, rather than drawing them from the sky to obey us.

"In truth," he continued, "they have no obligation, but their real forms consented to have their likenesses painted here. You know the principle of magical likeness?"

Traedis nodded. Two similar things were like mirrors, bound to each other; one could influence another if the similarity had enough magical significance. "It's mage's power, but I learned about many kinds of magic in the bardic college."

"Good," said the Quo'at. "That makes it easier to explain. These paintings open a doorway into a magical space where the connection is crystallized. The representations in your *falmyros* give you a right to be heard, but they will answer only if they choose." He fell silent for a long stretch; Traedis felt no need to fill it with words. Finally, he spoke again. "I have never heard of such a thing in all my lives; n'korreld magic giving itself over to one of another race. I think your fate must be entwined with my people, whether you are aware of it or not."

"I have no way to know." Traedis sat up and regarded him: the face of a child with the wisdom of an elder sage. "I haven't dealt much with your people. I don't know of any family connections." She shook her head. "It's as strange to me as to you that the Star Cavern has become so active in my *falmyros*."

"Whatever the reason," said the Quo'at, "it is in my heart to give you a gift. It is not payment for your actions, for that would cheapen them. But our way necessitates reciprocation when we have been met with extreme kindness or extreme cruelty. Most often it is reciprocal cruelty, which grieves me, though the anger of my people also pours through me. But when met with such generosity as yours, it is important to offer you the same generosity." He scooted forward and scuffed a toe on the floor. "Firstly, I name you a friend of my people. That is not an honor we give without great cause, but I bestow that title now on you."

Traedis swallowed hard; she was moved by the Quo'at's words. "I only give you back what is your own," she said. "It is certainly momentous for you to regain such a holy place, but it was never mine to keep from you."

"And that," the Quo'at told her, "is why the constellations have allied themselves with your *falmyros*."

Traedis nodded slowly. "I am honored."

"Then there is the matter of a suitable gift." The Quo'at gave her a grave stare. "Your uncle and his people have taken refuge in one of the n'korreld's ancestral homes, in the heart of the Kurtish Mountains. We are prepared to take him and to deliver him to your justice, should you so wish."

For an eternal moment, Traedis felt as if the entire world had suspended itself, like the motionlessness that Mardra had brought into her throne room. Traedis' thoughts balanced between the knowledge that this would be best for Tolin, and the terror that she must give Uncle Cordelayne over to Kenrydh's high justice.

She loved her uncle; even now, after he had imprisoned her for four years of her life, after he had hired her out of Tolin in a cold attempt to learn her capacities. He was also the man who had taught her to play the harp, who had brought her beautiful gifts from foreign lands, who had defended her as well as he could from her father. The secret wish of her heart had always been that she were his daughter instead of Linden's. He had filled that space in her life, and she was surprised to realize how much he still did.

Her throat closed, unwilling to let any speech pass the barrier of betrayal. She should accept the Quo'at's offer, but she could not. *A poor king*, she thought, *who cannot put aside her own desires for the sake of her nation.* But her heart refused, and her voice agreed with her heart.

The Quo'at leaned forward, an incongruous expression of gravity settling over his tiny features. "King Traedis, it is not my intention to grieve you. My offer is a gesture of goodwill. If it distresses you, something else can take its place."

"I – " Her voice still would not work. She cleared her throat forcefully, and squeezed the words out through a dry mouth. "It is something I must think on. I do not think I can either accept or refuse without deep consideration."

"Of course," said the Quo'at. "I think I understand why this gift may pose difficulties that I had not foreseen. We karrelds also value our kin-ties. We may speak of this later when you have had an opportunity to digest the matter."

"Yes," said Traedis, a faint trace of breathiness in her voice. "That would be best."

After leaving the Quo'at, she fled up the stairs as if chased by the Wild Hunt. Her heart battered itself on her ribcage, trying to exit her body. She ducked out of the building as fast as she could, hoping she would not meet Gavaya or any others of her family before she had made her decision.

Vandeyr joined her as soon as she left the library. Traedis did not look at her, but continued on her way back to the palace, hoping that her sister would not ask her about her obvious distress.

It was a futile hope. "Gods, Trae!" Vandeyr exclaimed as Traedis tried to avert her face from her sister so that she could order the chaos in her mind. "Are you all right? You're as white as Mother's best linens. What's the matter?"

"I am fine," Traedis told her from between clenched teeth. She did not meet Vandeyr's gaze. "I need to think about something."

Vandeyr snorted. "Do you think you're subtle? There's something really wrong, isn't there?"

A rush of stubborn anger impelled Traedis to lift her chin and glare at her sister. "Perhaps. But I'm not going to tell you what it is because I haven't made up my mind about it yet. Please don't ask me any more questions."

Vandeyr scowled. "Don't play the king with me. Sometimes I see why Mother is so dead set against you being ruler of Tolin. Go ahead and sulk in your rooms, like you've always done. When you deign to enlighten me, I'll be there awaiting your pleasure. My liege."

Vandeyr was obviously spoiling for an argument, but Traedis did not feel equipped for one just now. She shook her head. "I'll tell you later," she said shakily as they reached the palace doors. As soon as she could, she escaped to her apartments, where she could finally be alone.

Once in her sitting room, Traedis put her head in her hands, her thoughts churning in a chaotic mass of pain, anger, and despair. She knew that the Quo'at had no idea how his offer would affect her; he meant only the best toward her and toward Tolin. It was not his fault if Traedis' own weakness had stretched her near to breaking.

She forced herself to seriously consider what the Quo'at had offered. It would be the best step to take in terms of her relations with Telardur and Haven. Once she had Uncle Cordelayne in her keeping, she would have to surrender him to Kenrydh and execution in Telardur. Too many deaths lay between the City and Kenrydh's mercy.

Should that transpire, Traedis could expect no forgiveness from her family. Mitheira would never agree there was any justification for such an act. Already Otenemar would not speak to her. Vandeyr might withdraw her uneasy support, might even throw in with Daymet. Lang would be, at the least, angry and upset. Even Gavaya was unlikely to understand Traedis' reasons.

Her responsibility as king of Tolin superseded such concerns, though she could not force herself to ignore them. If it were the right thing to do, then she must do it, regardless of the personal cost. Even if the price was her family, it was not too dear for Tolin's freedom.

She would accept the Quo'at's offer. It was the right thing to do. She must not allow herself to be swayed by her heart, but must instead approach the question with logic and reason.

Firmly convinced that she had made up her mind, she started to rise from her seat. Then, flooded by the deeper love under her resolve, she sank back down.

Scenes rose to her mind; Uncle Cordelayne patiently guiding her hands on his own harp while she learned to play; his gentle tutelage in histories and literature; his forgiveness when she erred; his straightforward sympathy when she could not do what was expected of her. No one else in Tolin, not even Vandeyr, had ever treated her with such love and respect while she tried unsuccessfully to re-forge herself into someone the City would accept.

She knew it had been Uncle Cordelayne who sentenced her to four years in the terrible isolation of prison; who had tried to fly her like a falcon from the glove of the City in order to learn her secrets; who would have killed her if she had deliberately betrayed him. It did not matter. She loved him too deeply to order what would surely mean his death. She could not accept the Quo'at's offer.

By leaving Uncle Cordelayne free, Traedis knew that she might well be dooming herself, but she could not be as ruthless as he. It was not in her to destroy the person she loved most, even if he were also the person she feared most.

She felt hollow, an echoing emptiness like the aftermath of a storm of tears, though her eyes remained dry. She could not accept such a gift. Though Uncle Cordelayne himself would not respect her inability to take this advantage, she was not the woman he would have made of her. The gods had placed her here, knowing her many weaknesses; they must have known there were things she could not do. She hoped they, at least, would forgive her.

"I cannot accept your gift," Traedis told the Quo'at, barely keeping her voice from shaking. "Though it may be ungracious to refuse, my uncle is still my blood kin, and I cannot do such a thing."

They stood in the Star Cavern; the Quo'at was reluctant to leave it now that it had again become a temple rather than a storeroom. Traedis hoped that her refusal would not open a rift between them; the pride of a karreld was a touchy thing.

Instead, the Quo'at smiled warmly at her, light from the ceiling pooling around him as if to illuminate his holiness and wisdom. He hesitated for several long moments before he spoke. "King Traedis, it seems that I erred in making such an offer. I thought that it might be of worth. It was made in friendship only, and I did not intend to trouble you." He bowed his head in thought. "There is another offer I might make in its stead." He lifted his gaze level with Traedis' own. "Perhaps it would be a better token of friendship if I offered you knowledge of what your uncle and his people are doing within our halls. Would this be an acceptable substitute?"

Traedis felt her heart flutter for a moment with relief. The Quo'at was wise; this was an offer she could accept with gratitude. It might even be more useful than the first. Though Uncle Cordelayne was the greatest threat, he was not the only dangerous one who had fled from Tolin. Intelligence of all the rebels could be invaluable. Traedis' heart, her conscience, and her responsibility as king could be satisfied.

"I would be most happy to accept information on the rebels and their movements." Her voice sounded husky in her ears, but it worked, for which she was grateful. "And I thank you for your patience and good grace." She kept her gaze level, but stared into the space beyond the Quo'at's head, unwilling to see either pity or gentle understanding.

He gave her neither. "King Traedis, my gratitude to you is a deep well and a wide sky. We of the n'korreld do not forget those who have aided us."

Traedis felt a small laugh bubble up inside of her. "I suppose we could go back and forth politely thanking each other for the next several hours, but I suspect we would both hate it. Can we simply acknowledge that we are in each other's debt and end it there?"

The Quo'at laughed as well, a high, delighted sound. "Your directness is quite refreshing, King Traedis – many of my own people would be well to emulate it. I think sometimes the n'korreld lose something in our distrust of outsiders. But trust comes hard when it is betrayed too often, and our folk have misplaced it too many times for us to be comfortable relying on others." He shook his head slowly. "We can take this too far. There are those like yourself who are willing to aid us without thought of return. I have lived long enough to realize that anyone with gods-given free will may walk a path alongside ours." He smiled broadly. "In this case, my expectations have been greatly exceeded."

"May I continue on that path, then." Traedis looked up at the constellations, then back at the child who had seen the sky turn for thousands of years. The thought made her almost dizzy. "And may our people continue in amity."

"That is my wish as well," said the Quo'at. "The gods grant it may be so."

A week later, Traedis waited in her apartment's sitting room to meet with the spy promised her by the Quo'at. She had chosen the more private space so that the legion of house servants and even Vandeyr's guard would have few indications that she was seeing someone in an official capacity. She could not be sure that a spy had not wormed a way into her palace; her people had specialized in just such operations for centuries. To the staff who must know, word had been quietly spread by Vandeyr that Traedis was undergoing preliminary trade talks with an emissary of the Thane.

A knock sounded, and Vandeyr entered, a karreld at her heels.

It was Atchûk.

Traedis blinked, then relaxed as the young prince broke into a broad smile and bowed.

"Sit, please." Rising to greet him, she ushered him into a chair made for a karreld's comfort before re-seating herself. A small table laden with mead and small cakes stood between them. Vandeyr took a stance beside the door with an air of watchfulness; no other guards would be privy to this conversation.

She wanted to hear what Atchûk had to say; it was possible that he had come for another reason entirely, though given the n'korreld involvement in her affairs, she thought it unlikely.

He took the seat, scratched his sandstone skin, and brushed back a lock of hair. Gold flashed from a pair of tiny hoops in his ears. "Your Majesty, I am at your service, though not, perhaps, the service I had originally decided to perform."

He *was* the spy, then. Traedis was not sure if she were happy about this turn of affairs; she enjoyed having the karreld around. Still, she was relieved that someone she knew and trusted would take on this responsibility.

She poured him a tankard of mead, and took one herself. "I hope you're not tired of our hospitality," she said, part in jest and part seriously. "I wouldn't like to think we'd driven you off by our refusal to provide enough comfortable chairs."

Atchûk laughed. "You clearly have not spent enough time in the merchant quarter, Trae. They have seating for anyone from a brunaidh to an istronian, and some are adjustable – though not quite to that degree, I'll concede. If I have a strong desire to sit while strolling the streets of your beautiful city, I only need to aim toward the center, and I will find myself with dozens of chairs perfectly contoured for my frame." His expression changed from amused to earnest, and he leaned forward, his hands on his thighs. "But Trae, this is an adventure! It's been fascinating to visit Tolin and explore its differences from my homeland, but this is my chance to repay you for your hospitality and for remembering me when you uncovered the Star Cavern. To be the first karreld in thousands of years to see those stars shine is an honor beyond anything I could ever have dreamed of.

"And now a chance to revisit the now-abandoned halls of my people..." His eyes shone. "To use my skills and my mind to benefit a friend of the n'korreld? Of course I took the opportunity! And the Quo'at accepted my petition."

Traedis nodded slowly. She poured him a glass of mead before taking one herself; it gave her an opportunity to collect her startled thoughts. He accepted the glass and drank deeply, watching her at least as carefully as she watched him.

Tapping her fingers on the chair's arm, she decided to be direct. "I am surprised your father allowed you to take on this task – it's very perilous. My uncle is a dangerous man."

Atchûk nodded. "I understand, and I don't take that lightly. Please understand that my father would never ask me to cower in safety while any of my people brave danger. But don't fear too much – I grew up exploring every passage and crevice of those caves. I know them better than my own heartbeat. Besides, most of them are far too narrow for a human to fit. The place is honeycombed all over with natural peepholes, some of them through ells of rock. I'll be well out of their reach."

Traedis had to acknowledge his logic, but it made her no less uncomfortable. "I know this is intended as a goodwill gift from the Quo'at, but I put no conditions on n'korreld use of the Star Cavern. You are not obligated to spy for me because the Quo'at wishes it."

Putting down his mead, Atchûk's face grew serious. "There are layers to the situation that an outsider would not know," he told her. "Some might take offense at your words, but I don't, because you can't be expected to understand those layers." He picked the mead back up and took another long pull. "Firstly, amongst my folk, an act of generosity such as allowing our people access to the Star Cavern *must* be met with an equal act, or the scales are not balanced. We do not like to owe anyone, and when we are given something freely, we don't trust it. I don't say this to insult you, Trae, because I am certain that you have not intended to put us in your debt, nor does the Most Blessed Quo'at – but n'korreld history is full of occasions when other races have tricked us into allegiance or have given something to us, only to gain more for themselves. The debt is on our side, not yours, and we consider it a debt we must pay." He wiped his mouth with the back of his hand.

"Secondly, the Most Blessed Quo'at wishes it. Perhaps you don't comprehend the reverence we feel toward him. He is our star, our guide, and we look to him for lessons in what is good and holy and right. He is more than a man – he is a living path to the gods. If he says something is mete, few of our folk will gainsay him. We revere all the Reborn, but he is greater than the rest." He scratched his chin. "I don't think there is a human or faldren comparison. His desires are not for himself, but for all of us. To doubt him?" He shook his head. "We would as soon doubt the dragons."

Traedis listened with a growing realization that her words had been unwise, and might have offended the n'korreld seriously had she spoken them to someone else. Their sense of honor was often a brambly road for others to traverse. She nodded. "I understand, and I thank you for your patience."

"There is a third thing." Atchûk flashed his grin at her again before fishing a honey cake from the plate. "I volunteered to be the one to go. When I came here, it was because it promised to be considerably more interesting than sitting in talks with the fishermen about getting the right mushrooms to weave their nets, or wrangling with the stonemasons over how deep it's wise to build into the rock on Geltz Isle." He gave a light laugh. "Darg is the one who is good at sitting and talking with the patience of basalt. He's the diplomat. I'm the fellow who always has to be doing something, or I start wanting to bite the heads off seagulls. I haven't exhausted the possibilities for Tolin yet, but I can always come back. This is a one-time opportunity."

Traedis laughed; she could not help it. "Thank you," she said, the smile still curving her lips upward. "For explaining it to me, and for not taking offense." Her lips curved even more. "And thank you for saving the lives of countless seagulls."

Atchûk broke into a full belly-laugh, snorting and slapping at his knee. "There's a reason I like you!" He continued to chuckle for several moments before regaining his composure. "The seagulls will be safe for another day, as I intend to do an exemplary job of watching your uncle and his people."

A few more chuckles slid out before his expression straightened into a more serious aspect. "If I'm to do this properly,

I need some more information from you. Are there are specific conversations you want me to listen for? People you want me to keep a particular eye on? Code words or phrases that I might not know?"

They were good questions, and Traedis knew some of the answers. "Yes to the first two, I don't know to the third." She wrinkled her forehead. "For the first part, I would like you to listen for any plans to overthrow me as Tolin's ruler or to take the City by force. I need to know against whom they plan to act, when, where, and how. I need to know if they have spies in our midst." She considered the question further, wondering what sort of conversations Uncle Cordelayne might have that would *not* be important. "I think I am looking for plans, not whatever opinions they might express. That may seem obvious, but it's the best way I can narrow it down.

"As to the second question, there are a handful of people I would like to know about. I'm not sure if all of them are with my uncle, but if they are, their words will also be significant. My brother Daymet is almost as dangerous." A pang of guilt lanced through her stomach in a sudden cramp; she did not want to speak ill of either, but she had to be honest with the man who was risking his life to help her. "Lord Faylias and Lord Sedorin. One a small, neat man with a short beard, the other built large, with a ruddy face; both are middle-aged. They are the two other Council members who fled, and together with my uncle, the most important of the nine. Also, I need to know about anyone my uncle takes into his confidence, even if they are strangers to us." She shook her head as if to clear it. "Captain Atenel can brief you on anyone I've left out. She's far more likely to know who might be a danger."

Atchûk nodded. "In addition to those specifics, it seems to me that you are saying that I should use my own judgement." He wiped his fingers on a napkin, leaving honey-colored stains behind. "Which is a good thing, since I had already planned on doing just that. It seems, King Traedis, that we are in accord. Have I read that scroll rightly?"

Traedis inclined her head. "Indeed you have, Prince Atchûk. Indeed you have."

It did not take long for Atchûk to pack up his presence in Tolin, his departure as quiet as his entrance had been exuberant. Traedis found herself missing his cheerful presence, which had buoyed her spirits more than she had realized.

Atchûk's attitude had, she realized, reminded her of Kaelennar and the friends who had accepted her without family or standing or any knowledge of her at all. His openness recalled the freedom of Kaelennar's people. His irreverence was a tonic for the deadly seriousness of Tolin's crown.

The karreld had been gone three weeks, when a loud knock woke Traedis from sleep. She opened a bleary gaze to a room illuminated only by banked coals in the fireplace. Sitting up, she knuckled sleep-filled eyes, then took up the tinderbox on the bedside table and lit the candle which sat next to it. As the knock sounded again, louder, she rose, stuffed her feet into her slippers, and put on her dressing gown. Negotiating the space between desk, washing table, wardrobe, and bed, she opened the door beside the still-warm hearth.

Vandeyr stood there, in the outer chamber of her apartment. Traedis saw that her sister looked tense and worried, though perhaps no one who did not know her well would have noticed; Vandeyr's hair was perfectly combed and her uniform clean and pressed, but the faintest of dark circles underscored her eyes, and an almost invisible line traced the shape of her brow.

"What's wrong?" Traedis asked. "Something's wrong, isn't it? And what time is it?"

Vandeyr nodded. "It's an hour till first light. I'll tell you what happened while you dress."

Traedis nodded, the blood pulsing in her throat. She went to open her wardrobe, choosing a gray linen dress, plainer and more utilitarian than she usually wore to court.

"Captain Dorrell of the City Guard was wakened early this morning by a hammering at his door." Vandeyr's crisp recital of the facts might have almost seemed detached to one who did not know her. Her hand fell to her dagger; an unconscious gesture, Traedis guessed. "I suppose I don't have to say it was early." Vandeyr frowned. "When he went to investigate, he found a spearhead driven completely through the wood."

Traedis tried to calculate how hard a spear would have to be driven to pierce a solid wooden door. She thought it likely most spears would break first.

"Anyway," said Vandeyr, "he tried to open the door. He couldn't at first; there was a resistance to his pushing. When he got it open, he found out why – three dead men hung on the shaft, pinned there like joints of meat strung up in the smokehouse."

Traedis winced at the image. "Does anyone know how they got there?"

Vandeyr scowled. "We know, all right. Take a look at this." From her pouch she pulled a rolled piece of parchment, which she handed to Traedis.

Traedis opened it gingerly, uncertain of what she would see. She saw the writing first, and knew immediately the hand belonged to Uncle Cordelayne.

The note read: *These three men plotted the death of the King of Tolin, and therefore I have exacted justice.* Affixed to the bottom was the signature, *Cordelayne, Lord Atenel.*

Traedis stared at the parchment, reading it over three times before she could make sense of the words. She was not foolish enough to believe that Uncle Cordelayne's interference was a good thing.

"What does he hope to gain by this?" she asked, more to herself than to her sister.

"If I had to guess, I'd say he's showing his strength." Vandeyr retrieved the parchment from Traedis, refolding it and putting it back into her pouch. "By doing this he shows up the incompetence of the City Guard, keeps amateurs out of his game, and looks like a hero in the eyes of the City." She scuffed one heel angrily across the floor. "I'd say it was supposed to unnerve us as well."

Traedis pressed her lips together tightly and refrained from telling Vandeyr that Uncle Cordelayne's tactic was working. "Who were the dead men?"

"Now that's the other interesting part." Vandeyr impatiently brushed back her perfectly combed hair. "Two brothers and their friend. They were indeed planning to overthrow you. What wasn't on that Kyaan-cursed note was the fact that none of the three were competent enough to overthrow a cracked flagpole." Her voice grew taut. "I won't swear that someone didn't stir them up, either. Two tanners and a day laborer – an odd trio to suddenly decide to overthrow you. Uncle Cordelayne's hands have been all over this from its inception."

"What about the wall? Do you know how they breached it?" Traedis realized her fingers were tightly interlaced, and made a conscious effort to relax them.

Vandeyr shook her head. "Dorrell hadn't gotten around to investigating it yet. The old fool seems to think the trail won't go cold if he has his morning eggs first."

"Eggs," said Traedis. She frowned. "I should get something to eat now, because it sounds as if I won't have much time later. Send me a page when you go out, please. And I want to know as soon as you learn anything about how they got in."

"Oh, I will," Vandeyr told her. "I want to know as well. I can't do my job in the palace if Dorrell isn't doing his job in the rest of Tolin."

Traedis nodded, deciding to deal with that issue later. "And can you please send Ruth up here too? I'd like her opinion of this as well."

"Don't mind me." Vandeyr turned sharply to face the door. "I'm just here to run your errands. It's not as if I have anything important to do." She exited in a sharp motion which Traedis guessed had more to do with worry than with anger. Still, Traedis winced when the bedroom door slammed shut behind her. It was followed swiftly by the muffled slam of the hallway door.

Traedis opened the top drawer of her bureau and pulled out a rough blue-and-white stone the size of a large coin; its mate was in Atchûk's possession. Taking it to a chair, she sat, holding it between her cupped hands. If it worked properly, the karreld would feel his stone warm, and would contact her.

It was not long before it began to radiate heat, not enough to be painful, but more than it would gain from the heat of her hands. The amulet would allow Atchûk and her to speak mind to mind, though unlike Kenrydh's ruby, it would not enable them to see each other.

"Trae," the young karreld's clear voice said in her head. "Greetings. I have some news for you."

"And I for you," she responded. "As well as a number of questions. But tell me your news first, since it is possible that we may be holding two ends of the same rope."

Atchûk laughed. "Indeed, it is possible. I'll gladly tell you what I know." Traedis could hear him draw a breath. "About five days ago, a thick balding man with a clumsy tongue brought twenty-six others to these caverns. Your Lord Sedorin, I am quite sure. He and your uncle had a number of quiet conversations I couldn't get close enough to hear, though some of it sounded intense, maybe even contentious. His arrival set many of your rebels scurrying around like red ants with no one to bite but each other."

Uncle Cordelayne and Lord Sedorin had not always agreed in the past, and Traedis wondered how their new circumstances would affect that relationship. Once in charge of the rebels, Uncle Cordelayne would not want to cede authority to anyone, particularly to Lord Sedorin, whom he had once described in an unguarded moment as a 'stiff-necked unimaginative old bull.'

"That does not surprise me," Traedis said dryly. "What would surprise me is if my uncle and Lord Sedorin suddenly became the best of friends."

The karreld chuckled. "At the moment, I rather doubt that outcome. I've been scouting out some good places to listen from, and there's a fine spyhole right over where your uncle conducts his business. I can usually see what's happening, though hearing through it is harder. I can make out some of his conversations, and a fair number of his orders. And where I can't, I can make a good guess."

Traedis raised an eyebrow, realized that Atchûk could not see her, and lowered it. "Please, go on," she said.

"This morning, quite early, he was pacing back and forth as if waiting for something. He usually acts as if he would be most honored to fill the shoes of the gods, should they choose to step down, so the fact that he seemed tense made me watch and listen to learn as much as I could."

Traedis swallowed the impulse to defend her uncle against the karreld's words. Atchûk was risking his life for her; she had no business criticizing his opinions. Instead, she asked, "Past midnight and well before dawn?"

"Around then," he responded. "I couldn't give you a clearer guess without a view outside. Another man finally appeared – a long thin fellow with a mole on his cheek – and they were murmuring, so I only caught some of their conversation. I heard the words 'men,' 'captain,' and 'dark,' and 'wall,' but that's not going to be of much help. The phrase that caught my attention was 'the execution went perfectly.' That made me strain to hear more."

Traedis had the slightly hysterical urge to ask Atchûk which meaning of the word 'execution' he thought the man had meant, but she quelled it and clutched the communication stone closely "Did you catch anything else?"

"I did," the karreld said. "They got quieter after the first part of their exchange, so I thought I was wasting my time for a while. Then the second man said a little louder, 'everything went as planned.' That was the only other meaningful thing I managed to hear, but it sounded like it might be important."

"It might be extremely important," Traedis replied. She briefly outlined what had happened. "As you see, the conversation makes a great deal of sense, and gives me something to hunt for. I need to know if the wall was breached magically. There are supposed to be safeguards on it, but if anyone would know how to circumvent them, it would be two Council members."

"I will keep watching to see if I can find out anything more significant." He paused. "I'd be happy if someone would shout their plans up to me so I can take notes when I'm perched in a stone hole not much bigger than a ferret, but I suppose it's too much to hope for."

Traedis could hear the smile in his voice.

"But more seriously," he continued, "if I can give you little scraps of knowledge, you may be able to boil them together and make a decent stew. I understand it's how these things work."

"It is," said Traedis. "And thank you. Be careful."

"I will. Until we speak again, Trae."

Traedis' stone immediately cooled, even though she still held it between her palms.

Atchûk's news was not entirely a revelation; Traedis already knew that Uncle Cordelayne was behind the assassinations. Though she had not known Lord Sedorin was with him, it was not a surprise either. The potentially important information was the possible breach in the magic of the walls. She could not tell if there were more.

Later, as Traedis ate breakfast with Ruth, a sharp rap at the door interrupted them. Traedis sighed, knowing it must be Vandeyr. "Come in."

Vandeyr swept in like a thunderstorm. "I have some news about how the wall might have been breached." Her tone said that she would prefer to tell Traedis alone. Traedis almost smiled; the delicate shades of meaning in Vandeyr's subtle speech would have put most of Kaelennar's bards to shame.

"How?" she asked Vandeyr.

Vandeyr made a fractional glance at Ruth and back to Traedis, who had no intention of telling Ruth to leave. Vandeyr sighed.

"One of the crystals on the wall is cracked," she said shortly. "You know the ones I mean? They're set into the top of the stone to give a warning should hostile magic cross. It's not much of a crack, though, and it's awfully hard to find – I took a look at it myself. The mage who inspected it said that the wall might have had difficulty determining whether the rebels were hostile or not, especially considering their errand. Of course, if the City Guard had been doing its job, no one would have gotten through anyway, but half of them are layabouts, and the remaining few don't know what on Coran's black earth they're doing. You should really have a talk with Dorrell, Trae. He needs to straighten his people out and get them working the way a City Guard ought."

"I'll consider it," Traedis said mildly, not willing to argue the subject. "After we make sure nothing like this will happen again."

"The mage is waiting on your word to repair the crystal," Vandeyr said. "Mine is apparently not good enough. I've got people scouring the wall inch by inch for any other weaknesses."

Traedis thought about Uncle Cordelayne's resourcefulness and her palms began to sweat. She hoped there were no other gaps in their defenses, but if there were, he would know them.

She could not match wits with him, but perhaps there were small deceptions which might draw him into an error of judgment. "Don't repair the crystal."

"Don't repair the crystal?" Vandeyr glared at her. "It's a

weakness and an enticement for Uncle Cordelayne and his people to try something else. Has Kyaan taken your wits, or are you trying out a fashionable new trend in stupidity?"

Traedis glared back. "It's a small crack, you say, and hard to find. Who's to say we found it? If Uncle Cordelayne thinks we've gone slack, he won't expect us at our best."

Vandeyr's expression turned thoughtful. "That's not such a bad idea," she said. "I suppose even you can come up with one once in a while. I take it back. You've got a few of the Atenel wits after all."

Ruth said, "I think it's a good idea. Why not put a couple of extra guards on the gates as well, to give the impression that you think they got in that way?" She picked the remains of the sausage from the fork and licked her fingers clean.

Vandeyr moved a half-turn to look at Ruth. "That's not a bad idea. I suppose."

"See to it," Traedis told her, wiping her mouth with a napkin. "Let me know if there are any developments."

"Very well." Vandeyr turned and left the office, her footsteps lighter than they had been when she had entered.

Traedis returned to her rooms, leaving instructions that she was not to be disturbed for anything less than an emergency. Entering her bedchamber, she shut the door after herself, removed her hairpins, and lay down on the bed, fully clothed. Closing her eyes, she felt for the webwork of connections between herself and

Tolin, the pressure of the City on her body, swathing her and running through her veins like blood.

She used her affinity to see the walls, their massive stones buttressed with two thousand years of magical fortifications. Knowing what she sought, it was not difficult to find the cracked crystal which had weakened the structure. It felt like the hairline break in a dish or teacup, nothing great in itself, but increasing the wall's vulnerability. She did not know if Uncle Cordelayne would use it again, for though it left its mark for the City's wardens to see, it was also the thin spot in Tolin's defenses.

Like a woman spinning thread, she strengthened and twined the link between her and that section of wall, tying its awareness into her mind where it would flare to sudden consciousness if anyone tried to exploit the weakness. Advising it that the rebels worked toward the City's harm, she felt its relief that she had made the distinction; the wall had been hard put to distinguish between friend and enemy, when both were of Tolin. Then she backed out of the *falmyros* carefully, trying to avoid falling into its pull and forgetting herself in the land that already felt like her ribs and her heartbeat.

Chapter Nineteen
Foxes

Her stomach cramping with nausea, Traedis watched her mother smile across the dinner table at King Kenrydh. "Your Majesty," Mitheira said, "I am most intrigued by the quality of the clockwork coming from your people in the last year." She gave her brightest smile, and though Traedis could see her mother's look was somewhat brittle, she did not intend to mention it. Her mother had already committed one intentional act of extreme rudeness.

Spring had cast its earliest green mist over the trees when Kenrydh made his first visit to Tolin. It was a state affair, and it had been Traedis' hope that it would go smoothly. But her mother would not have forgiven Traedis if she had not been invited to the dinner, and Mitheira's status in the City entitled her to a seat at the table. That meant Telardur's king was close enough to see Mitheira's hair, styled around a hard bar with heavy knobs at both ends that could be used either as a blunt weapon, or pulled apart to reveal a wire garotte. Clearly, Traedis' mother intended to make the statement that her true loyalties lay with Old Tolin.

Kenrydh nodded solemnly and speared a square of meat-filled pastry. "I confess that I find some of it miraculous myself." Sipping at his wine, he continued, "I was recently treated to a demonstration of a novelty, a clockwork town that took up half a room. Its citizens moved about, each performing a different task, some even climbing into carriages pulled by tiny mechanical horses. I was astounded by the complexity of the whole, and the time it must have taken to fit the gears."

The artificial conversation grated on Traedis. She knew Kenrydh would not hold her mother's conduct against her, but she felt sick, nonetheless. The tentative peace between their nations was still so new that Traedis feared some of her citizens, or possibly the rebels, would find some way of overturning it.

The dinner had been carefully arranged by Traedis' oldest brother Lang, who had learned statecraft from their father and from Uncle Cordelayne. Though Lang seemed resigned to accepting Traedis as king, she knew there were many matters on which they disagreed.

She was wary of her entire family, except perhaps for Gavaya. Traedis could not afford to trust, so she watched Lang as carefully as she watched Otenemar, though from closer quarters. At least she could feel the presence of Vandeyr and Ruth, both of them determined to keep her safe.

"How extraordinary!" Jahn Greymont, head of his Council house since his elder brother had died during Toledru's uprising, raised dark eyebrows at Kenrydh. "I would find it fascinating as well, and though it seems frivolous, I am sure the philosophy of clockwork has been much advanced by such endeavors."

Traedis gritted her teeth to hold her immediate response back. That comment had been an insult disguised as a compliment, and Kenrydh had to know it. She hoped he did not think she was completely incapable of handling her own subjects; she was not sure she could.

On the other hand, her childhood training in etiquette had been honed in Kaelennar; she knew how to redirect a conversation. "My brother has arranged a tour to the Council Spring," she said, keeping her tone light and friendly. "It is our own new marvel; when the old Council building collapsed, a pure spring broke through, and now provides us with a second source of water so that we do not need to wholly depend on the river. Its wholesomeness has washed out Toledru from under the earth as thoroughly as he has been scoured from the City." Or more so, she thought, her thoughts nimbly skirting the horror of the demon's memory.

Her gaze flicked to where Kenrydh's Haven guard stood at attention. Arlen Longspear stood at the wall behind his king's seat; the alliance was sufficiently new that neither side wanted to take chances with Kenrydh's safety. Two others of the Haven guard flanked Arlen. One of them was Elben Tallforest.

Elben was a tall, lean man in his early thirties. Red sifted through blond hair that he wore in a short tail; he sported a red military beard which ran down his long jaw and over his chin. A straight nose and a curl of humor in the lines of his face sent a not-unpleasant shiver over Traedis' skin.

She had grasped, albeit tardily, that Elben's letter was a polite attempt at courtship. She had told herself repeatedly she should have known he would come. He was Arlen Longspear's second-in-command; of course he would be included in a high-risk and important endeavor. She must determine what to say to him, preferably sooner than later; he deserved that courtesy. But she was unused to being courted by anyone who seemed to have true regard for herself rather than for Tolin's *falmyros*.

Wingblade's curse made her loath to entertain any suitor she might learn to care for. His voice seemed to blow through her memory, carried on a feral wind: *Who will lose their love to the storm?* Now that she had defied Mardra, there was every chance that any situation to which the words could possibly apply would be held against her. She could not afford to love.

She returned her attention to the table, realizing that the discussion had shifted, largely due to Lang and his wife Alluve, both of whom seemed to have deftly wrested the conversation away from Mitheira and Jahn Greymont. They now inquired politely, but with clear interest, into Kenrydh's dealings with the n'korreld. Traedis ran the last few lines of the exchange through her head, and realized that Lang and Alluve had managed to block several verbal sorties made by her mother and Jahn. Her brother and his wife were a formidable pair.

Hoping that her brief inattention had not been too obvious, Traedis dipped back into the flow of speech. "I have had few dealings with Thane Bi'ia, but his son Prince Atchûk is a fine man." She knew better than to explain what activity Atchûk was involved in, as she thought it possible that some of her family might betray his presence to Uncle Cordelayne. "But I know the n'korreld have a great deal of pride, and a well-earned mistrust of other peoples. How do they take to your *falmyros*?" Telerdur's experience might help prepare Traedis for the flood of karreldish pilgrims who had come to the Star Cavern in a steady stream since the Quo'at had repainted it.

Kenrydh replied gravely, "They have been gracious with me and do not seem to find my rule too burdensome. I treat them with respect, King Traedis, so they do the same for me. I do not condescend, I do not believe or act as if my sovereignty gives me the right to command them beyond binding them to my laws. The air dragons sacrificed their own lives to give free will to the secondborn races, and I do not take that lightly. Before the gods, those races are as worthy as any other."

Traedis gave a genuine smile, not one of the false expressions she had learned to paste on her face to give the semblance of cheer. Though she was still intimidated by Kenrydh's presence, she was beginning to think he was also a man she might like very much. He was honorable and just, and the fact that he would not permit Tolin to continue in their old path did him credit rather than otherwise.

Alluve leaned forward in apparent interest. "You make no distinctions between the firstborn and secondborn races?" It was clearly not a challenge, but an honest question. "Despite the difference in how we were made into thinking, choosing peoples? I know some philosophers believe that the gift of the gods weighs more heavily than the dragons' gift, but others hold that, as the dragons do the will of the gods, there is no inequity. It sounds to me as if you take the second position."

Traedis looked at her fondly. Alluve had always been kind to her. She was a pleasant, plump woman with large eyes, soft features, dark brown skin, and a cloud of thick black hair pinned up neatly. She had a mind equal to anyone in the City, and was a fine scholar. Though she was not from a Council family, even Mitheira had never complained about the match. Well-liked throughout Tolin, Alluve and Lang were devoted to each other.

"I fully believe the dragons do the will of the gods." Kenrydh stopped to take a draught of wine before continuing. "Though dragons, like any created beings, may fall into error, when such a monumental sacrifice is made, I consider that the gods have accepted it and the change was willed by them." He stroked his beard. "Perhaps it was the gods' plan from the beginning, and perhaps not, but that it has become their plan I have no doubt."

Lang looked at him as if considering his response. "I see that the faldrim and the City have very different ideas on the will of the gods." He frowned, though it seemed less in disapproval than in thought. "I would like to talk with you further about these matters. My mind has been more challenged these last four months than in the four years preceding them."

"I would be honored to hold a deeper discussion," Kenrydh replied. "It would bode well if our countries were to grow in mutual understanding."

When Traedis looked at her mother, Mitheira's expression was perfectly blank.

Three main courses and a dessert later, Kenrydh retired to his chambers, leaving Traedis free to seek her own. Vandeyr trailed her without speaking; Traedis could almost feel darts in her back. The food she had eaten sat in her stomach like lead. It was a relief to slip into her apartments, letting Vandeyr post herself outside, her stiffness implying she did not trust anyone else to guard her sister against the faldren king – especially his Haven guard. Ruth, at least, had been persuaded to take some time off while Traedis practiced her harp.

Traedis slid out of her satin court gown and donned a more comfortable and looser linen frock, pulled a dressing gown over it, then slipped her feet into her comfortable fur slippers. It was not late, but she wanted leisure to practice, and to examine some records that Gavaya wanted her to read. She looked wistfully out the window at the purple shadows already creeping across the mountain peaks, then settled herself at her desk.

The sound of voices at her door did not surprise her; Vandeyr was captain, so her lieutenants would need to seek her out for orders. But one of the voices caught her attention, though she had not heard it for months. She sat up, trying to discern the words.

"Can the fox come out to play?" asked a man's voice. Elben's.

Traedis felt her heart bang against her chest. She did not know if she was prepared to face him. On the other hand, if she did not, she was reasonably sure Vandeyr would find some pretext to send him away, and Traedis was not prepared for that, either. Not sure what she intended, she opened the door.

A large red fox sat outside on its haunches, looking at Vandeyr with an intelligent expression. Traedis blinked; she had seldom seen Elben in his other form when she had not also been in hers. Despite her ambivalence, she felt a smile stretch across her face. "Deputy Captain Tallforest," she said.

The fox turned toward Traedis. "Do you want to come out and play, Your Majesty?" he asked, laughter in his voice. "It's a fine evening out if you have fur. I think I spotted a good place for tag in the courtyard."

Traedis laughed in spite of herself, unable to resist Elben's casual playfulness. "It sounds like a wonderful idea." She regretfully shook her head. "But when I turn to fox, I'm truly a fox. I wouldn't know how to play tag. I probably wouldn't even know who you were."

Elben's tail swished from side to side. "Every fox knows how to play tag." He cocked his head cheerfully to the side and looked up at her. "Besides, I can tell that you need some time away from the concerns of your land and of our visit. You look exhausted."

Vandeyr stiffened just enough for Traedis to notice. "It would not be seemly for the King of Tolin to frolic with a Haven knight, and it is not your place to make personal observations about her."

Traedis glared at Vandeyr. It was true that it would not be seemly to frolic in the courtyard with Elben, but she sorely needed a respite from the anxiety that accompanied King Kenrydh's visit. Elben's form sat appealingly in her doorway, and Traedis felt a strong desire to lay down the burden of kingship for at least a few hours. She certainly was not going to allow Vandeyr to dictate who she associated with, or how she spent her time.

"Perhaps you're right," she told the knight. "Perhaps that's what I need." She ignored Vandeyr's silent seething, and nodded slowly. "Yes. I'd love to come out. I'm not doing anything urgent at the moment."

"Come out, then." Elben turned quickly and made for the stairs, his russet coat glinting in the late sunlight which still poured through the hall windows. Traedis went after him, followed by Vandeyr.

The air was chill, common enough in the mountains at this time of year, and a cold wind knifed from the mountains. The sun shone in a darkening azure dome marred by gentle drifts of cloud and a slice of slowly greening sky.

It was harder to see the fantastical shapes of the mountains over the palace walls, especially shrouded as they were now in the beginnings of darkness. Still, she could feel them leaning into Tolin's border, an itch of overwhelming power straining against its boundaries. They gave her a strange feeling in her stomach, as if she stood beside a high cliff. She tried not to let herself think too hard about what powers lay adjacent to Tolin on that side of her *falmyros*.

The courtyard lay alongside a garden hedged with early-budding snowdrops and strewn with small bushes and trees flushed with the faintest shadow of green. Leaves of daffodils and primroses poked through a thin layer of snow. Soon they would be joined by the blue of wood hyacinth and cilla, like the blooms of Ymre. Carefully tended rosebushes held still-bare branches upward, as if beseeching spring rain to fall. The scent of cooling earth enriched the odors of snow, stone, and the juniper hedges which bordered some of the paths.

Elben sat on his haunches and began to wash his face. "Here," he said. "I know you don't like tight spaces, but you can hide under the bushes where you'll feel safe if you need to. Some of them are quite thick."

Traedis smiled sadly. Elben had cause to know her fears, since she had displayed them publicly in Faldrohaven. He was kind to think of her comfort, but she wished he did not know how vulnerable she could be.

Standing before the hedge, she breathed in its aroma and thought fox thoughts to encourage herself to change. The safety of briars; the dark, delicious taste of mice and shrews; the freedom of a wild creature in her own element; all ran through her mind, tantalizing and tempting her into the form which hid Traedis even from herself. It was easier to be a fox than a human. The fox could not be held accountable for errors and misjudgments.

She was no more aware of the change than of the transition from wakefulness to sleep. One moment she stood on two legs, convincing herself to become a fox; the next she ran on four legs, smelling the wind and tasting the myriad scents that hung on the late winter breeze. Her ears pricked up at the distinctive squeaks of baby mice; somewhere under the bushes was a mousehole. Among the multitude of scents and sounds, all of them captivating, ran the musky tang and the swish of fur that spoke of healthy male fox.

Traedis hovered between the fox and mouse, uncertain which was more appealing.

The red fox came bounding through the hedge, ears and whiskers quivering with laughter. "Chase me," he said, and though she did not understand his words, she knew the language of his body, the invitation to frolic. He disappeared back through the hedge, the tip of his tail flicking through the branches in a shimmer of white.

Somewhere behind a fox's sensations and instincts, Traedis knew that this red fox was no danger to her. She turned to the chase, delight overriding a fear which she did not now understand.

He lay just out of sight under another portion of hedge. She reached him easily by scenting his trail and hearing the slight rustle of his fur on the bushes. Slipping up behind him, she prepared to nip him gently. But before she could reach him, he jumped up, laughed joyously, and streaked away through the thick of the bushes, disappearing under a curtain of newly budding branches.

She followed him, her senses more than keen enough to trace him even through the disorienting cascade of smells that distracted her nose. Most of the scents were neither pleasant nor odious; they tasted neither of danger nor of food. Losing the trail for a moment, she discovered it had doubled back on itself and returned the way it had come. His sleek form reappeared beside her and licked her mischievously on the ear. She sprang after him, nipping his flanks with playful abandon.

He began to tussle with her like a cub wrestling with its

littermate. She felt a thrill through her body, heightening all her senses and telling her without language that the two of them were connected. The tension which underlay her every action ebbed, though it left a ghost of fear in its place, an unwelcome reminder that she was more than her mind could currently encompass.

Time meant nothing, except in terms of warmth and chill. The sun dropped precipitously behind the horizon, covering her with comforting shadows. She felt an unfamiliar sense of deep delight, which a fragment of her true self told her was rare. She wanted something from Elben she did not entirely understand, rooted both in her fox's form and beyond it, in the part of her which waited for the return to human shape and intelligence.

Human scent poured over her suddenly. She shied, recognizing the odor of her sister. Cowering, she looked for cover.

"Damn it, Trae," Vandeyr's voice said impatiently, raising the gray fox's hackles. "I'm not going to hurt you. Do you have to act like I eat foxes for breakfast?"

Not understanding, Traedis made a dash for the nearest part of the hedge, ignoring the tug of twigs in her fur. The red fox did not follow her, but turned to position himself between her and the feared human.

"You're a fox, too, Haven knight." Vandeyr's tone was cross enough to make Traedis crouch even lower. "Can't you get her to come out? She needs sleep, and she has a full day ahead tomorrow. Since this is your doing, you might as well help me mend it."

The red fox spoke in human words which contained no

contrition. "She's relaxed considerably. I can coax her to human form any time now, unless she's frightened again."

Vandeyr sighed. "Very well, I'll withdraw. But she'd better be human again soon, or I'm bringing out a mage to change her back." She turned and left the garden, her footfalls quivering lightly but distinctly on the ground. She did not, in fact, go far; the gray fox could hear the steps cease and the low breathing continue, and though downwind, human odor still lingered in the frost that was rapidly collecting.

The red fox sat on his haunches, all play gone from his demeanor. "Traedis?" he said softly. "You need to be a human again. I'm going to talk to you and help you remember who you are. You're not truly a fox. You're a woman, and the ruler of this city. You need to know that now."

Traedis crept slowly out from beneath the hedge, swiveling one ear backward for any sign of her sister's return. It was clear that the red fox no longer wanted to play. Instead, he spoke to her in words she found both alarming and soothing, though she could make no sense of the contradiction.

He continued to speak in a soft, comforting voice which reminded her of human life and existence. Lulled by its comforting cadences, she reached for her harp, then stared, momentarily confused, at the five fingers of her hand. Looking down, she saw herself clad in a linen dress decorated with leaves, twigs, and a considerable amount of dirt.

"Oh dear," she said, the pulse in her throat quickening. "I

really can't be seen like this, can I? I look like I've been traipsing around in the woods for half the day."

Elben's form moved and flowed back into his tall human shape. He also was stained and decked with foliage, but he was dressed in practical leather garments, and looked more like a woodsman than a forest spirit. Affection rose in her chest, which she attempted to quell. She did not want to give him false hope that she would return his feelings when she was not even sure what those feelings were. Her thoughts were tangled with confusion and churned in her belly.

"You look like a fox who has been playing in the garden." Elben brushed dirt from his sleeves and shook a leaf from his hair. "I had a marvelous time. I hope you enjoyed yourself as well. '

Traedis could not deny that frolicking with Elben in the garden had been one of the most enjoyable experience since she had received the *falmyros*, but she felt guilty for avoiding her responsibilities and shirking her duties, even though none of them had been urgent. "It was nice," she said unwillingly. "I shouldn't do it again, though. I have duties, and I haven't practiced harp. I should be more available than usual while your king is here for a state visit."

"Even King Kenrydh allows himself some personal time," Elben said mildly, managing to avoid sounding as if he were giving a lecture.

Traedis smiled weakly. "I need to look over whatever has accumulated on my desk since this morning. Please excuse me."

"Of course, King Traedis," Elben said as she turned back toward the palace.

That stopped her short. She looked back to see the hint of a grin shine through his red beard. His eyes gleamed. His presence was a banked fire.

"Don't call me 'King Traedis,'" she told him firmly. "After today I hardly feel as if we are strangers. 'Trae' is how I am known to my friends."

"I am honored by your friendship." Elben's curve of a smile broadened. "Trae."

Traedis smiled back, then hastened back inside, enumerating in her mind all the things she had neglected which must be done before bedtime.

In her chambers, Traedis sat, wakeful, staring at the wall, books of old City laws spread before her. She could not concentrate. The romp in the garden with Elben had stirred something in her; a longing for love and security. He was not interested in gaining power and influence; as a Haven knight he was above such things.

She must marry and have heirs, or everything she had tried to accomplish would be undone. If the kingship went to Uncle Cordelayne after her death, Old Tolin would be restored, and secured so that no one would be able to change it again. Gavaya would not accept any summons to rule, and Traedis did not know what Lang's course would be, left to himself. Then came Daymet and Otenemar, and that did not bear even considering. No, she must have heirs, and teach them what she needed them to know.

The best she could do within the City was Parmo Faylias, who was handsome, two years older than she, and had a disarming honesty which had caused him to tell her, "I am no more in love with you than you with me, but I am willing to work together to fashion the new Tolin." It had been, at least, a unique approach, but Traedis feared that it simply implied that Parmo was more subtle and therefore more dangerous than his counterparts. She would not marry Parmo.

Those from outside Tolin were little better. Scheming lords and a single esch nobleman: the qualities of those who wished to rule the City through her were dubious at best. Likely they were insincere, given that they were proposing marriage to a woman they had only just met.

Elben was different. He had met her when she had been only a rebellious daughter of Tolin, not a king. As a Haven knight, he was incorruptible, and he spoke to her as if she were a woman he was courting, not a political alliance.

It was not close to midnight, and Traedis knew she would not get to sleep just yet. On a mad whim, she dressed herself, put on her shoes, grabbed Rose's case and a cloak, and headed out of her apartments. Tethyn and another followed, their movements as devoid of curiosity as Vandeyr's would have been full of disapproval.

Kenrydh occupied a suite of rooms in the east wing. When any of his Haven guard were not actively on duty, they stayed in a smaller suite adjoining the larger. It was to this door that Traedis found her feet straying, despite the impropriety of seeking out someone she barely knew.

A pair of Haven guards were stationed at the end of the wing: a woman with a short black braid that reached to her collar, and a man with a military beard similar to Elben's. Two parallel scars marked the right side of his cheek.

"King Traedis," said the woman in obvious surprise. "How may we serve you?"

For a brief moment Traedis felt like answering, "Can the fox come out to play?" but quelled the urge. She did not want to act too young and frivolous before a Haven knight, and enjoyable though the afternoon had been, she was glad to be back in her native form.

Her presence might make them nervous, but if so, they hid it well. She gathered her courage and said, "I know it's late, and if Deputy Captain Elben Tallforest is asleep, I don't want you to wake him. But if he is not, and he is off duty, I'd like to speak with him."

"Certainly, Your Majesty." The woman's courtesy did not flag. She shot her companion a glance, then retreated down the hall. She was back in moments, followed by Elben, clothed not in his Haven greens, but in a loose linen shirt and trousers. His hair was free of its tie, and his face and posture were relaxed. "King Traedis?" he asked, clearly surprised. "What can I do for you?"

"I wrote you that if you were ever in the City, I would show you the sights. If you aren't busy, I can take you to see the Star Cavern."

Elben's eyes widened. "I would be most honored. I'm off until mid-morning. Please wait a moment..." He disappeared back through the hall, reappearing in a warm cloak and a pair of boots.

She donned her own cloak, pulling up the hood to hide her bright hair. They went on foot, boot heels clacking on the polished cobbles of the street. Several lengths behind, her guards followed.

The nights were still cold, though spring was dawning, and snow stained the edges of the roads in gray-and-brown clumps where dirt had been kicked by horses and boots. Traedis looked up to see the brilliant clarity of the stars; she could make out the constellation of the Twin Lions in its late-night ascension, and the heart-star of the Northern Dragon blazed over night's domain like a ruddy beacon. A stiff wind blew downslope from the higher reaches of the mountain, but she did not feel cold. Holding onto her hood, she flashed a grin at Elben, more than a little pleased at her own daring. This was the woman she had been in Kaelennar; not a timid, fearful king, but a bold girl running into adventure as if to a magnificent banquet.

Elben let the wind tear his own hood from his head; his hair blew back, strands tangling together in elf-knots. He laughed. "I didn't expect to see the sights at this hour. I imagine my friends are wondering whether I'm a fool or a genius, to let the King of Tolin spirit me away under the ground."

"And which are you?" Traedis asked with a nighttime boldness that her daylight hours seldom saw.

"A genius, of course." He swept one arm toward the heavens. "Look, Dragon's Heart is shining on our escapade!"

"Not for long," Traedis told him. "Here's the library now, and the Northern Dragon isn't one of the constellations below."

They hung their cloaks and headed through the books to the back staircase. A candle flickering in the direction of Gavaya's office told Traedis her sister must be working late. Lighting the lantern, Traedis opened the old door and began her descent, the other three trailing her.

Elben looked around with fascination, exclaiming out loud when the walls changed from stone blocks to seamless granite threaded with spider veins of quartz. Traedis was glad of the extra light, for it had begun to feel close and stuffy, though the crosswind from ventilation shafts breathed over them constantly. She wiped sweat from her forehead, then put her hand against the wall to steady herself as she descended. She focused on her physical sensations: Elben's quiet breathing, the sandpaper rock, the feel of the lantern handle against her hand.

In the antechamber of the Star Cavern, Traedis put the light down. "Wait outside," she told Tethyn and the other. "I want to see if we're the only ones here."

They were. Traedis held the door for Elben and ushered him inside.

The knight's astonished gasp was worth the trip. Traedis watched him stare upward, his eyes drinking in the shining star-whorls. "The Southern Dragon, the Bowl, the Firebrand, the Twin Lions, and the Great Road," he said, naming them in a tone of dazed wonder. "How can something so symbolic look so much like the stars themselves?"

"It's a mystery of the n'korreld." Traedis sat down on one of the reclining benches. "You don't have to crane your neck. We have furniture."

A bark of laughter escaped him, but he took her advice and seated himself on one of the other benches, leaning against the cushioned back and continuing his wide-eyed staring at the ceiling above them.

Under this artificial sky, Traedis did not feel trapped. She let her eyes accustom themselves to the darkness, then looked up, feeling the presence of the constellations and their magic in her *falmyros*. It was a strange sensation, like an echo in a space that should not have carried sound. She greeted the stars silently, and they drowsily replied, aware of her presence, but groggy with the sleep of millennia.

She compared the painted sky to the real one outside. It was different, she decided; she could not consider this supreme exhibit of artistic magic to be an inferior thing, but it could not hold all the power of the truth that lay behind it. Indeed, her entire *falmyros* could not have contained that power. The karreldish nature of the paintings tugged at her mind as if it half-contained a distant memory.

"What do you think of the City?" she asked Elben, finally able to relax under the luminescent spirals. "I know you haven't seen much of it yet, but does it match your expectations?"

Elben nodded. "Some of Tolin really does remind me of Haven. The older architecture is very similar. I feel quite at home." He laughed. "As far as Haven is home, anyway."

"Isn't it where you're from?" Traedis contemplated his dim profile, wondering how he had found himself among the company of holy knights.

Elben's voice seemed to smile. "I'm from nowhere special. My father is a minor lord with a hold in the Southern Forest; in practical terms, he's lord of acres of trees and some passable farmland. A backwater near a small town."

Traedis felt silly; she had never considered that a Haven knight might have a past and a childhood. She had always thought of them as though their dedication to the gods set them apart from ordinary mortals. Perhaps, she thought, once she had decided to despise the City, she had transferred some of that reverence to Haven. Of course Elben had come from somewhere, and there was no real reason it had to be the island state.

Elben cleared his throat. "Obviously, you were raised here, but you haven't said much about yourself in your letters. Did you grow up in the palace?"

"No." Traedis thought about her mother's home, the ancient Atenel estate that would one day be Lang's, as Gavaya had no children. "The original owners fled when I gained the *falmyros*. Wisely, I think. But they're not likely to come back, and the manor was perfect for my purposes. Since it was unoccupied, I made it into my palace." She tasted bitterness under her tongue and heard it creep into her voice. "There was quite a scramble amongst some to get out of Tolin as fast as they could load a pack."

"I didn't mean to overstep my bounds," Elben said after a moment's pause. "It isn't my place to pry. I want to know you better. I still don't know much about you at all. That is, I know a few details of your history – I must in order to do my job. But I don't know what it was like to be born here, what caused you to run away, why you were imprisoned, how you took up the harp, and what your favorite fruit is. It's not my right to know, and if you don't choose to tell me I won't harbor any hard feelings."

His voice was musical, a clear tenor without a hint of rasp; the best kind to train, as it had few bad habits. Traedis' bardic master would have loved it.

She chose her words carefully. "I understand that you're not trying to learn my secrets. You're a knight of Haven, and I know that you live by an honorable code. I simply don't trust people easily. Not when half of my family would rather put me back in prison than accept my rule."

Elben made a choked sound in his throat. "I knew you were in prison, but I'm not clear on why." He looked as if he were about to speak, then he shook his head in a rueful manner. His voice broadened with a back-country accent that nearly made Traedis laugh despite her discomfort with the subject. "Or should I only discuss the weather with your majesty? The sky seems fair set for a spot of snow tonight."

Traedis appreciated his lightness; it left her free to answer or not as she chose. She opted for honesty. "The charge was desertion. It might have been a capital offense, but – I am an Atenel."

"Desertion? How old were you?" Elben sounded shocked.

Traedis swallowed. "Fourteen."

Elben breathed out in a long sigh that Traedis suspected was an attempt to keep himself from saying something impolitic. His silence lasted long enough that Traedis found herself shifting uncomfortably on the reclining bench.

Finally, he said, "Desertion? You were a child, not an assassin. How could they hold you responsible for something you did before you even reached your majority?"

Traedis shivered; the darkness seemed to thicken around her like mist. She was suddenly aware that she was surrounded by heavy stone, and not under the true sky. To combat the stifling memories, she spoke carefully, trying to keep her focus on the words rather than the heaviness of the cavern. She leaned into the embrace of her *falmyros*, letting it remind her that she had sovereignty in this place, and could not be trapped while that connection lasted. The ghost of Toledru gibbered in a distant corner of her mind.

"You don't understand," she told him. "It's not like it is in Telardur, or I expect, Haven." She caught a lock of hair and twisted it nervously. "The City lives, or used to live, under strict discipline. Leaving without permission is – was – desertion. They let me live because of who my father was, and my uncle."

Elben's silence this time was even longer. Finally, he said in a subdued tone, "You hear things, of course. Haven is full of rumors about what the City of Assassins does or doesn't do. But I didn't expect those particular rumors to be true. To imprison a young girl just for running away from home..." His voice trailed off into silence.

Traedis felt an obscure need to defend the City, despite its behavior toward her. "It's not quite like that. I mean, it is, but the City doesn't think of it that way. We've needed that discipline to further our aims and goals." She rushed ahead before Elben could respond. "I never agreed with those goals, but for those who did, hard choices were necessary. Don't make the mistake of thinking that the people of the City were any less dedicated or committed than those of Haven, even if that dedication was to something Haven abhors." She felt her voice waver and strain to force the words through her teeth.

Tethyn popped her head through the door. "King Traedis, Captain Atenel is looking for you. She needs to go over the duty roster for tomorrow."

Traedis sighed. She could not have the freedom even for such a short excursion as this.

"Would you escort me back?" she asked Elben. "Unless you want to stay for a while."

Elben's silhouette nodded. "I would be glad to escort you," he said. As they rose, he offered her his arm. "In fact, I'd be honored."

"So would I," said Traedis automatically, before tasting the truth of her words. "So would I."

Kenrydh nodded graciously to Traedis, who returned the gesture, saddened that the visit had been so short. Surrounded by her own citizens, she had almost come to believe that the convoluted machinations they delighted in were the right and proper way to behave. Kenrydh was hardly foolish or unsubtle, but his natural straightforwardness reminded her of her own better nature, and that Tolin's way was not the only one. She would have to keep that in the forefront of her consciousness when he was gone.

"I hope that you will allow me to return your hospitality, and receive you in Faldrohaven," Kenrydh said. "When you last were there, it was not under happy circumstances, and I would like to remedy that. Queen Duinedh would be most gratified if she could host such a gathering."

"I would like that," Traedis said, finding that she meant it. The memories of Faldrohaven were dark. But not entirely: she had been trapped between the City's imperatives and her own sworn word, but she had been supported by her friends, and those in Kenrydh's service had offered more understanding and compassion than anyone in Tolin.

Her gaze sought Elben, to find that he was looking back at her with a steady and warm regard. Though they had been unable to find more time to spend together, she was heartened by his promise to return Tolin on some of his rare leave. She mentally traced out the map of his face, the long, strong jaw, the high forehead, the lips that could quirk in amusement as easily as thinning in anger. His eyes were a different green than her own, darker and more opaque, sparkling beneath long, fringed lashes.

She did not lose track of what she was doing, and brought her attention back sharply to Kenrydh to exchange formal farewells. He was only one Haven knight among many now. She could not expect that a private leavetaking was possible.

Later, when Traedis retreated to her chamber, Vandeyr swept in behind, shut the door firmly, and glowered at her. The expression on her face reminded Traedis of a mountain cat ready to pounce.

Traedis frowned at her sister. "All right," she said impatiently. "You're acting as if you sat on a scorpion or ate a nest of ants. What's bothering you? Is it Elben?"

Vandeyr half-turned, every muscle in her body expressing fury. "Is it Elben? What else would you expect it to be?"

Traedis felt muscles go rigid. "I know he doesn't make you happy. But Haven knight or not, I have the right to choose my own friends without consulting you beforehand. Or at all."

"Tell that to someone who isn't your sister." Vandeyr hit the wall lightly with her fist. "Why didn't you just send him packing? Do you know that he sent us all guest gifts? Me, Mother, Lang, and Gavaya. He tried to cozy up to us too, though Mother managed to let him know what she thought well enough. Are you lacking the sense you were born with? – never mind, I know you weren't born with any. If you had been, you would never be so foolish as to encourage a Haven knight, of all people."

Traedis felt her anger fall away into confusion. Guest gifts were not strictly necessary when someone was courting, but they were a formal courtesy, and Traedis would have thought that Vandeyr would at least appreciate Elben's manners. "What sort of guest gifts? Were they inappropriate? Why shouldn't he have given them?"

Vandeyr stared at her. "Are you blind? Or simply so stupid that you can't see what is right in front of you?"

"Assume that I am very stupid," Traedis told her slowly. "I really don't understand. I know you don't like Elben because he is a Haven knight, but what else do you have against him?"

"What else?" Vandeyr threw her hands out in a gesture of futility. "What else? Isn't it enough that a Haven knight is courting my sister?"

Traedis was beginning to be frustrated at the interrogation. "Yes, he's courting me. But at present, he's a friend, which is more important by far. Do you really think he's trying to control Tolin through me?"

Vandeyr snorted. "You think he isn't? The loyalty of your precious knight is spoken for, and it's not to you. Haven has wanted to determine our course for centuries. This is an opportunity they can't afford to miss. Can't you find *anyone* suitable from here? Lelis Mastery? Parmo Faylias? Ketrantar

Ammas? I can understand if you don't want to put up with a Shefferie or a Quill, but even someone below your station would be better than this!"

Traedis slapped the arm of her chair. "Vandeyr, I am not going to marry someone and then fight them for the crown. You know that's what every single one of them wants. Is it so ridiculous to find someone attractive who wants Trae the bard, not Traedis the King?" She shook her head, angry tears crowding her eyes. "I am sick to death of this whole charade; I am so very sick of the men who see me as a jewel for their arm or a dynasty for their house. Elben has the good grace to be interested in me, rather than my position. He's even a lord's son. Isn't that suitable enough?"

Vandeyr turned her head and stared out the window as she said bitterly, "You believe that. Don't you see how insidious this suit is? Yes, he is attracted to you, because he's not blind and half-witted. Yes, he likes you, admires you. Do you think Haven would send someone you could see straight through like a clear pane of glass? That makes him more dangerous, not less. They know their job in Haven, and his genuine attraction for you makes him an apt tool."

Traedis shook her head. She refused to believe that Elben's gentle humor and clear regard were weapons in Haven's arsenal. Of course, she also did not believe that the Haven which Emmen ruled would mandate such a courtship. Vandeyr was demonstrating her own prejudice, not showing Traedis the folly of her choices. Traedis smoothed her skirt with an unwontedly shaky hand. "I don't think we're going to agree on this."

What frightened Traedis was the intimacy Elben wanted, not his interest. It was hard to trust when trust had been repeatedly betrayed, first by her family, then by the entire City of her birth. And there was the curse, of course: *Who will lose their love to the storm?* But she must then struggle with the question of whether to accept that her love might doom someone – Elben, perhaps – and whether she was prepared to make a cold marriage alliance. She was sure only that she was prepared to do neither.

Which lessened some of the force of Vandeyr's argument. Traedis squared her shoulders. "I will marry no one unless I am sure of them." The callouses on her fingertips caught a tuft of silk, teased it out of its weavework, leaving the snagged thread peeking from the warp and weft. "Heir or no heir, I'm not ready to marry. Not *anyone*, Vandeyr. I will promise you this – I will not accept anyone until I am sure of them. Tolin, Haven, or denizen of some unheard-of northern isle – no one. I will not be ruled. Not by you, not by Elben, not by Mother or Uncle Cordelayne, or the Council families. I have been given Tolin, and by the gods, I will keep it. But if I choose Elben, you will not overrule me."

She watched her sister's muscles relax from the angry tension. "You are the king," said Vandeyr. "I have accepted that. But you are also my little sister, and if he hurts you, he will end with a dagger in his heart."

Traedis closed her eyes. "Just don't put one through mine as well."

Spring burgeoned into an unusually lush growing season, then blossomed into abundance and the promise of an early summer. Traedis could feel the land rejoicing in its freedom as it put up lavish spikes of wheat and grass, lupines and lettuces. New ivy embraced the woodland trees and clambered up chimneys with thousands of tiny feet. Healthy lambs graced farms outside the City, and heifers dropped strong calves. Tolin had not seen such abundance for generations; priests considered this the sign of a prosperous reign.

Others felt differently. Traedis was losing what popularity she had with the nobles, and even the tentative support of those who had earlier thought to control the City through her had dissipated. The ordinary citizens were split in their allegiance; some seemed glad of the changes she had made. Others held to the old traditions, grumbling that not only would the king ruin the land, but that having a king to begin with was already destroying the character and morals of Tolin. It was like climbing a staircase, only to discover that half the treads were missing, and those remaining contained face-up nails. No matter how carefully she trod, she would either miss a step or injure herself.

Near the end of the spring month of Unicorn, Traedis was rousted from a comfortable sleep by a loud knock on her bedchamber door. Dragging herself out of bed, she threw on a dressing gown and slippers and opened the door, wondering what could not wait until at least the light of dawn.

Vandeyr padded into her room as if she were a leopard or panther. "Get dressed," she said shortly. "We've got a problem."

"Uncle Cordelayne?" asked Traedis. The stiffness in her sister's spine, a suggestion of alarm in the twitch of Vandeyr's fingers over her dagger hilt, told her something beyond Tolin's ordinary troubles was involved.

"None other." Vandeyr jerked her head to the west. "The gate guards caught six men nailing someone to the City gate. There was a skirmish – none of our people were hurt, but one of theirs was wounded. They all got away from us, though."

"Whom did they nail to the gate?" Traedis asked, acidity spreading in the pit of her stomach. "Was there a note? If not, how do we know it's Uncle Cordelayne?"

"No note." Vandeyr scowled. "Do we need one? It's exactly what he did to Captain Dorrell's front door. So far, we haven't identified the dead man – he wasn't left recognizable, I understand – but we'll get it figured out. He's a karreld, fairly young. There aren't any karrelds reported missing, though, and it's not as if we have so many we wouldn't be able to trace one. I'd say he wasn't from Tolin at all, except why else would they nail him to our gate?"

Traedis felt her breath stop for an extended moment. "A karreld?"

Vandeyr gave her a long look. "You don't think...?"

"I hope not." Traedis went to her bureau and retrieved the stone which she used to communicate with Atchûk. Holding it in her palm, she concentrated hard on reaching the young man, hoping fervently that her fears were groundless.

The stone remained cold, unwarmed by the heat of her hand. Traedis focused on it, bringing the image of Atchûk's face, his bantering, light speech, his warmth of manner, into the forefront of her mind. The stone remained silent. As she bent all the energy she could muster toward connecting to the prince, she felt hope slipping from her heart, each moment leaching more of it from her mind. Finally, with a sound of distress, she set it down.

"I'd better come down and look at the body," she said, still clinging to the hope that she was wrong. Uncle Cordelayne would have no mercy on a spy; his ruthlessness in serving his idea of the City was absolute.

"Very well." Vandeyr paced out a circle on the floor. "You know Prince Atchûk better than I." She slapped her hand angrily against her thigh. "Damn Uncle Cordelayne, anyway. What in Kyaan's name does he think he's doing?"

"I would think you'd know," Traedis replied shortly. The sensation in her stomach was progressing to full-out nausea. "You're the one who studied with him. Is this normal for him?" She scrambled into a plain linen dress, put on her boots, and combed out her hair from its sleep-drenched tangles, braiding it quickly down her back.

"Not precisely." Vandeyr grimaced. "But he's never been in this position before, and neither have we. He's sending stronger and stronger messages to you, and I'm getting worried about where this might end." She fingered the hilt of her dagger. "Why doesn't he go found his own little city if he's unhappy with the way you're running this one? That's what Toledru did. The gods gave you Tolin – he's not going to change that."

"Let's go," Traedis said, cold seeping into her veins. She knew her sister was right; Uncle Cordelayne's actions were more than simple harassment. Between his time as an assassin and his time on the Council, he had a mastery of both sweeping strategy and precise tactics. Traedis herself had no experience with which to fight him. She had hoped that he might come to accept that she had received Tolin's *falmyros* from the gods, but she had never expected it.

"All right," said Vandeyr. "If it's the Thane's son, we'll have enough problems to keep us busy for the next year. Kyaan take Uncle Cordelayne's thrice-cursed sense of duty!"

As soon as she saw the body's sandstone-hued skin and tall form, Traedis knew that it was, indeed, Atchûk. She felt her hopes shift and slide like an unstable hillside under a torrent of rain. His face was disfigured, and his limbs contorted, not only with the spikes that had been used to pin him to the gate but with signs of obvious torture. He had been taken down from the main gate and moved inside the City Guardhouse onto an empty cot just beyond the door.

The air was thick and hazy with pipe smoke and the fumes of torches; Traedis felt her eyes water and sting. She could almost convince herself that it was only the smoke that blurred her vision.

Atchûk's face had been lacerated and burned, and rope marks seared deeply into his wrists and ankles. One of his hands had been completely smashed, and his flesh was covered with livid bruises. Traedis could not immediately make out other injuries, except for the nail holes, which had been made after death. His eyes had not been touched, but were wide and staring, as if he watched something no living soul should see. She reached out a hand to close them, but his body was rigid, and the lids would not move.

Vandeyr bent over the body closely, peering at the nail holes, the bruises, looking into the corpse's mouth, now filled with a swollen tongue. She minutely examined his eyes, then pulled back his shirt to look at his chest. She turned down Atchûk's collar, and though Traedis could see nothing amiss, grunted as if she saw something she had expected. It might have felt ghoulish, had Vandeyr not been wearing the professional face of a captain: composed, alert, and extremely dangerous.

"What is it?" Traedis asked.

"Look at this." Vandeyr pointed to a spot on Atchûk's neck.

Traedis peered closely, but could still see nothing odd. "What am I looking at?"

"No, look more closely." Vandeyr described a small circle on the skin with her index finger.

Traedis leaned forward and stared, trying to make out what her sister had indicated. She could barely see several tiny, raised dots. Red and puffy, they looked like a rash, or a collection of insect bites. Traedis looked back at Vandeyr, her brows knotting. "Those spots. Is that what I'm supposed to be seeing? Did Uncle Cordelayne use drugs as well as force?"

Vandeyr nodded shortly. "A professional job all around. A combination of physical torture, drugs and probably magic, though Tagg is the one who can tell that, not I. I doubt if the poor boy even remembered his own name after Uncle Cordelayne got through with him."

An icy prickling began in Traedis' head and spread down through her body and limbs. Atchûk's suffering was horrific, and he had undergone it because of her. Guilt tugged at her chest, stifled her breath; the young karreld should have lived for decades, not had his life extinguished in unimaginable agony.

Uncle Cordelayne could have done exactly the same to her. He could have destroyed her, body and mind, when she was in prison. Perhaps he wanted her mind intact, but she might have escaped Atchûk's fate by the thinnest of margins. The suffocating dark of her prison cell settled around her like a smothering mantle, narrowing her vision to a small circle of brightness directly before her.

"I need," she said, hearing her own voice like a distant disturbance, "to contact the Thane. This is his son; he needs be told as soon as possible."

"I expect he does," Vandeyr said, an unusual catch in her words. "Traedis, sit here while I check with the guards to see what else they can tell me." She made an angry and frustrated sound.

"What did he think he was doing? This is going to be more trouble than it warrants."

A stab of fresh guilt lanced through Traedis' throat. If she had accepted the Quo'at's original offer of assistance, Atchûk would not have died. She was responsible, and she could not evade the consequences, however harsh.

"Get me Tagg," she said, the distance between herself and the guardhouse buzzing remotely in her ears. She took several deep breaths, holding them, letting them flow out of her in measured increments. Neither her sight nor hearing was yet normal, but she was Tolin's king, and she must act. She would deal with fear and guilt when she had time, but now it was necessary for her to function. She could not afford any kind of weakness.

A short time later, Vandeyr returned with Tagg. The round little man was missing his usual good humor, and his lips were tight and grim. He looked at Atchûk's body, then knelt by the young man's side. "If you wish, your majesty, I can see what magic was used on him. I can almost smell it, and it reeks of the assassin corps." His eyes were somber.

"Please." Traedis felt a burning coal of anger ignite amidst her shock, horror, and fear. "I need to know what happened. The Thane will most certainly want to know."

Tagg nodded. Placing his stubby hands lightly on Atchûk's chest, he slowed his breathing, and his pupils dilated. Traedis could feel the sensation which meant magic was active, its lightning power dancing through the air like a symphony of notes, its whole greater than the aggregate.

Finally, he sighed and moved his hands from the body. "Yes, there was magic used. Interrogation magic, as I thought, but also magic which mingled with the poison they gave him, and made each thing they did to him more painful even than it should have been. It is a terrible use of power, and though I was taught it, I long-since delved into other pursuits to make myself less suitable for an assassin's job." He turned toward Traedis. "Your majesty, there are many who have reason to be grateful that you put an end to the City's practices. I have two friends, mages, who were conscripted, and they suffer constantly from nightmares to this day."

Traedis nodded, not taking in the entire sense of his words in the face of the terrible event. She laced her fingers together. "I need to send a messenger to the Thane. I don't know if he will want me to go there, or if he will want to come here, but he should have the choice. I must face him myself." Her voice did not crack, though she felt that her heart might.

"Send me," Vandeyr said. "I'll let him know the facts, and leave the explanations up to you."

Traedis nodded. "Gate Captain Atenel to the house of the Thane Bi'ia," she told Tagg, who nodded. "If the Thane wishes to return with Captain Atenel, offer your services to him; he may prefer to use his own people, but you should ask. Other than that, take your orders from Captain Atenel."

Tagg made a sound of assent and touched Vandeyr lightly on

the arm. The two of them vanished immediately, leaving the barest trace of an afterimage which disappeared almost as soon as it became noticeable.

Traedis retrieved a pair of silver eagle coins from one of the guards and placed them over Atchûk's eyes to hide their wide-eyed stare of death. She did not want to face Thane Bi'ia, but it was her responsibility, and the death her fault. She would fulfill her responsibilities. Sitting in a smooth wooden chair by the cot, she folded her hands in her lap, waiting for Vandeyr to return.

The torches had barely burned a finger's width before Vandeyr and the mage appeared back in the guardhouse. Vandeyr's color was slightly higher than usual, but she seemed composed. "The Thane will be here presently," she said, and moved into position just behind Traedis' left side.

Traedis flinched involuntarily; she did not like anyone to stand behind her. When Traedis had been a child, both Daymet and Otenemar had taken great pleasure in catching her unaware, and Traedis had never managed to shake the fear she felt when exposing a vulnerable side.

Shortly thereafter, Traedis felt a *whuff* of displaced air, and Thane Bi'ia appeared among a small group of n'korreld, all of whom appeared as grim and watchful as if they stood on a battlefield.

The Thane's expression was a mixture of intense pain and blazing anger which Traedis could almost feel like a fire at her face. "Tell me who did this," he commanded with dreadful intensity, not seeming to notice he stood on City land and faced guards twice as tall as he.

Now that she could act, Traedis found her voice steady. She met his gaze squarely. "This was done by my uncle, Cordelayne Atenel," she told him. Explanation or apology was too superficial for the depth of a father's grief.

The Thane nodded and approached his son's body, taking

Atchûk in his arms as if cradling a newborn child. Tears spilled from his eyes, but his voice was the slow, harsh grind of stone on stone. "I swear by Lord Coran," he said in a low, even tone which sounded to Traedis more dangerous than the passion of hatred, "that I will wash my hands in Cordelayne's blood." He smoothed a lock of Atchûk's hair back from the dead karreld's forehead.

Looking up, his eyes focused on Traedis. His mouth worked for a moment in silence. Finally, he said in a subdued tone, "I cannot blame you."

Holding Atchûk close to his body, he gestured to one of his men. The entire retinue vanished.

Vandeyr let out a long, slow breath of air. "You can count yourself lucky that he still remains an ally," she said softly. "He was that close to swearing a blood feud upon the Atenels if I'm any judge. The City may be up to the challenge, but it's ill-advised to underestimate the n'korreld. Doing so generally brings regret on its heels. They may be small, but they've been known to carry grudges for centuries. Father always said that anyone who dismissed them was thrice a fool and deserved what they got."

Traedis nodded, still unnerved by the Thane's odd mixture of intensity and calm; Vandeyr's words spoke to her of what she instinctively knew. "I think Uncle Cordelayne made a mistake."

"I do, too." Vandeyr gestured toward the door. "We'd better get back to the palace. I expect there are going to be a number of unpleasant consequences coming our way before long."

Traedis knew that she had brought this on the City by her

inability to harm Uncle Cordelayne, and she must be willing to accept what came of it.

She would also need to tell Kenrydh. He would not be happy that in her attempt to protect her rebel uncle, she had agreed to mount a spying expedition in his country without his knowledge or permission.

Words welled up in the back of her mind, words that, as a bard, she could twist tens of ways to hammer their harsh syllables through her heart. *Fool* and *coward* were the first, followed swiftly by *selfish, stupid,* and *useless.* They spoke in a dozen voices, all of them her own. She used their viciousness to goad her into courage, their deadly sting a reminder of what she had vowed to change.

Taking out Kenrydh's ruby, she summoned his image in her mind. He soon appeared, richly dressed despite the early hour. Looking at her sharply, he said, "King Traedis? What is it?"

"I have some important news," she told him, her throat feeling as if a stone lodged within.

"Just a moment." He spoke a few words to someone before turning back to her. "I have some time. What is wrong?"

Traedis found it easier to stare through the faldren king than to meet his gaze. Feeling like a child admitting guilt to her disapproving father, she said the words quickly so that she could be sure they would come. "Prince Atchûk, second son of Thane Bi'ia, was murdered this morning by my uncle and his people." To her own ears, her voice sounded hollow, spoken into a distance.

The skin of Kenrydh's face stretched taut. "Why? How?"

"The fault," Traedis told him, "is mine. the Quo'at would have delivered my uncle over to me, in gratitude for my allowing the n'korreld free access to the Star Cavern. I did not assent." She straightened her neck and raised her head in a sort of defiance, though whether against Kenrydh or against Tolin she was not sure. "He offered me, instead, intelligence of my rebels. This I accepted, and Prince Atchûk put himself forward as a spy in their midst."

His demeanor deceptively mild, Kenrydh asked, "Where were your uncle and his people?"

This was the hardest part. "In a cave system at the edge of the Kurtish Mountains."

"In Telardur." A muscle jumped in his cheek.

"Yes." No matter how harshly he judged her, Traedis would not disclaim responsibility. She must do her best to mend any breach with the n'korreld and with Kenrydh.

"I gave you no leave." His chin was rigid.

"No," she admitted. "You did not."

Kenrydh swallowed, exhaled slowly, and frowned. In a gentler voice, he said, "Why did you not ask me? Did you fear I would have said you nay?"

Traedis started to answer, then realized that she was not sure she knew. "I..." She shook her head. Perhaps it was because she had spent so many years keeping secrets that she did not know how to put real faith in anyone. Now she must rely on Kenrydh's goodwill if she were not to risk a serious breach.

Her voice was soft as she spoke. "I do not trust easily. Not even – especially – my own family. During my years in Telardur, I was forced to hide my origin. When I was returned to Tolin, I knew things that I did not dare tell the City. I'm very good at *not* giving information. I'm terrible at knowing who I can rely on. And only a few months ago, the two of us were considered enemies."

It still sounded to herself as if she were making excuses. Steeling herself for an even deeper honesty, she told him, "And I felt ashamed that I could not bring myself to accept the Quo'at's first proposal."

Narrowing his eyes, Kenrydh seemed to search her for further signs of deception, his gaze boring into hers so long that Traedis wondered if he had seen some other falseness there of which she was not aware. After what seemed like years, he nodded. "I believe you. But, King Traedis, we cannot afford to let such fears crack us apart. You, Emmen, Bi'ia and I must be united in our purposes – there are enough malign forces which wish to widen a fissure into a chasm. We have greater enemies than each other."

It was a gracious concession, and one Kenrydh need not have made. "Thank you, King Kenrydh," Traedis said. "In token of my good faith, I'm now willing to answer your questions about the entire affair. This time I will keep nothing back." Any discomfort to herself was well-earned. Now was the time to plant her feet in the track she intended to walk.

"Thank you," Kenrydh told her, a trace of surprise tinging his tone. "If you will, please tell me about what the Quo'at said to you, and how this entire situation came to pass."

Traedis made a tale of it; she found it easier that way. Not sparing herself, she told him everything up until Thane Bi'ia's arrival and departure with the body of his son. Kenrydh listened quietly, a line furrowing the space between his brows.

He held her gaze for a long moment of assessment; Traedis felt it like a weight pressing against her mind. Then he nodded, and Traedis felt as if a spearpoint had turned aside. She had never before crossed him in such a way. She was uncomfortably aware of his nature as a high faldro, which conferred greater power on him than she could ever hope to match.

He let out a tiny puff of air, and Traedis realized in some surprise that he might also have been nervous about the confrontation. Lifting her chin, she asked, "What do you need me to do now?"

"I think," said Kenrydh, stroking his beard, "that we need to come to an understanding. King Traedis, you are chosen by the gods; I do not intend to force your hand, unless you intend to give Tolin back to the assassins. I have no desire to rule what I have not been granted."

Traedis felt her lungs expand in relief. Kenrydh had answered the question she had not asked, and she was glad to have it spoken between them.

"Thank you," she said. "It is good to know honor is alive in my allies."

"We are allied because of your own honor," Kenrydh said. "May it continue to be so."

At midmorning the next day, Traedis sat in her top-story workroom. Here she could play as loudly as she needed without disturbing anyone but servants and pages, and those only if she opened the door. The room was well-insulated from sound and from magic.

She turned her head sharply as the door banged open to let her sister in. A pale wisp had come loose from Vandeyr's severely tied-back hairstyle and trailed over the top of one ear. She carried a piece of parchment with a broken blue seal.

"You opened it," Traedis said foolishly.

"Of course I opened it!" Vandeyr turned a glare on Traedis that could have stripped paint from the walls. "Did you think I was going to allow you to unseal a letter that might contain extortion, poison, magic? That's part of my cursed job, keeping you safe. Most of it, in fact."

Traedis was beginning to understand that Vandeyr's tempers often had little to do with fault, and everything to do with fear. "Where did it come from?"

"That is," Vandeyr said, "a question indeed. It was affixed to the front door of the palace with a nail. And we know who is fond of driving sharp objects into doors, don't we?" Her breath hissed through her teeth.

"Let me see."

Vandeyr handed it over to her. It contained only two lines, followed by a signature. *King Traedis, you are being judged. If you are found wanting, I will come.*

It was signed *Cordelayne Atenel.*

Traedis could hear her pulse in her ears, and little else.

"He's trying to frighten you," Vandeyr said through the rushing of Traedis' blood. "You know that, don't you?"

Her gaze half-focused, Traedis looked back up at her sister. "He's succeeding," she said quietly. Somewhere behind her conscious thoughts, a tune was forming, its beat in time to her heart. Its minor scale was oddly disquieting.

Vandeyr muttered a curse under her breath. "He knows how scared you are of him. What he does isn't going to be affected by what he tells you."

"I am aware of that." Traedis took three deep breaths, trying to clear her mind enough to concentrate on what was really important. "I see what he's doing, but it doesn't help. He must be counting on that."

Vandeyr looked at her, her expression blank. "It's not honorable of him to use his knowledge of your fears against you. I don't like these tactics. It's one thing to use all the weaponry you have against a professional target, but it's another thing entirely to use them against family. I don't like much of your stirring everything up like a child playing in mud, but I don't approve of Uncle Cordelayne's actions, either. In case it matters."

"It does to me." Traedis looked at the broken seal: the Atenel wyvern. Though she was king, Uncle Cordelayne was still head of the family, and seemed intent on reminding her of that. She shook her head, trying to dismiss the fears from her mind. "I'm *not* going to turn aside. He may know what I was like years ago, but he doesn't know me now. Not all of what I have learned is from the City."

"You always were the stubborn one." Vandeyr gestured at the parchment. "I could have told him not to try forcing your hand. He should know that already. He probably does. But I expect all he's really trying to accomplish is to throw you enough off balance so that you'll make mistakes." The muscles in her hands bunched. "He can't be traced through the letter, either. We've already tried."

Traedis felt her pulse diminish to a more normal beat. The initial impact of the message was wearing off, and she was determined not to allow her uncle to intimidate her. In the shock's wake a surge of anger sent a searing trail through her body. "He's made a serious error if he thinks I'm going to give in because of Atchûk's death."

Vandeyr sighed. "No, of course you won't – you'll be more mule-headed that you were before. I don't know what he was thinking. It's the closest thing to a mistake I've seen him make in years." She paused. "Except for letting you out of prison. I'm glad he did, but for him it was a mistake. Especially considering what's come of it."

"Yes." For a moment, the room darkened and Traedis was left alone in her cell, comfort and companionship beyond her dreams. She shivered. Then she knew it was morning again. She tore her thoughts away from the memories with the same determination that had kept her from madness in those terrible four years.

Traedis raised her chin. "It's time to find out who in the family is behind me, and who isn't. I need to talk to Lang."

"I'll send him a message." Vandeyr examined Traedis' face. "Doing better?"

Traedis gave her sister a wan smile. "Some better. Thank you."

"Well, let's get back to work, then."

Traedis felt her lips curve in shaken amusement. Then she picked up her harp and followed Vandeyr out the door and down the stairs.

"Coup in three moves," Lang said to Traedis as they bent over the hexagonal gameboard. He had suggested they play a game of King's Crown while they talked, and it was a sufficient change from her routine that Traedis had agreed. Now, her wooden kingdom surrounded by enemy soldiers, she felt more relaxed than she had since returning to Tolin.

They sat in a small private room on the first floor of the palace overlooking one of the gardens. Lang seemed genuinely at ease, as he often did. Taller than Daymet, his features were regular and not as fine. He had a remarkably sweet smile. His red-brown hair was just long enough to need a trim, and his clothing was of the clean and simple style that valued cut and quality over ornamentation. His shrewd blue eyes watched his sister at least as much as they did the game.

Traedis saw the strategic trap and avoided it; Lang was a better player, but she was not a novice. She smiled. "You'll beat me, but I won't make it that easy."

Lang looked at Traedis' face rather than at the board. "I believe you," he said before moving the right flank of his cavalry into a stronger position.

Lang was much older than Traedis and she had not spent time with him much as a child; she was closer in age to his oldest daughter. She was still not sure how far she could trust him, and she wanted very much to be certain.

"You haven't tried to undermine me in Tolin," she said, shoring up her castle wall. "I was afraid you'd take as much against me as Daymet and Otenemar, but so far you've honored my will. Thank you." She checked her archer's positions before ceding her turn.

Lang spoke as he studied the pieces. "Let me be honest with you," he said. "There are a number of things I would do differently. I don't agree with many of your changes, and I think your assessment of the South Quarter's stability is lacking in information." He reached for a piece, then drew back to take a second look. "I would like to sit down with you and make some suggestions that would help keep peace among the merchants, and I think one of the minor lords is hoarding food. I don't love the temper down in the West Quarter's Coran church, either.

"Coup in four moves."

He stopped and looked up, his gaze boring into hers. "But, Traedis, you have done far better than I would ever have guessed, and you've taken care with even the smallest details that affect the City. I was not given the rule, and that tells me that the gods wanted something other than what I have to offer. Daymet and Otenemar are wrong. I would be a fool not to understand that."

Traedis looked back at the gameboard, largely to keep her composure. This time, her brother had maneuvered her into a situation she could not salvage. She reluctantly handed him the crown piece. "Thank you," she said, her voice husky. "I know you would have inherited Uncle Cordelayne's seat on the Council if it hadn't been for me."

Lang sat motionless for a moment, as if trying to make up his mind. Slowly, he said, "I would have done my duty, of course. It's what I was trained for, when it became clear Gavaya would not sit on the Council. But – I didn't want it, Traedis. There were too many things broken, and not enough people interested in fixing them." He twirled the crown piece in his fingers. "Gavaya and I both knew that. We also knew we could do nothing about the situation."

He gave the ghost of a smile. "I would have followed Father's example, would have advocated for the best of the City, not the worst. But I never liked how we broke the people who didn't fit. Like you. It's not the way things ought to be."

Traedis straightened, startled; she had not expected this confession. Then, dampening the instinctive trust, the question she had not asked her mother rose to the surface. "Why didn't you visit me in prison? Don't tell me you were unable. That's true for Vandeyr, but I know it wasn't for you."

Lang dropped a blue gaze to the table, then raised it again. "Yes, I could have. I allowed myself to be persuaded by Cordelayne, and I shouldn't have. I knew how much he cared about you, and so I thought he must be right, that his course was the best." He squared his shoulders. "I was wrong, Traedis. *Entirely* wrong. I'm sorry."

A single tear squeezed itself from Traedis' eyes and tracked down her cheek; she believed him. "You didn't just – abandon me?"

"Never," said Lang with clear sincerity.

Traedis thought she understood. It had been only her constant inability to live up to her family's standards that had made her challenge the City's mission. She looked at her brother, assessing his knowledge and his honor. "I value your experience," she said softly. "I know you've always done your best to be ethical. I know you've never wanted power for its own sake – but neither does Uncle Cordelayne, and that made me question. I'm sorry I doubted you."

"I would have doubted me had I stood in your place," he responded. "Traedis, there were many things Gavaya and I disliked about the City as it was. We spoke of things we would like to change – but quietly, where no one could overhear. She chose to step out of a Council role; she left that to me. And I was content because I could at least count on having a voice." He hefted the crown piece, then set it in front of Traedis. "I did not have the courage to challenge our beliefs, and I didn't think I could make a difference." He swept the rest of the pieces toward Traedis. "And that, little sister, is why the gods chose you to rule, and not me. You have more courage. If I want to teach my children to stand up for what's just, I have to honor it in you."

Traedis blinked several times. Lang had thoroughly surprised her in a way that even Gavaya had not. "What does Alluve say?" she finally managed to ask.

"The same. And when you gained the *falmyros* she had words

with me about my laxity in supporting you." He shook his head. "I was confused. You overturned everything in the space of a few days, and it caught me off guard. I wasn't sure what my position should be, and Cordelayne and Daymet were whispering sedition into my ear. Add Mother's alarm at your behavior to that whole pile of flaming dung and I was so busy smelling manure that I couldn't tell it from my own chamber pot." He chuckled. "It was Alluve who said to me, 'You don't have to agree with her, but she's your liege, and unless there's something you forgot to tell me, the Atenels aren't gods.' That woke me out of my dithering on what I should do." He hesitated. "I have not yet formally sworn to you, and I would like to."

He rose from his chair and dropped to one knee. "Traedis Liori Eisel Atenel, I swear fealty to you before the gods and their steward Lord Shoriantemeth, and accept you as my liege. I swear to be faithful to you and to your rule, to obey your laws, and to defend you at the cost of my own life."

Traedis caught her breath; this was more than she had expected. She leaned down and took both of Lang's hands in her own. "I accept your fealty," she said, her tongue thick in her mouth, "and swear that I will be a good king to you, will protect you and yours, and will keep faith with you. This I swear before the four gods and Lord Shoriantemeth, King of the World." She tugged at him. "Now, get up before I start crying."

She returned the pieces to the board, setting them to their starting position one by one. "You've put my mind at ease. Lang, I have something to ask – I need a viceroy, and I can think of no one better than you. Your experience and knowledge are greater than mine, and I – I trust you to put my will above your own. Will you consider it?"

Lang regarded her shrewdly before a wide smile stretched across his face. "I would be honored." He rose to his feet. "Little sister, I have much to make up to you."

Several weeks of settling disputes in open court had begun to take their toll on Traedis. As she sat in the Great Hall, sweat slicked her forehead, despite the cold late mountain spring. This was partly due to the large fireplaces, and partly to the tension of dealing with so many people who hated her. She was grateful for Ruth's presence at her back, and Vandeyr's at her side.

A disagreement between two farmers was trying her patience while she forced herself to pay attention to the mind-numbing petition.

"But Your Majesty," said one of the two, a red-faced man with a supercilious smile. "His cow came into my pasture, got fat on my grass, and drank my water. That makes her mine."

The other, who looked a like a wheat sheaf, tall and thin with a haystack of golden hair, scowled. "Your grass isn't worth spit, and it's everybody's water. That's like saying my child is yours because she ran into your house. It's nonsense. You just want something for nothing."

"Speak to me, not to each other," Traedis said firmly. If the two farmers could have mended their quarrel by themselves, they would not need her to resolve it. "It is true," she said to the first man, "that your grass is worth something, but it is not worth the price of a cow. This is my judgement: Goodman Sharm will pay you a copper drolys for each week his cow has pastured on your land, and he will build a fence at his expense to make sure that this does not happen in the future. From what I estimate, the fence will cost forty copper drolyses. Should he fail to build the fence, he will owe you that sum as well. The cow remains with him."

Neither of the men seemed particularly happy with Traedis' ruling, but both of them did seem relieved that they would not go away empty-handed. They bowed low and began to exit just as the chime sounded that announced the end of petitions for the day. A handful of people behind them, mostly tradesmen, sighed and turned away.

Traedis gathered her skirts and stood, suppressing a yawn as she picked up her harpcase. It was only noon, and she still had a full day ahead of her. She needed to review quite a number of written petitions, meet with Fors Mastery about some crumbling foundations in the business quarter, hone her fighting skills with the new armsmaster, and practice her harp. Then she must prepare for a delegation from esch lands, which was expected next week.

The last was a headache she did not want; she had enough insincere suitors attempting to gain control of Tolin's invaluable assassins. As there was neither an official treaty nor a state of war between the City and the esch nation, it was up to Traedis to define their relationship. She intended to wait until Tolin was stronger to openly declare the City's refusal to ally with King Llyrach or any of his subjects.

Vandeyr followed her through the vestibule behind the throne and around to the main flight of stairs to the second floor. Traedis' room was not far, and she needed to change into leathers and boots. Ruth turned toward her own quarters. Vandeyr was flagged down by a guardsman; she held up a finger to Traedis, who nodded and left her sister to deal with her own business.

A maidservant approached her; one of the housekeeping staff, not a page. The woman held a sealed missive in her hand.

"Your Majesty?" she said timidly. "A letter came for you."

Traedis smiled the practiced smile that she had held all morning in court. "I would rather letters were sent to my office, but since you have it here, I'll take it. Thank you." She reached for the envelope and scanned the wax seal to see who had sent it.

In an instant, the woman whipped out a fist dagger and tried to thrust it between Traedis' ribs.

Immediately, Traedis' training took hold. She twisted away from the knife, which ripped across her sleeve. In the same twist, she rounded, pulling up her skirt to allow for a solid kick to the woman's hand. It connected with a smack, and the maidservant cried out.

Still clinging to the knife, the woman slashed at Traedis' chest. Traedis swayed back while the blade tore into the cloth on her bodice. It caught in the silk of her gown; the woman pressed forward. Traedis shoved at the woman's jawbone, but could not find good leverage without risking impalement.

With lightning speed, two daggers flew out of the air. One slashed squarely across the woman's hand, opening it to the bone. The second stuck in the woman's wrist. Blood spattered across the bodice of Traedis' ruined dress. The maidservant cried out and finally dropped her knife, clutching at her wrist.

In another moment, she sank to the ground with a white-bladed dagger in the back of her knee. Two guards materialized from down the hall, one pinning the attacker's arms, the other bringing a sword to her throat. Ruth appeared beside Traedis an instant later.

Vandeyr was already there. "Who sent you?" she asked in a low monotone that managed to convey the chill of her anger.

The woman grunted in pain as her blood dripped onto the stone floor of the hall. "She's a traitor," she said in a barely audible voice. "And so are you. Consorting with Haven." Her eyes moved toward the letter which Traedis still clutched. "Someone had to take a stand."

Traedis felt her anger rise as she realized how close she had just come to death. She lifted the letter up to examine the seal again, knowing that this must have been what had precipitated the woman's attack. Expecting to see the royal sigil of Haven, she was surprised to see instead the twining Tallforest trees, drops of blood staining their branches.

"Bandage her arm and take her to the prisons," Vandeyr said

expressionlessly. "And send for Lieutenant Tethyn and four more guards right away. I want a full investigation of this incident."

One of the guards crudely bandaged the woman, then pulled out a pair of manacles from his belt, while the other continued to level his sword at her throat. Once they had restrained her, the second guard lowered his sword, pulled out a heavy silken cord from a pouch on his belt, and hobbled her, tossing Ruth's dagger onto the floor. They dragged the would-be assassin off toward the second-floor guard post.

Traedis held back a shiver, recognizing how angry her sister was. Ruth flashed her a quick, reassuring grin and retrieved her weapon. She pulled out a cloth and wiped it down, but did not place it back in her belt.

"Let me see the letter," said Vandeyr. Traedis handed it to her without objection. After scanning it briefly, Vandeyr handed it back. "Let's get you to your room." Her gaze darting in every direction, she accompanied Traedis down the short section of hall which led to the royal apartments.

Guards were always stationed at Traedis' door, whether she was inside or not. Vandeyr nodded at them with her chin and gestured for them to follow her into the sitting room. Traedis dropped into a chair and pulled Rose out of her case, her hands shaking with reaction.

Vandeyr quickly set a pair of women to watch the hallway. More guards investigated the whole of the sitting room, then made a sweep of the entire royal apartments. Traedis did not move while they searched, certain that her sister would not allow her to move until the rooms were deemed clear. Instead, she patted Rose, who sighed a descending chromatic scale as soon as Traedis set her on the floor. Ruth stood beside Traedis, knife at the ready.

Traedis broke the seal on the letter carefully so as not to sully the inside with the blood that painted its exterior. Inside was another beautifully calligraphed page, illustrated with grey and white gamboling foxes. Harps that spiraled into vines wrapped the text in color and intricate design. Traedis raised her eyebrows, quite aware of how long it must have taken the Haven knight to create a work of art out of a simple message. She had a fine hand herself, but she was no scribe, and would never have been able to pen something this exquisite.

The words, however, were simple.

To King Traedis Liori Eisel Atenel of Tolin, from Elben Tallforest, Haven Deputy Captain of King Kenrydh's royal guard in Faldrohaven, Greetings.

I most heartily enjoyed my visit to Tolin, though I was on duty for much of it. The best part of it, as I am sure you can guess, came from the time I spent with you, though I am perhaps forward in saying so. Our speech together was not only enlightening, it warmed my heart that you were willing to speak as freely as you did.

Traedis was interrupted by the arrival of several more guards in the sitting room. Following on their heels was Tagg, his portly figure a welcome sight. "Your Majesty," he said. "I am going to search your rooms for dangerous magics. I expect you will feel this in your *falmyros* if I understand the situation rightly. I thought I should warn you, so you won't be alarmed if you feel me tugging at your protections."

"As long as you leave them in place." Traedis looked down and realized that she had flipped the letter over so that no one could see its contents. "You'd better start with this letter. Though I know its sender means me no harm, someone else might have tampered with it."

"I already checked it," said Vandeyr, her voice taut. "Do you take me for a fool?"

Traedis shook her head. "Of course not." Though her sister had no innate magic, she did carry a number of enchanted artifacts that assisted in her duties. "Which ring is it?" It was a guess, but Traedis knew that if Vandeyr had magically assessed the letter, it had been accomplished by simply taking it and handing it back.

Vandeyr held up her left pinkie, which held a thin band of unornamented silver. "This one," she said, and tapped at it with her right forefinger. "There's no magic in the letter, just a waste of paper and ink." She turned to Tagg. "I'm going to want a sweep of the entire palace, but I'd like to know first that there is a safe place to stow King Traedis while we investigate."

"Vandeyr," Traedis said, "I know you want to be thorough, but it seems unlikely that the servant planned this, much less left poison or magic for me to find. I think she saw the seal, recognized it, and decided to do something on the spot."

"That's what I think, too." Vandeyr shook her head impatiently. "That doesn't mean I'm not going to investigate."

"Then let Tagg examine it," Traedis retorted sharply. "An object isn't as flexible as a living mind. That's one of the first magical principles they teach you, whether you're a mage, a bard, or a healer. And stop being so bullheaded that you insist on doing the work of the entire palace *and* City Guard all by yourself. No one is that perfect."

Vandeyr opened her mouth, then closed it again. She took a deep breath. "You're right," she said, softly enough that it would be hard for even her soldiers to hear. "There are things that are not in my power to accomplish. But I promised myself and you that I would do everything that *was* in my power to keep you safe, and I meant that.

"This scared me, Trae. I lost you for six years. I don't want to lose you again."

Traedis felt a deep ache in her chest, and tears stung the backs of her eyes. She had not expected this vulnerability on Vandeyr's part, and she did not know how to respond. She had always envied her sister, who had the approval and admiration of not only the Atenel family, but the City itself. Now she began to wonder if the appearance of perfection was as much of a burden as failure. Tenderness bloomed in Traedis' chest, and she reached out a hand to touch Vandeyr.

"I've lost too many people already," Traedis said to her, just as softly. "Don't let the next one be you."

Later that day, Traedis set to with a less-than-perfect will and attacked paperwork and policy alike with frustrated determination. She was grateful for the distraction, so that she need not yet examine the events of the day. Likely, the knowledge of how close she had come to death lay in wait, seeking to catch her in an unseen snare as soon as she allowed herself to feel it. She tried to ignore the warning of her body that she was building up tension which might force her into her fox shape.

It was late evening; a lit candle on her desk provided the only light, and the window's glass mirrored the room back to her, as insubstantial as a phantom's recollection of life. For one moment, Traedis felt her heart struggle against its rhythm as the walls seems to flex inward, threatening to crush her. She gasped and clutched at the edge of her desk, trying to remind herself where and when she belonged. The *falmyros* answered her in a wordless rush of comfort. Its imminence quelled memory, and Traedis relaxed warily back into the space between her body and the land of Tolin.

"Vandeyr?" she called through the door, her voice less than steady. "Are you there?"

The door opened promptly and Vandeyr strode in. "What do you mean, am I there? Did you think I was going to leave you alone after what just happened? If I have to sleep at your bed's foot like a hound, I'm sticking with you." She looked sharply at Traedis. "You've been working a long time, you know. Through supper and into the night watch. Should I order some food brought up?"

"Mice," Traedis' fox self blurted out without thinking. Vandeyr's forehead wrinkled, and Traedis heard the echo of her words in the air. "I mean..." She trailed off and made a low, semi-hysterical laugh.

"Cooked or raw?" Vandeyr asked, as calmly as if Traedis had ordered goose. "Or would you rather prepare the meal yourself? I can order the carpet taken up in your sitting room."

"Uh... no." Traedis knew that such a slip meant that she needed to return to her fox shape, but she did not like the lack of control. "Veal will do. Cold is fine. Perhaps a potato or two. And I don't need to kill either of them myself."

Vandeyr stepped out the door and said a few words, presumably to whatever guard or page stood ready in the hall. Traedis heard retreating footsteps.

Leaning back in her chair, Traedis stretched like a cat. A yawn caught her unexpectedly, filling her lungs with air and her mind with clarity. She looked at the stack of papers she had just finished, and at the considerably smaller stack she still needed to study, and decided that she was too tired to finish tonight.

Vandeyr returned, looking as fresh as if she had recently woken and bathed.

Realizing that her sister was the only one threatening to sleep at the foot of her bed, Traedis looked around in concern. "Where's Ruth?" she asked.

"She may annoy me, but she's devoted to you." Vandeyr

leaned her back against the door, though she was obviously not relaxed. "She's consulting a priest about what other dangers may lie in wait for you. A few dozen, no doubt." She stood back up as abruptly as a coiled spring. "Curse it, Trae, you could have died this afternoon, and it would have been my fault. I wasn't there."

Traedis laced her fingers together. "You're wrong. If it hadn't been for you, I would have been in such poor training that I might not have fended her off. You're the one who restored my ability to defend myself. And you and Ruth were both there just moments after the attack."

"That's easy enough for you to say." Vandeyr folded her arms. "You're not the one who was dealing with stupid administrative matters while her sister the King was attacked." She scowled. "Ruth is your friend, not your guard captain. I'm the one who left you on your own in a public area without protection. You'd be within your rights to send me packing, though hopefully you won't do anything that stupid."

Vandeyr's logic was enough to make Traedis' head spin. "You know I won't."

"You should." Vandeyr seemed in a contrary mood; Traedis was not sure her sister would agree that the sun traveled through the skies.

Rising, she went to look out the window at the stars, which wheeled through the upper air without a moon to dim them. She knew them passingly well; the Harp, the Firebrand, and the Dragon were ascendant, while the Bowl and the Fisherwoman had already dropped below the horizon. In the breast of the Northern Dragon shone a red star brighter than anything else now in the sky: *Dragon's Heart.* It was an exquisite gem on the ceiling of the world.

"I'm grateful to Ruth for asking the gods," she said, taking in the pattern of the stars. "And I'm grateful to you for saving my life."

Vandeyr shook herself like a dog shedding water. "After you eat your dinner, I'll put you to bed myself if you won't go on your own. Mice! You're not in any shape to continue working right now."

Traedis grinned wanly. "Perhaps not. I accept your judgement."

A corner of Vandeyr's mouth finally curled upward. "Then stop working and get to bed."

Ruth came in the next morning, her normally cheerful face graven with serious lines. Vandeyr was right behind her; she held herself rigidly, her jaw tight.

Traedis was attacking a plate of venison and eggs with a single-mindedness that suggested she had still not mastered her fox side, though she had managed not to change during the night. Perhaps she should cancel open court in an effort to prevent herself from becoming a fox in public.

Ruth pulled up a chair and hopped onto it. "I've got some serious news," she said, her voice laden with worry. "I'm not entirely sure what it means, but I have an answer from the gods about what threatens you most, and it's not a stray assassin or even your family. It's from a different quarter entirely."

Traedis suddenly lost her appetite. "Gods, there's something else? It's not the Dance, is it?"

Vandeyr seemed to stand straighter, and she fixed a stare intently on Ruth's slight form.

Ruth shook her head and shadows of worry played under her eyes. "Not that either." She picked up a spoon and spun it between her fingers. "It's from the n'korreld."

"The n'korreld?" Traedis' stomach sank. This was terrible news; the alliance she had just tentatively formed must be in ruins from Atchûk's death. "They've decided to repudiate me?"

"Not exactly. This is what Lord Coran told me." Ruth tapped the spoon on the table's edge. "Let's see if I can get this right. *'From the dangers the* falmyros *brings, Traedis cannot be entirely freed except by breaking the strictures of the gods, by madness, or by death. From the danger of Cordelayne Atenel, all she need do is wait. The Red Man of the n'korreld will be called, and will come for him. That will bring an even deeper peril to her and to the realm of Tolin. To defend Tolin, she must first stop the Red Man. Should her realm survive, she will face other perils, but this is the most immediate.'* That's all I got, except for a sense of overpowering urgency. I don't know what it means, but I'm worried." She dropped the spoon with a clank.

Traedis felt her heartbeat speed up. "What does that mean, the

Red Man? What kind of danger is he? And why, if someone is calling it on Uncle Cordelayne, is it a danger to me and to Tɔlin?" She did not doubt the god's words, but making sense of them was another problem.

"I thought of that." Ruth puffed out her cheeks. "I went ɔo talk with your sister – " She gave Vandeyr a cursory nod. "Not that sister. Lady Gavaya. She did a little research for me."

That was good; if there were anything to find, Gavaya would find it. "What did she say?"

Folding her hands, Ruth leaned forward. "She couldn't find out anything about a Red Man of the n'korreld, but she did come across references to red animals that were associated with n'korreld blood magic. They seems to be a very rare sort, and there weren't a lot of details on how the n'korreld called them forth."

Traedis felt her stomach sink. Blood magic – rightly – had a bad reputation for being both brutal and effective. She cleared her throat. "What sort of red animals? What did they do?"

Ruth knotted her brows. "The two she could find out anything about were a red wolf and a red bear. The sources didn't seem to know if they were of demonic origin, but they doubted it. It might not matter. They were certainly called by a karreldish blood curse under circumstances where the n'korreld people had been wronged." The creases in her face deepened, making her look older. "The important part is, that once called, they rampaged through everyone who stood in their way, one laying waste to an entire city, the other to the better part of a country. Gavaya speculated they might destroy anything with a blood link to their target."

The breath caught in Traedis' throat. The import of Ruth's news was clear; someone intended to call this force upon Uncle Cordelayne. Perhaps her uncle deserved to die in such a way, though it would be wrenching. But if the power followed links of blood, his death would likely prove deadly to the entire House of Atenel. That was bad enough, but given two thousand years of intermarriage and bastardy, it was possible that almost everyone in the City was linked by blood, even if the link was tenuous or distant. Blood magic could devastate the entire City, and even the surrounding countries might suffer. This was a threat greater than the curse Traedis had lifted.

Vandeyr stilled. "How can the n'korreld wield such power?"

"They are made of the earth's bones," Traedis answered her. Many considered the n'korreld a pathetic, weak race, fit only to serve others. She knew this to be folly. Their enchantments were slow growing but powerful, like the tides of the earth building to a great quake. Traedis knew almost nothing of their blood magic.

She pressed her lips together. "Thank you, Ruth. I might otherwise have waited too long before learning the truth. You're a good friend, and you've proven it to me over and over again."

Vandeyr rested her fingers over her dagger. "What are you going to do?"

"I don't know." Traedis shook her head. "I don't know what to do."

Immediately clearing her entire agenda, Traedis debated frantically how to proceed. Both Vandeyr and Ruth stood in the hall just outside the door, three other guards sharing their watch. Rose whispered music into the air while Traedis rummaged through the papers in her office, selecting everything that had to do with the n'korreld and their disposition toward Tolin. In addition, she had ordered some history books from the library, which were brought in by a pair of sturdy pages, one with skin and hair the color of mahogany, the other so pale he looked like an old man. The two seemed relieved when they were able to shift their burden onto Traedis' desk. She thanked them and watched them retreat while she wondered what degree of relation they might be to her, and whether they were in danger from Thane Bi'ia's wrath.

She wished that she had Atchûk to guide her through this labyrinth of n'korreld vengeance. But it was Atchûk's absence that was the problem: that, and the reason for it. She missed his cheerful confidence and optimism, and most of all, his sense of humor. Cursing herself for agreeing that he should spy on her uncle, and indeed, for taking the Quo'at's second offer instead of the first, she wondered if a direct appeal to the Thane would be effective.

She doubted it. Though Bi'ia had said he did not blame Traedis, he was taking no pains to keep her safe. It was quite possible that, now he had time to consider what had happened, he nursed anger against her as well as Uncle Cordelayne.

The door handle turned and Vandeyr entered. "Trae, a

messenger arrived for you. Do you want to see him here, or downstairs?"

Sudden hope caught Traedis' heart in a double beat. Was this some missive from the Thane, telling her that she need not fear for Tolin? He *had* told her he did not blame her. Perhaps she had been wrong about him.

"I'll come." She smoothed a creased page, then followed Vandeyr out into the hall, down the great staircase, and into a small, less formal reception room. The karreld who sat waiting had skin like marble with streaks of green. He stood as she entered, bowing low.

"Greetings, good courier, and welcome to my house." Though Traedis was anxious to know what he had to say, she would not omit the proprieties, especially now. "What is your message?"

The karreld looked at her with eyes the same green as the streaks in his skin. "King Traedis, I bear greetings from the Quo'at. He salutes you, and requests you come to Kurt where he must speak with you at length."

Traedis' blood sounded in her ears; if the Quo'at needed to speak with her, things must be dire. Gavaya's worst suppositions rang in her head.

"Of course I will come."

Traedis felt her ears pop as she, Vandeyr, and a small party of n'korreld arrived out of the *blork* into the karreldish capital. Though it was full summer, the air was moist and chill; they had come in an instant from the light of day to a false night punctuated only by lanterns and lamplight.

They stood in an enormous cavern, vaster than any Traedis had ever seen – big enough that it swallowed the entire city. She looked around in fascination and wonder at the bustling karreldish place. N'korreld in all the colors of stone walked the streets, hawked wares, and strolled together; children darted into the wide streets, playing around low goat carts. All wore tunics in brilliant patterns and colors made of the shiny fabric they wove.

Here, in the middle of the city, it was possible to see how it was patterned. Beehived buildings, constructed of varied types of rock, were round rather than square, huddling low to the ground like clusters of squat toadstools which had sprung up in the damp. Streets swirled around the dwellings in wide arcs that spiraled inward toward the heart of the city. Nowhere could Traecis see a straight line.

The city's center was occupied by the abode – Traecis could not think of it as a palace – of the Thane. This edifice was bigger than any other, spreading over what seemed to be the rounded equivalent of a Tolin city block. Its grounds were walled, but a row of high windows lined the domed roof. Traedis could not tell if they delineated a second story, or whether they were simply vents to allow more airflow. They would certainly be useless for lighting purposes.

That was not where they were headed. Their karreldish escorts, led by a high official in a frog-patterned tunic, took them through several turnings during which Traedis lost track of the cavern's entrance, the palace, and her entire sense of direction. Buildings edged close to the street, giving Traedis the sense that they were leaning toward the travelers. Fungi of all sorts climbed the structures or grew from cracks in the streets, and pale white lichen draped over large stones like bedsheets. The whole place smelled of damp earth and must, closed in, but not rotten.

They took a final curve, and found themselves in front of a wall built higher than Traedis' head out of an astonishing assortment of rocks of all sizes. None of them appeared to be mortared together, though the wall was obviously solid and immovable. Traedis spotted granite, limestone, agate, and feldspar, even the occasional glint of rough-cut ruby or topaz.

The karrelds guided Traedis and Vandeyr through a low, arched gate, into a courtyard. Two armed guards, half Traedis' height but well-muscled, joined them at their approach. They sported livery of red and black, instead of the red and brown of the royal house.

It did not take great perception to see that they stood before a church of Coran, the god of earth. The structure before them rose in a half-sphere, rather than the more hivelike slope of other n'korreld buildings. It was constructed of basalt that had no visible seam or roughness, smoothed to the texture of water-polished rock. A door of curved black metal could only be seen by the higher sheen on its surface.

One of their escorts spoke in his own tongue, and the larger of the guards nodded, his chin expressing a disdain that Traedis guessed was directed at herself and Vandeyr. The second guard said something sharp, which the official quelled with a formidable glance. The first guard opened the gates, allowing them inside.

More guards appeared as they entered the church grounds, three of them splitting off to follow their small party. Traedis was surprised to see a sort of garden, planted with crystal stalagmites and burgeoning with fungi of more colors and shapes than she had ever guessed existed. More lichen lapped over the church's foundation like fine lace. She gave a cry of delighted awe, and was rewarded by a pale smile on the second guard's face.

Servants escorted them into the building and seated them in a room that reminded Traedis of one section of a pie, walls and ceiling of the same smooth basalt as the exterior, floor set with irregularly-shaped agates all colors of the rainbow. The seats were wide enough, but too low for human comfort. Traedis thought of the Quo'at kicking his feet in oversized chairs and relaxed, trying to keep her feet out of the way. Vandeyr remained standing, her posture wary but calm. Their escorts also stood, with the exception of the high official, who took a seat opposite Traedis.

One of the servants gave a sharp call, and a page appeared, a sturdy young lad who looked older than the Quo'at by several years. He gave a quick bow and darted back out of the room. Shortly thereafter, a ranking priest joined them; his status was denoted by a sumptuous clerical coat with designs of red and black, ornamented with threads and beads of copper. His ashy gray hair split into three braids, each of them beaded with copper and rubies.

The priest held a short conversation with the guards, who responded in terse but polite tones. Traedis wished she spoke karreldish; she hated not knowing what was said.

Finally, the priest turned to Traedis. "I am very sorry, King Traedis, to speak so that you cannot understand, but we have few guests, and karreldish is the only language known to all of us." He glanced at the guards, then back at Traedis. "I am Ett, the chief priest of this city of Dinyc, and I welcome you in the Quo'at's name. He has given instructions that he wishes to see you as soon as you arrive. I have sent a page to let him know you are here. Fear no one in this church; you are under his protection, and these guards will defend you with their lives."

"Thank you." Traedis was more worried about what the Quo'at wanted with her than whether his people would harm her. A chill shuddered through her. What did the Quo'at know about the Red Man? What if she could not stop its manifestation, whatever that might be? How was she to protect Tolin from a blood curse that had destroyed nations? She had her land's power, but even that had limits.

The priest left the room quickly. Vandeyr did not seem overly nervous; Traedis was glad someone was calm. Her nerves jangled at every movement or sound, even so slight as the shuffling of a foot.

Traedis' thoughts were dark with the blood that would be shed if she failed. She did not know what passed through Vandeyr's mind; silence stretched between them like shadows at sunset.

Finally Traedis heard the sounds of booted feet, and the Quo'at appeared, guards as well as priests at his back. He wore a simple robe the color of blood; a pendant consisting of a single copper nugget encircled his neck. Tension etched his face; his mouth was firmed in a line. He approached her, his step leaden.

"King Traedis," he said in a voice as strained as his face. "I am very glad you have come." He gestured, and one of the priests brought a perfectly sized chair that he sat in without difficulty. His feet were on the floor, Traedis noted. Waving the all the guards away, the Quo'at lowered his voice. "It is unusual for us to consult with outsiders, but you have rightly earned our friendship, and I cannot honorably agree with my thane in the course he has taken."

"How can I help you?" she asked. "It is my doing that Atchûk became a target of my uncle – "

"Bloody guano!" the Quo'at said, reminding Traedis so much of Atchûk that her heart ached. She closed her mouth as the Quo'at continued. "This happened because several people made mistakes, not excluding Atchûk himself. You, me, Atchûk, even the Thane – all of us contributed to what happened, and it's no one's fault other than your uncle's. You need not take responsibility for the stars in the skies or the tides of the earth.”

Vandeyr actually broke into a brief smile before setting her jaw again.

Traedis blinked. “Did you just swear?”

“You forget my age.” the Quo’at shook his head. “Though my keepers would prefer me to act excessively dignified and suitably reserved – ” he beamed a smile at them clearly intended to bring them into the joke, “ – I have no desire to be other than what I am. When I hear foolishness, I confront it. And blaming yourself is foolishness, King Traedis.”

Traedis took a deep draught of the musty air. “Why have you asked me here, Most Blessed Quo’at?” Sick dread weighted her belly. “Lord Coran told my friend that the Thane would call the Red Man of the n’korreld.” Her trained memory supplied her with the exact words, which she repeated to the Quo’at. “All anyone could find about this was a red wolf and a red bear, and I don’t know if they are the same.”

The Quo’at’s smile faded, and his brows lowered. He sat quietly for several moments before speaking. “Thane Bi’ia is set on a course which may be disastrous for Tolin, but also may have deadly repercussions for our own land. The Red Man – the Bear, the Wolf, the Bull, the Hawk – belongs to another age, one in which we had no friends, and no justice we did not exact ourselves.” He gripped the edge of his seat with tight fingers. “Understand, King Traedis, the Red Man could destroy your City, and might gravely affect Haven as well – two thousand years is a short time to the elemental spirits of our people. Telardur would also be affected."

More silence followed, broken only by the sound of their breath. Finally, the Quo'at continued, "I have not been able to persuade the Thane to reconsider his course of action. King Traedis, Coran has spoken to me also, and his words were thus: *Break not your alliance, lest the n'korreld find themselves truly alone. The Thane must swallow his blood, or he will do untold harm to the world. You must speak to Tolin's king if you wish to avert disaster. Only your joint cooperation can turn Bi'ia from his course.*" His eyes glittered, and Traedis thought she saw the sheen of tears.

"I don't understand." A melody murmured through the room; Traedis laid a finger on Rose, who stopped immediately. "Swallow his blood? What does that mean? And is it true that whatever arcane spirit or demon Thane Bi'ia is going to call will destroy everything with a blood link to my uncle?"

The Quo'at nodded. "Though I will correct your words to say, 'has already called.'"

Traedis' heart knocked against her chest. "If it is already called, how does one avert it?"

"One does not. Only he who called it may even contain its damage." the Quo'at's tone was heavy with ancient grief and wisdom. "I can promise you nothing except the opportunity to plead your cause to the Thane. He will not hear me, though I explained to him my belief that you are one of our own, clothed in the flesh of another people."

"What must I do?" Even if this killed her, Traedis knew she had to follow the Quo'at's advice.

"Come with me to the ancient stone circle of Tatek'h, where the Thane even now awaits the arrival of our blood-called spirit of vengeance. Talk to him. Remind him that he will destroy far more than the one who killed our prince. Remind him that you are also a person, one who has done good for our people." He shifted in his chair. "I don't know if you *can* persuade him, but my own words have been futile."

Traedis swallowed. "I understand your intent, but will that not simply make him angrier? That I could stand before him and beg clemency, even though it was my error that condemned his son?"

"My error also," the Quo'at gently reminded her. "I have spoken to him – at length – and if he will not heed my words, whose will he heed? The god moves in me, and I believe that you are a necessary part of this."

That was that; Traedis could not gainsay Coran. She bent her head. "I will come with you, Most Blessed Quo'at. I see no more alternative than do you."

"Thank you," he said simply. "May Lord Coran look favorably upon you as upon me."

As soon as Traedis rose to leave, Vandeyr began to follow. The Quo'at raised a palm to stop her.

"I'm not leaving you," Vandeyr told Traedis. "As your guard

captain, I cannot allow you to venture into dangerous territory without me." Her jaw was set and rigid. "Didn't you learn anything from that assassination attempt?"

The Quo'at shook his head. "The Thane will see King Traedis only. As it is, he wishes to speak with no human, nor suffer one in his presence. I am stretching that command because I believe she has the soul of a karreld. She will suffer no harm, upon my honor, but Captain Atenel, you must stay here."

"I am not – " Vandeyr began.

Traedis shook her head, cutting Vandeyr off. "No," she said. "We *cannot* offend the Thane. The Quo'at has given me an assurance of safety, and I will abide by that. I don't fear murder – only failure."

Color brushed Vandeyr's cheeks, then vanished. The expression on her face disappeared, and she nodded. "Yes, King Traedis. As you will it."

Traedis had the distinct feeling that she would have to deal with a furious sister later, but that did not matter now. If Traedis did not succeed, it might not matter at all.

She shouldered Rose, stood, and followed the Quo'at. Two karreldish soldiers fell into step behind them, making Traedis feel uncomfortably like she was going to her own execution. They were met on the far side of the door by a karreldish woman in a deep blue gown, a jeweled pendant hanging from her neck, with her hair hidden in a voluminous scarf. She bowed to them and spoke in karreldish, her voice deeper than was usual for a woman of her people.

The Quo'at raised his hand in benediction and responded in the same tongue. Turning to Traedis, he said, "She is a mage, and will carry us to Tatek'h. It is another of the holy places of our people, and though it would normally be sacrilegious to bring a human, Coran has directed me to you, and I grant you the freedom of Tatek'h just as you granted us the freedom of the Star Cavern."

Nodding her head, Traedis waited for the touch of the mage's hand, as necessary to a *blork* spell as kneading dough was to baking bread. The disorientation hit her hard and she struggled with momentary dizziness.

They stood on the western slope of a mountain, already in shadow, though it was not late. Jagged purple crests could just be seen peering around this peak: the Dragon Mountains, farther here than from Tolin.

As her eyes adjusted to the dimness, she could see dark shapes, rough stripes painting the sky with shadow. Rising high over her head, she saw that she was outside a circle made of coarse-grained dark stone which soaked up what little light remained. She felt as if eyes watched her from cracks in the rock. There was still enough light to see that the stones were made of blue or black granite, any color fast waning with the day.

The Quo'at put a hand on Traedis' wrist. "The Thane waits for moonrise. There is still time to speak to him." Somehow, though he was smaller than anyone else there, he stood tall and powerful. Traedis took a deep breath and looked around her.

Thane Bi'ia sat inside the ring, legs crossed, before the southmost facing menhir. His face turned blindly toward them like an aboveground mole.

Traedis stared at him, shocked. Since coming to retrieve his son's body, Bi'ia seemed to have aged by decades. His face was drawn and gaunt, and bore lines that had not been there on his brief trip to Tolin. He seemed far too old to be the healthy, middle-aged karreld whom she had seen just weeks earlier. His tunic was unadorned except for laces that tied it against his chest. At the Quo'at's nod, Traedis walked toward him, kneeling in the hard-packed dirt and ragged grass of the stone circle.

"Thane Bi'ia," she said, her voice scratching against a dry throat. "I have come to speak to you about the Red Man."

Slowly, the Thane's eyes focused. Eyes that looked out of deep hollows turned an uncomprehending gaze on Traedis' face, looking through and beyond her. He did not speak.

A deep sorrow came over Traedis, flooding her with compassion for this man who had trusted her with his son's life. "Thane Bi'ia?" asked Traedis again. "I grieve for your son. Atchûk was my friend, and I mourn his loss, though I know my grief is nothing compared to yours. He was a fine man."

The Thane's voice, when it finally came, was low and monotone. "He was."

Heartened by even this pallid response, she continued. "I understand that you want vengeance for his death. I don't blame you. But what you have called goes beyond simple vengeance.

Would you make others suffer for what they did not do?"

The Thane looked into the air behind her head. "Soon the Red Man shall come, and all will be done."

A chill wind blew down from the mount, numbing Traedis' face. "If you call the Red Man, many of my people will die. People who had no hand in Atchûk's death."

Bi'ia's gaze finally seemed to recognize her. He frowned. "It does not matter. I will avenge him with my heart's blood, and my son Darg will rule."

Traedis felt as if she argued with that same mountain wind which swept inexorably downslope without acknowledgement of dispute or petition. She summoned her gift of words, searching for some that might sway him, or at least reach far enough into his darkness of spirit that he could hear her. "I have a niece who is two years old," she said. "Should she suffer for my uncle's actions? Save your vengeance for the one who deserves it."

The Thane straightened in his seat. "My son was innocent."

"He was." Traedis' jaw tightened in frustration. "Would you avenge one innocent life with the blood of many?"

"I will avenge him with my blood." The Thane lifted his arms toward Traedis, wrists upward. As his sleeves fell back, Traedis could see livid wounds, scabbed over, but white and puffy with infection. "I have already called the Red Man. It only remains to complete the summons, and the curse will be fulfilled."

Traedis felt a shock go through her, like lightning striking her bones. "I beg you, sire, send him away again. Is there nothing which will sway you?"

"There is nothing." The Thane's voice weakened. "I cannot send him away now. At moonrise he will come. My son Darg will take my place, and I will go on to another life. It is already accomplished."

Traedis looked at the rapidly darkening sky with dread. "You will give your own life," she whispered. "Your heart's blood to call him – that is what it takes. You have already spilled your blood, and prepared the way. Am I right?"

Off to one side, Traedis heard the Quo'at's uneven breathing, but she was too focused on the Thane to acknowledge it.

"That is how he is summoned," said Bi'ia as if explaining to a child.

"Is there no way to stop him?" Traedis felt the seeds of panic sprout in her chest. "To turn him aside, so that he does not harm the innocent?"

"I do not wish to turn him aside." The Thane leaned back against the stone and closed his eyes.

Chapter Twenty-six
The Red Man

Traedis rose and joined the Quo'at. The child-man's eyes were shadowed, and his face in the dim light was full of bleakness. He shook his head slowly. "I do not know of a way to turn the Red Man without Bi'ia's help. It will be a touchy matter at best, even if he fully cooperates. Once that spirit has tasted your uncle's blood, he will take his due." His voice was husky and low.

"How soon is moonrise?" She glanced into the air, where streaks of orange-gold were turning red against the mountains. Above her it was deep, royal purple. She wished she knew some magic that would hold back the sun, keep the moon from leaping into the sky: prevent the Red Man from coming.

"A quarter turn of the hour." The Quo'at's voice seemed deeper now, older.

It was a fool's hope to wish away the danger. "I will stand against him," she told the Quo'at. "I will stand against him, whether I fall or not. But first, I will beg him for the lives of my kin."

Giving her an enigmatic look, the Quo'at spoke into the silence. "The Red Man is not a spirit reason can reach. He is our blood, our need for vengeance, our answer to helplessness. He is not a man as you understand it." He expelled a long breath. "To my sorrow, I long ago called the Red Wolf down upon the country of Isbayaen. We were a tiny band fleeing from captivity, and crossed their lands, having no other place to run. Like wolves, they hunted us in a pack, stripping us of our food, our water, and our lives when they could."

He laced his tiny hands together. "I was angered beyond measure. They were wolves on two legs, so I called the Red Wolf, spilling my heart's blood on their soil to deprive them of life." He looked up at the stars which had begun to emerge from the fabric of night. "Most of that country died. King Traedis, I was young, and I was angry, and full of outrage that we could not even flee without someone taking from us." He shook his head. "That was many, many lives ago. I would never call that spirit into this age; many died for me to gain such wisdom. But vengeance runs in our veins and wells up in any injury we suffer. Bi'ia has suffered a mortal injury, and he believes only blood will suffice to mend it." He clucked his tongue. "It may seem odd that he must spill his heart's blood to mend that same heart, but it is one of our people's ways."

"How can I make him hear me?" Traedis asked, loath to squander any more remaining moments. She had few encugh of them left.

Rose sang out one high, clear note.

The Quo'at actually smiled. "What is the best way you know to make someone listen?"

Feeling foolish, Traedis lifted Rose, strapped the instrument over her shoulder, and placed her fingers on the strings. She started with a simple melody, a lullaby, words older than the City. The lines were not hard to rework so they called for mercy upon the children of her homeland. She was responsible for them, after all; not only her nieces and nephews, but all the innocents who would suffer if the Thane did not do – whatever it was he must do – to turn the Red Man aside.

The Thane rose to his feet, turning slowly, his face twisted with anger. "I sang my son lullabies. I rocked him to sleep. I taught him to hunt, I allowed him as much freedom as I could grant a prince of our people. Why should your kin live and mine die? All to fulfill a debt to you, a *tsurra!*" Traedis did not recognize the word, but she could guess from the meaning.

She kept her fingers moving on the strings, trying to reach the blighted place in his soul, frantically pulling from her mind anything else which might dissuade him. He cared neither for her people nor his own life, yet he was avenging a dearly loved son. Perhaps there *was* some way to impress upon him why he should turn aside his vengeance.

"Your son Darg will inherit," she said slowly. "And you have another son as well, do you not?"

"I do." The Thane's eyes remained closed.

"Do you not fear what this blood curse will do to them?"

The Thane opened his eyes. "They share no blood with Cordelayne Atenel. There will be no harm."

Traedis tried to quiet the flutter of her heart. She quickly sorted through what she knew of blood curses; she had cause to have studied them in recent months. Mardra hated her, and would do what she could to further the n'korreld revenge. Searching her memory, she said, "Blood curses are not simple things. They have a way of rebounding on the ones who cast them."

The Thane's eyes snapped open. "What do you mean?"

Traedis summoned her courage to make her most telling argument. "You will not suffer for it, but your surviving sons may."

"Do you threaten me?" The karreld stiffened his spine and narrowed his eyes.

"I threaten no one." She softened her voice, used her training to let him hear the sincerity in her tone. "Curses are unchancy. When they can, they cut their maker's hand. They twist the curse into something that is felt on both ends. And she who authors them is angry about the Star Cavern."

The Thane lifted a trembling arm. "My sons will take my place. My heart's blood will suffice. It is all that is needed to finish paying the price."

The sky had been darkening as they spoke, royal blue shading into the majesty of full dark. The stars shone chill and crystalline above. The wind slackened into a breeze which teased Traedis' hair into fierce tangles. As she looked east, the first curve of a nearly full moon surfaced over the horizon.

And the Red Man came.

Like the pulsing of a giant heart, the earth contracted and expanded, sending Traedis scrambling for balance. She caught herself before falling, but Rose had grown silent. The stone under her seemed to exhale a figure the size of a karreld.

Exactly the size of a karreld: a familiar one.

A naked Atchûk stood at the center of the circle – but it was not Atchûk as Traedis had known him. He was illuminated by a dead, sourceless light as pallid as a corpse lantern. The shape was his, the bearing, the face: but this figure poured with red, as if bleeding from every orifice and pore. Even his eyes wept the color of heart's blood, streaming constantly and leaving a dark stain on the ground. No expression animated his face, and at first, he moved no muscle.

Gazing on him, Traedis felt her heart hammer wildly in her chest as if it might burst and send her own blood spurting out into the night. A miasma of horror surrounded the Red Man, not the otherness of *demonfear*, but the immediate, visceral terror of spilled blood, torn flesh, death laid bare. The iron smell of blood assailed her nose and her stomach turned over.

After an age, he slowly turned to face the Thane, gazing on him with eyes that could not possibly see. Dread clutched at Traedis' throat, choking off her voice. It was more terrible to see the grotesque parody of her friend's face than it would have been to see a monster. He did not move like Atchûk, at least; he had none of the grace and enthusiasm that had once animated the young man's entire self.

The Thane stepped forward, his eyes almost as unseeing as the creature who wore the face of his son. From his belt, he took a long obsidian blade sharpened to a translucent edge. He fumbled with the laces of his tunic.

Rose shrilled several chords at the top of her range, earsplitting notes screeching an alarm. At the sound, the Thane dropped his knife, which clattered onto the rocks. Traedis felt her entire body jerk as if struck, and her breathing quickened. The Red Man remained motionless, though his blood began to pour at a greater pace.

She jumped at a touch on her elbow: the Quo'at. "Sing," he told her. "Sing for your life, and the lives of your kin. I will help you if I can."

Traedis nodded and tried to gather her breath. It was a beginner's exercise, drilled into her at the bardic college, reinforced by the almost trancelike state she had perfected in prison. Even with the Red Man's proximity, she felt her inhalations stabilize, her exhalations smooth. Rose began to sing before her strings were plucked, segueing effortlessly into the pull of Traedis' fingers. The melody was an old one, a plaintive, haunting tune that caught at the mind and could not be easily dislodged.

Atchûk's stolen form did not move swiftly; it turned like a sluggish river, swollen and inevitable. Traedis could almost feel the weight of his feet against the mountain stone, heavier than guilt. He took a step toward her, sniffing like a hound on the scent. For a single instant, Traedis' vision shone dull red. She felt malice turned toward her, implacable and deadly.

The Thane, still groping among the stones for his knife, grunted. The Red Man turned back to Bi'ia, but the malice lingered. Traedis felt as if spiders crawled along her spine. How could she possibly fight this abomination?

She danced back, threading power onto her spellwork like embroidery floss. She leafed through her mind for magics of constraint and holding, anything she could use to prevent the relentless progress of the ancient n'korreld spirit. He must be bound. Taking strength from Rose, she wove a tight net of song and age-old story: the wizard disenchanted, the giant felled, the demon thwarted. Words fell from her lips in bright clusters measuring the warp and weft of the music; old, strong words to catch and hold fast.

But the Red Man was blood, pulsing with the power of the massed n'korreld people, and blood could not be captured in a net. He washed through her civilized magics as if they were not there, pausing only for Rose's *sagathas*-laced power. If Traedis had tried to carry a mountain on her back, it could be no harder an effort. She needed something – anything – that could enable her to fight.

Rose let out an almost human sigh; Traedis suddenly felt a wash of power enter her. Her *falmyros*, knowing itself endangered, surged into her magic, filling her with Tolin's stubbornness and stone-deep refusal to yield. All of her precious country, the country that loved her beyond measure and justice, flooded Traedis. Rabbits and squirrels, veins of quartz-laden granite, quarrelsome nobles, and cross-grained cattle farmers swarmed through her veins. The net strengthened into a dam, rising to meet the surging river of blood. Traedis felt stretched from within as the land filled her.

It would be enough; it must be enough. The dam shifted, but held. Traedis continued to pour out Tolin's power as she strove to force the Red Man back into whatever nightmare he had stepped from. She could feel it working.

With a crack like lightning, her dam split in two, shaking Traedis to the cornerstone of self. The deluge of blood from the Red Man had formed great pools from which a turgid stream was converging. It sounded stifled, deadened, heavy, not the bright plink of spring water.

Traedis continued to play, pinned by the *falmyros* and Rose's *sagathas* spirit, but her best defenses had disintegrated. Tears of fury and futility leaked from her eyes, though she kept them from her voice. It seemed that even the might of Tolin was not enough to defend against a spirit that had fed on blood since the morning of the world.

Desperation clawing at her insides, Traedis cast about for anything else that could give her an advantage. Her head throbbed. The moon had soared above the mountain peaks; it was the color of old blood. She did not have much time. She had not felt this helpless even when Mardra had tried to reinstate Lord Foli's curse.

The Star Cavern. Traedis felt hysterical laughter rising to her lips as she remembered the constellations which lay in her *falmyros*. They were n'korreld work; they were what she needed to combat the Red Man. Her fingers twitched, ready to call forth the Southern Dragon; the Firebrand; the Twin Lions; the Bowl; the Great Road. She took a breath to sing them awake.

And hesitated.

She knew they were n'korreld work, and perhaps they might help her. But she had no right to use them against their creators; some things transcended even survival. It was her responsibility to lead Tolin down the right path, and this was not it. At the same time the Thane found his knife, she let go of any thought that she might force the constellations to her purpose.

In that moment, standing under the blazing stars, she knew what she must do.

She dropped her all of her current spellwork, letting it trail off and die into an echo while she began a much simpler, more heartfelt song. Tears dropped into and thickened her voice as she started a keening lament for Atchûk. Bi'ia looked up at her, seemingly startled out of his lethargy; his eyes grew wide. Traedis used the dregs of her power to remind him who his son had been, using the truest magic of a bard: to change hearts. Atchûk was not the terrible red figure, eternally dying, but the quick, clever karreld with a joke for his friends and a wry assessment of his talents.

The Thane looked again to the Red Man, then down to his knife. He shook his head. "No. I will not surrender my vengeance." His voice was almost too low to hear. He raised the knife.

Even that had not been enough. Hope finally abandoned Traedis, though she continued to play with the tenacity of despair she had learned in prison. She barely remembered the Quo'at until he said quietly, "Bring the inspiration of the god, shining through me, into your spell. You can do that, yes?"

"Yes," Traedis breathed, afraid to hope further, but unable to stop herself. Her great skill – the chording which could blend magic with magic, or with the voices of the gods – was the only weapon she had not used. With a pulse beating so strongly in her throat that it was hard to sing, she opened herself up, letting the Quo'at guide a whisper of Coran through her song.

It was like opening to the warmth of summer earth, memories of clean grass and ants finding their way into new soil. The god supported, but did not alter her spells, allowing memories of the Quo'at's earlier life to sink into the harpwork. The stone under her feet seemed more present, and every note she played more real.

Now there was not one figure in her inner vision, but three: Atchûk and his two brothers. Sometimes rivals, sometimes friends, they all strove to make their father proud. And proud he had been, of serious, thoughtful Darg, of adventurous Atchûk, of brave Bekk. The Quo'at, much older than his new self, had seen Bi'ia's overwhelming love for his children, and knew that the Thane would do anything for them, with one exception: he would not sacrifice one for the other.

And that, Traedis realized, he might do if he freed the Red Man.

The Red Man had stopped again, his crimson streams like dark water in the moonlight. His eerie figure stood motionless, perhaps waiting for the Thane to finish the summons with heart's blood.

Amidst the *falmyros*, Rose, and the presence of Coran, Traedis barely remembered herself. She was a voice and a conduit for greater powers. But with the Quo'at's memory, she felt a sharp pang of her own envy; Atchûk had come from a caring, if undemonstrative family, and had always known he was loved. His father would call down the most terrible scourge of his people in order to avenge him.

Her own father had died without ever reconciling with Traedis, and she knew he would never have admitted any fault. Uncle Cordelayne, close as a father, intended to bring down her reign. The bond of family she had known bore no trust. Atchûk had been blessed in those who had loved him.

Without realizing it, Traedis had pooled those feelings with the memories of the Quo'at, aching for herself as well as the Thane, and knowing that they were each as lost as the other. Guilt was a common chord in all of them: the Quo'at over calling the Red Wolf; Traedis for the memory of the way she had left her father; the Thane knowing that he had allowed his son to go to his death. Rose amplified the pain, brought it into harmony, until all of their separate notes were in accord, the Quo'at a steady bass line that anchored the song.

The Thane was no longer fighting them. Clean grief and understanding was beginning to replace the calcified guilt that had called forth the Red Man. Traedis felt the Quo'at interject one idea: that Bi'ia's other sons might suffer if the ancient n'korreld spirit were allowed his way. It was the same idea that Traedis had tried to broach, but now the Thane heard. He stopped, and Traedis heard him take sobbing breaths as the moon flooded down upon them.

"Darg," he said in a voice that sounded as if it had been ripped from the bottom of his soul. "Bekk. They must live. And Darg's son Yuo." He rose to his knees. "What am I doing, Ashkin?"

"Call him off," said the Quo'at, gently as the touch of a feather. "Call the Red Man off his scent. You are lost, but your sons are not. Give over your vengeance and let there be peace."

The Thane bowed his head. "Go! I will do what I must, Ashkin. Take King Traedis and go. I and no other will accept the consequences of my actions."

"May your next life be bounteous." the Quo'at's sounded immeasurably sad. "Come, King Traedis." He took her hand and led her to where the mage waited to take them back to Dinye.

Traedis cast a single look back. The last thing she saw among the dark stones was Bi'ia embracing the bloody form of his son for the last time.

Rose finally stopped singing as the mountain vanished.

Chapter Twenty-seven
The Blade of the Knife

Traedis paced up and down the paths of the rose garden, which had exploded into early summer bloom. Every variety that some past gardener had been able to grow in the mountains flourished there, from simple single-rowed flowers to ruffled blooms the color of sunset. Sweet but not cloying, their perfume permeated the air; a bee, dressed in his dinner jacket of yellow and black, landed on a blossom the size of Traedis' fist. On a low stone bench, Ruth lay stretched out on her stomach, reading a book.

Vandeyr stood at the end of the path, glowering at Traedis. "You're doing it again. I hate it when you do that."

"Doing what – " Traedis realized a moment later that Vandeyr meant she was again pacing out the confines of her cell. She stopped in the middle of the path. Reaching out a finger, she touched the petal of a rose the velvety crimson of heart's blood.

Vandeyr straightened an already straight back. "I know you're anxious. I know we haven't heard a thing from the n'korreld since the Quo'at dropped us all back here. I'm anxious too." Her expression softened. "But Trae, you succeeded. You – and the Quo'at – talked Thane Bi'ia into calling off the Red Man. If he'd changed his mind again, the Red Man would have already come."

"I know," said Traedis miserably. "And he was going to die either way. But I can't help feeling responsible, and I wish I knew what happened. For all I know, they'll never tell me, and I'll wonder my whole life how bad it was."

"Not," said Ruth without looking up, "as bad as having him die *and* losing this entire corner of the world." She turned a page and Traedis heard it flutter against the wind.

That was fair. Traedis still had more guilt over Atchûk than over his father; she might never be free of it. It nestled with other guilts: the last parting with her father; giving her uncle's name to Kenrydh; her inability to please her mother. Sighing, she relegated it to the corner of her mind that held so many unresolved feelings that it was a bruise on her heart.

A faldren page approached from farther down the path. Traedis consciously dropped her hands so that she would not seem to be fidgeting, arranged a smile on her face, and lifted an eyebrow. "What is it?"

The page dropped her gaze. "There is a party of n'korreld to see you, Your Majesty." Her voice was barely audible.

Traedis felt a weight in her stomach. "Who?" she asked, keeping her tone neutral so as not to terrify the poor child any more than necessary.

"N'korreld, Your Majesty. They're in the Silk Room. I'm supposed to find out what you want to do."

"I don't bite," Traedis said mildly, though her nerves stretched taut. "Tell the steward I'll be with them..." She assessed the state of her attire; she was clean, dressed well, and her hair was braided up. "As soon as I can get there."

The page bowed and whipped around to disappear back down the path. Ruth was already rising, one finger marking her place in the book. Vandeyr squared her posture, becoming the silent guard rather than Traedis' temperamental sister. They started down the path, passing the profusion of roses without a glance, weaving through the two other gardens which teemed with bright colors and foliage.

It was not far from the door to the Silk Room. Traedis swept in with cramping muscles and a fixed grimace on her face. The first person she saw was the Quo'at in his dollhouse chair, his retinue around him. Though a table full of delicacies was spread before him, he did not eat. A bag the length of his arm was clutched in his fists.

She might not be able to ward her expression, but she would give no offense she could avoid. She nodded respectfully. "Most Blessed Quo'at, welcome back to my home. Though our last meeting was full of grief, your presence brings joy." That might be a stretch of the truth, but it was required for hospitality.

The Quo'at's smile was tired. "King Traedis, I am glad to see you again. I am sorry that my errand is one that brings no such joy as you have professed, but it is important to us all." His mournful expression was not unexpected.

Traedis seated herself carefully and invited Ruth to join her with a grave smile and a nod. "You have my heartfelt condolences on your grief, Most Blessed One." She barely kept her voice from cracking. "Is Thane Darg well?" It was hard not to ask what she truly wanted to know: whether the Red Man were indeed gone. On the other hand, the Quo'at was presumably here to answer those questions. She tried not to stare at whatever he carried in the sack, and focused instead on his face.

"I thank you for your condolences, Your Majesty." The Quo'at blinked, unshed tears in his eyes. "Though Bi'ia will come again, it will be in different flesh, and who knows if we will meet again?" He shifted the bag on his lap. "Thane Darg is indeed well, though his sorrow is great. I think he will make a fine leader – he is wise, and he understands that we live in a world where we must work together with other peoples in order to further our welfare. It is not a stance all n'korreld take, but in my judgement it is necessary."

Her throat dry, Traedis reached for a teacup. "I am glad of that. Is it, in your judgement, a good time to send an embassy? Or would that be precipitous, given my part in his father's death?"

The Quo'at rubbed his temple. "King Traedis, you were *not* responsible for Thane Bi'ia's death. His choices were his own, and he chose to call that ancient spirit of our people when he could have sent his own assassins to find your uncle, or to declare a bounty on his head. He was not ignorant of the consequences. He chose to ignore your generosity and what your rule means for all of us. Do not take that burden on your heart."

It was too late for that, but Traedis did not say it. Instead, she sipped her tea. "Is it then your counsel that I should send an embassy to the new thane?"

"Yes." The Quo'at smiled, though sadly. "He is willing to receive you and yours – and unlike his father, Thane Darg does not blame you at all for the deaths of his kin. He knows how daring Prince Atchûk was, and how much his father's reason was unseated by the loss." He sighed. "But there is another matter I have come for."

He reached inside the bag and gently drew out a knife; a stone hilt with an ivory-colored blade the length of Traedis' hand. It clearly consisted of bone, and fresh bone at that; it did not have the dry, yellowed appearance of a weapon made long ago. A shudder ripped through Traedis.

The Quo'at nodded. "You begin to understand. Yes, this is made from Thane Bi'ia's breastbone. Once the Red Spirit is called, he *must* taste the blood he was called to devour. *Nothing* can send him to rest without it. This bone, taken living from its flesh, is that which must spill the heart's blood of your uncle."

Traedis heard a roaring in her ears. She could not move.

A tear finally spilled down the outside corner of the Quo'at's eye. "Bi'ia was too far gone for reason or for mercy. He had spent too many years defending the n'korreld from our many oppressors, had imbibed too many tales of impotence and grief. He wished to make you suffer as he had." Suddenly his voice sounded the same age as his body. "King Traedis, I would have spared you this, but it is your hand which much wield the knife. With this blade, you must spill the heart's blood of your uncle."

The roaring grew more intense. As if she had no connection to her body, Traedis watched herself stretch one hand slowly toward the Quo'at. She could not feel the hilt of the blade when he placed it in her hand, but a shock like distant lightning sparked through her hand, up her arm, and into her own heart.

"How long?" she asked finally, her voice a croak.

"A year and a day." The Quo'at looked at her with a gaze so compassionate she would have wept herself if she had inhabited the shell of her body. "If it has not been accomplished by then, the Red Man will come again, and nothing will hold him back."

Beside her, Ruth reached out a hand to steady Traedis. "There is no other way?" she asked.

The Quo'at shook his head. "There can be none. I am sorry."

Wingblade's voice echoed in Traedis' ears: *Who will love their love to the storm?*

His curse, reinforced by Mardra, had never weighed more heavily.

The light over the mountains burned, clouds in the eastern sky reflecting the flame of sunset, rapidly darkening to the color of heart's blood. Traedis felt as if she were burning inside, the strain of Bi'ia's charge consuming her like the phoenix. She would be nothing but ash by the time she must take up the Thane's knife.

"I must find another way," she forced through a constricted throat and rigid jaw. Her unwillingness to betray family was another layer of guilt weighing down her heart. She had thought herself ready to give up those she loved to cold justice, but faced squarely with its imminence, she was not. No matter what he had done, she would always love Uncle Cordelayne.

As the sunset shaded into a cold, clear blue behind the shadowy mountains, her determination crystallized. She would do what she must, even if it meant Uncle Cordelayne's death; but if there were any other solution, she would find it.

Her dreams that night would be full of black wings.

Inspired by authors such as J.R.R. Tolkien, Lloyd Alexander, and Madeleine L'Engle, Beth determined to become a writer when she was still in grade school. Deciding to focus on her writing, she began to publish fantasy short stories in various magazines and anthologies. *The Herd Lord*, a novella about a war among centaurs, was published in 2011, her first full-length novel *Etched in Fire* was released in 2015, with its sequel *A Gift of Flame* following in 2018 (hardback editions are available through Amazon.com and Infinite Realms Bookstore irbstore.com), and her short story anthology *Seeing Green* came out in 2017. Beth's ideas are sparked by music, artwork, designer coffee, and the question, "What if?" But it is her children who keep her striving for excellence, so that she can make them proud of her.

Seeing Green
Fifteen spellbinding tales open a gateway to other worlds full of love, betrayal, and the cost of magic.
Because sometimes, when you seek magic, you get your wish.

https://www.amazon.com/Seeing-Green-Beth-Hudson-ebook/dp/B0741HJTY6